An Apology for Roses

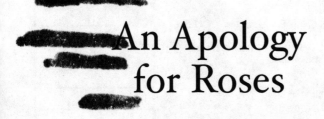

An Apology
for Roses

John Broderick

THE LILLIPUT PRESS

This edition published by

THE LILLIPUT PRESS LTD
62–63 Sitric Road,
Arbour Hill,
Dublin 7, Ireland
www.lilliputpress.ie

First published in 1973 by Caldar & Boyars Limited

A CIP record for this title is available from The British Library.

ISBN   978 1 84351 6927

The Lilliput Press receives financial assistance from
An Chomhairle Ealaíon/The Arts Council of Ireland

Printed in Ireland by ePrint

ACKNOWLEDGMENTS

The John Broderick Society wishes to acknowledge the contributions of many
people who have helped keep the John Broderick legacy alive since the Rotary
Club of Athlone organized the first John Broderick Weekend in 1999. The
following are not listed in any particular order but have all helped by their
moral and/or financial support:

Athlone Municipal District and its predecessor Athlone Urban District Council
with special reference to the naming of John Broderick Street, Desmond Green
particularly for his help in getting a selection of the non-fiction writings of
John Broderick published (under the title Stimulus of Sin), Billy Galvin,
Paddy Galvin, Maureen Doherty née Hunt, Cait Browne née Hunt, Dr Patrick
Murray, two late-lamented supporters Christy Bigley and Aidan Heavey,
Gearoid O'Brien, Senior Executive Librarian at the Aidan Heavey Public
Library, Senator David Norris, author D.J. Taylor, author Colm Tóibín, Mel
O'Flynn, Desmond Egan, Rev. Patrick Lawrence, Harry Meehan, Cllr Aengus
O'Rourke, author Madeline Kingston, Sheila Buckley Byrne, John Devins,
Joanne O'Connor, Angela Blacoe, Mary D'Arcy, Peter Cooke and others.

John Broderick:
a very provincial novelist

I grew up in the Athlone of the 1960s when John Broderick was emerging as a novelist of promise with the publication of *The Pilgrimage* (1961), which was promptly banned on publication, *The Fugitive* (1962), *Don Juaneen* (1963) and *The Waking of Willie Ryan* (1965).

As a teenager when I showed a keen interest in creative writing my father arranged for me to meet our local author. This was the early 1970s and John Broderick was on the dry. I was invited around for high tea and graciously accepted although I felt quite nervous. Arriving at the front door of 'The Moorings' I rang the bell. Unlike John Broderick, when he rang Samuel Beckett's doorbell in Paris, I actually waited for a reply. His housekeeper invited me in. I was fashion-conscious then with my long hair, flared trousers and loud ties and was rather taken aback to discover how a real writer looked. When John greeted me in his three-piece pinstriped suit with a gold watch-chain drawn across his waistcoat he looked every inch the provincial squire.

I was introduced to his mother and plied with tea and confectionery from the family bakery before being asked to sit in an armchair for a relaxed chat. I was facing John across a great Victorian fireplace. Apart from the physical space there was a cultural chasm between us that gradually filled over the coming years. He was cultured and sophisticated. I was gauche and shy. I was of Athlone and he was on the periphery wishing he could be part of it. He admitted to me that he was dreadfully out of touch with things and was by then largely dependent on his housekeeper, Mary Scanlon, to bring him home the news from town.

Some idea of his generosity might be gleaned from what happened next. We were talking about the Leaving Certificate and when he heard that we were studying *Wuthering Heights* he became animated. He waxed lyrical about the book and drew my attention to some of his own favourite passages. He proceeded to expound his own theories about Heathcliff and his relationship to Mr Earnshaw. I was, to say the least, interested in what he had to say and told him so. 'Do you think other Leaving Cert students in Athlone would be interested in my views?' he asked. When I said that they would he agreed to give a free lecture for the students. I got the venue and he gave the lecture.

An Apology for Roses came out in 1973, the year I was sitting my Leaving Certificate, and its publication caused quite a stir. Firstly we were attracted to the cover of the hardback edition, which was designed by our glamorous young art teacher, Anne Murtagh, and depicted a typical Athlone scene. We were even more intrigued when we learned that one of the principal characters, a fornicating priest, shared the same name, both Christian name and surname, as our school principal – himself a cleric. We knew however that the two Father Thomas Morans were clearly unrelated. John later apologized to our Father Moran for this unfortunate coincidence.

An Apology for Roses was a daring book by any standards. In 1973 it was considered a 'dirty book' and was as much in demand with my school friends as the infamous *Little Red Book* of Mao Tse-tung then banned by the school authorities if not by the censorship board. Its reappearance in 2016, forty-three years after being first seized by the customs and submitted to the rigours of the censorship board, is refreshing. Unlike *The Pilgrimage* it emerged unscathed from the censor and possibly even benefited from adverse publicity. It sold over 30,000 copies in the first week of publication and went on to have record paperback sales.

Ireland has come a long way since the crippling days of literary censorship of the 1960s. Having lived through myriad cases that rocked both the Catholic Church and the country we have emerged as a more broad-minded and tolerant society. In his time some critics admonished Broderick for his references to homosexuality, fornicating

priests and dark insights into the crippling nature of Irish
provincial life. John Broderick ploughed a fine furrow
and many Irish novelists followed in his wake. I think he
would be both surprised and delighted to know that this
book is being made available to a whole new audience,
without any apology, by The Lilliput Press.

GEARÓID O'BRIEN

Senior Executive Librarian,
The Aidan Heavey Library,
Athlone, County Westmeath
June 2016

Money, which represents the prose of life, and which is hardly spoken of in parlours without an apology, is, in its effects and laws, as beautiful as roses.

R.W. EMERSON

Oh, it's a snug little island!
A right little, tight little grocers' republic.

adapted from THOMAS DIBDIN (1771 - 1841)

CHAPTER ONE

He slowed down as he approached the speed limit outside the town. Creeping suburbia: petrol stations,
lounge bars, crazy pavements and a half-clipped
poodle. The sky shone like painted enamel, and even
the fallen leaves on the sparkling road seemed to reflect the light of the October afternoon.

His spirits lifted, as they nearly always did when
the weather cleared and the secretive countryside
through which he had to drive revealed itself with a
sort of primeval abandon. Roofs, trees and spires that
had been shrouded for days stood out clear and
glistening against the metallic horizon. It was a shadow-
less land and no mountains gave shelter against the
sky which reared over it, vast, capricious and
enveloping.

He hummed to himself as he turned by the railway
station onto the road that ran between the river and
the military barracks. The great stretch of water,
broad and polished between its two bridges on his left;
on the other side the sick-horse field where the Duke
of Wellington's mount had been buried by the red-
coats, and the cannons outside the massive iron gate.
Across the road, the tree-lined promenade, the rows
of painted boats, and the falling leaves drifting over
the water like fish in a tank.

He turned into the market square in front of the
great heraldic church that dominated the bridge and
confronted the lowering bulk of King John's castle
across the way. The unicorn and the toad. The river
swollen by the recent rains seemed hardly to move, yet
beyond the weir-wall it had inundated hundreds of acres
below the town, wiping out miles of the low-lying country
roads like a wet cloth applied to a chalk map on a
blackboard. In that silent land the river was mistress:

placid, seductive and uncontained.

He got out of his car and returned the nods and greetings of familiar faces.

'Don't tell me you're locking your car, Father.'

He grinned and put the keys in his pocket. The townspeople were friendly; easy-going and garrulous; much given to forming little knots for an idle gossip. Difficult to know like moods of their river goodess, shrewd and grudging in their praise; experts at the age-old Irish game of saying a lot and giving nothing away. The tricolour flapped damply above the castle walls. A garrison town, given to service and cynicism. It had always been a cross-roads between east and west, unimpressed by strangers and servile to them; but yielding to no enthusiasm.

He visited the bank; bought a tube of tooth-paste and a fruit-cake in a super-market, where piped music was tuned to a wildly incongruous Spanish rhythm, and women walked with an Irish slouch. Back in his car he edged his way across the bridge in low gear, for it was jammed as usual with trucks and trailers on their way to Galway.

On to the Longford road, where a few large houses surrounded by high stone walls broke the pattern of suburban villas on either side. He stopped in front of a white fluted gate, opened it and drove up a curving avenue that led to a big yellow Georgian house with amber windows blinking over a garden ablaze with the tawny fires of autumn. At the bottom of the lawn a clump of holly trees were already speckled with red, and the plumes of pampas grass waved gently in the breeze: the flame and smoke of late October.

He got out and stood for a moment admiring the golden radiance of the fading beeches, and the stubborn grace of tall feathery ash trees. On the broad stone terrace in front of the house the hydrangeas in their green tubs were still unbrowned by frost; and a lazy puff of smoke coiled about one of the high chimneys. No ripple disturbed the quiet luminous trees; and the house might have been uninhabited but for a faint light glowing deep within one of the upstairs windows.

Then he put his hand into his inside pocket, felt in

his wallet, patted his chest and walked slowly to the
wide front door.

CHAPTER TWO

After tea the four of them, Father Moran, Mr. and
Mrs. Fogarty, and Marie, went into the drawing room
for a little chat. The older couple sat on the sofa, while
their daughter settled herself in an armchair facing the
priest with the blazing coal fire between them.

'I hope you're not cold, Father,' said Mrs. Fogarty,
touching her blue hair with a thin spotted hand. She
peered at him narrowly and raised her sharp shoulders
as if she felt a draught. 'It's the turn of the year, and
there's a cold going.'

'How could anyone be cold with a fire like that,'
laughed the priest, grasping the arms of his chair and
raising himself a little. Then he pushed himself back
against the cushions and felt a little easier. No matter
how much deodorant he applied, or how much powder
he dusted over his body before visiting the Fogartys
he always began to sweat after he had been a few minutes
in the house. Except on the hottest summer days the
central heating was always turned up full blast and a
raging fire kept going in the drawing-room.

'All the same,' she murmured querulously, looking
at her husband for support.

Pat Fogarty grunted and folded his arms across his
plump belly. His wife usually assumed that he agreed
with her in company. At the moment he was looking
slyly at his daughter out of the corner of his eye. Cool
and composed, her dark hair glinting in the firelight,
she sat with her eyes lowered, her plump white hands
folded on her lap. As if aware of her father's scrutiny
she raised her eyes, looked at him impassively, and
turned her face to the fire. Pat Fogarty fingered the heavy
gold watch-chain that stretched tightly over his waistcoat and transferred his side-long look to his wife.
Sharp bony profile, flat chest, yellow skin and twitching

hands that were never really occupied except when clutching her rosary, she sat with her thin legs pressed against the bottom of the sofa, watching the clock on the mantelpiece. Ten minutes small-talk and then it would be time to get ready for Mass at the friary.

'Frost at night,' she remarked amiably. 'We'll have to bring in the tubs this week. I'm not sure that I'll put them out again next year. Hydrangeas. Everybody has them now. I see them in all the suburban front gardens. The new rich -' her voice trailed off, as her husband stirred uneasily beside her. Mrs. Fogarty considered herself to be one of the 'old crowd' in the town. Whereas her husband had been born on a small farm in the west; started life as a junior clerk; and accumulated enough money to start his own wholesale business by the time-honoured method of cooking his employer's books.

'I like hydrangeas,' he said in his thick, rumbling voice. 'The nuns' garden is full of them. Isn't that right, Father?'

'Do you know,' said Father Moran heartily, 'I've never been in the nuns' garden. I say my Mass, take my breakfast in the parlour, and that's all I see of the convent. Of course I only fill in if one of the local curates is sick or something.'

'That's right,' said Mrs. Fogarty brightly. 'I keep on forgetting that you're not in the parish. Don't you ever wish you were in the town?'

The priest smiled and looked down at his shining boots. He had large feet and big peasant hands; but the former were well shod, and his nails were carefully manicured.

'I never think about it,' he said slowly. 'That's the bishop's business.'

'Ah, the poor man, how is he?' Mrs. Fogarty took up a box of chocolates, opened them with a crisp flurry and offered them to her guest. He shook his head, and patted his flat stomach, not without a certain air of self satisfaction. Mrs. Fogarty chuckled and looked enquiringly at her daughter.

'Just one,' said Marie, turning down the corners of her mouth and selecting a caramel cream.

13

Father Moran did not think it necessary to reply to
his hostess's question about the bishop. The old man
was seventy-five, half-blind, and rarely moved out of
his palace. There was nothing to say about him that Mrs.
Fogarty did not know already, except that most of the
diocesan business was now in the hands of his secretary,
a close friend of her guest.

'Pat?' She held out the box to her husband. He
swallowed hard, raised his hand, and then hesitated.

'I shouldn't,' he mumbled, with a greedy glint in
his eye. 'I'm on a diet.'

They all knew that; but before anybody could say
anything he had reached out, grabbed a couple of
strawberry whirls and crammed them into his mouth.

Marie swallowed, cleared her throat and covered
her neck with her hand.

'Daddy,' she said in a loud clear voice, 'you'll kill
yourself. You know perfectly well what the doctor said.
Mummy, you shouldn't tempt him like that.'

Mrs. Fogarty simpered and closed the box without
helping herself.

'Oh, well, Marie, one or two won't do him any harm.
Are you sure you won't have one, Father?'

'No, thank you ma'am.'

Pat was sucking his sweets noisily, with a sly,
half-guilty expression in his small moist brown eyes.
The priest looked at him with an indulgent smile.

'Perhaps breaking a diet now and again is good for
you,' he went on, covering his knees with his hands.
The black hairs on his wrists glistened. He always
wore his shirt rolled up over his elbows.

'That's what I always say,' said Mrs. Fogarty with
an eye on the clock. The hand was poised over the
hour. They all waited as it struck seven. Immediately,
there was a light knock on the door and Mrs. Fogarty
stood up.

'All right, Nelly,' she called out. 'I'll be ready in
a moment.'

The cook's red moon-face appeared round the edge
of the door. She smiled and bowed her head at the
priest, who nodded back.

'How's the form, Nelly?' he asked easily, looking

over his shoulder with a sudden flashing smile that revealed strong yellow teeth, and a dimpled cleft in each cheek.

'All right, Father.' She took a step into the room, and pressed herself against the wall as Mrs. Fogarty went out to collect her coat. 'The Pope is better,' she said earnestly. 'Had a good night and is resting quietly.'

Father Moran resisted the urge to tell her that they were not worrying; but instead he nodded solemnly, and his face grew grave. Nelly dwelt on terms of intimacy with the great, and had to be humoured; since in most other ways she was dangerously sane; and an intimate friend of his own house-keeper, Miss Price. They shared a half-day on Sunday and spent it in the cemetery, exchanging gossip and performing the corporal works of mercy.

'I'm glad to hear that, Nelly.'

'A frail pair of shoulders to carry the weight of the world,' went on Nelly. Pat lumbered to his feet, and belched, clapping his hand over his mouth.

'Sit down, sit down,' he rumbled, flapping his wrist as the priest stood up. Father Moran smiled and remained standing. They all knew their parts in this weekly ritual. In a few moments Mrs. Fogarty would return, hatted, gloved and coated for the evening devotions; Pat would go out into the hall to put on his coat and hat; and at ten past seven precisely they would drive off, bringing Nelly with them in the back of the car. Mass began at half-past seven but the Fogartys liked to be well on time.

'Well, are we all ready?' Mrs. Fogarty rustled back into the room with her jerky puppet-like steps, warmly clad in a fur coat, and a flat religious hat. 'I hope you don't mind us rushing off like this, Father. Maybe you'll wait until we come back?'

Father Moran shook his head and frowned thoughtfully as he always did when she made this remark every week without fail.

'I'm afraid not, Mrs. Fogarty. I have a lot of work to do tonight yet.'

'Well, don't let Marie bother you with too many questions.'

15

'You're too good-natured, Father,' puffed Pat,
shaking his head with grateful intent, as he waddled out
to the hall. Nelly bounced after him, and Mrs. Fogarty
lingered for a moment looking uncertainly at her
daughter.

'Are you all right now, Marie? Do you want us to
bring you back anything?'

The girl raised her head and looked at her mother.
Her eyes were like her father's, small, brown,
flickering. But she could on occasion invest them with
a baleful glare, blank and steadily hostile. Under this
calm, contemptuous inspection Mrs. Fogarty flinched,
bit her lip and plucked at her sleeve with her gloved
hand.

'Will we bring home the evening papers, or anything?' she went on nervously, looking to the priest for
support. Father Moran was looking at his boots.

'You always bring them back, don't you?' said Marie
with a little chuckle. 'You like to read them. I'm all
right.'

'Good, good,' burbled her mother, with a sigh of
relief. 'I must be off now. Mustn't keep Nelly waiting.
Good-night, Father.'

'Good-night, Mrs. Fogarty,' said the priest in his
deep slow voice.

The front door closed, the car started up, and gravel
crunched on the avenue. The two in the drawing-room
were left in a pool of silence, broken only by the
delicate ticking of the clock and the dull crackle of
the fire. Marie looked at the priest, her warm brown
gaze gliding from the top of his raven-black head to the
toe of his shining boots. Although he was a big man
with powerful shoulders, his broad chest, heavy thighs
and thick legs curving outwards below the knees gave
him the appearance of being stocky. As if aware of her
scrutiny he sat down abruptly, crossed his legs and
rubbed his chin with his fingers.

'What am I going to do with you,' he said sadly,
looking at her with narrowed eyes.

Marie shook her head, smiled and stood up. She
raised her elbows, and stretched her arms, digging
her fists into her plump breasts. She was inclined to

put on weight and had her father's greedy appetite; but violent if sporadic dieting had kept her waist small and her hips under control. She had long shapely show-girl's legs and neat arched feet.

She looked at the clock, stifled a yawn, and walked out of the room with lithe cat-like steps. The priest did not look after her, but was aware of her fresh, spring-like scent, so curiously at odds with her personality. Yet she possessed, he knew, a streak of pure pagan innocence.

CHAPTER THREE

He looked at the clock on the mantelpiece and checked the time on his wrist watch. It was now twenty past seven. Marie's books, a pile of German biographies and histories, in the reading of which he was supposed to help her, were heaped on a small table by her chair. During the last year she had taken up German, bought herself a set of Linguaphone records, and borrowed some books from the German cultural centre in Dublin. For some reason which she never explained she liked the idea of Germany, and Father Moran on the strength of three holidays spent in that country, was supposed to be an expert on the subject.

He stood up. Mass usually lasted half-an-hour, after which the Fogartys did the Stations of the Cross, and came home about eight-thirty, leaving Nelly behind to complete her evening in the company of whatever cronies she could pick up in the church porch; after which she walked back to the house alone.

The priest went out into the hall. The house was big and rambling. An outer hall, an inner one, and yet another at the bottom of the stairs. There was also a breakfast-room, a study filled with books bought by weight at auctions, and a huge cellar underneath, unused except for the heating plant. He went up the stairs following his shadow, which blended with his dark silent body as he turned the corner, and trailed along behind him as he mounted towards the landing.

Marie's room was around the corner adjoining the bathroom. It was small-and low-ceilinged; but she preferred it to the larger rooms opening off the landing because it gave her a sense of privacy, and was near the bath, where she spent long delicious hours soaking herself in hot scented water. Her parents, true to their upbringing, regarded baths as faintly indecent as well as injurious to the natural oils of the body, and washed themselves once a month and on the eve of feast days.

As usual the curtains were drawn when the priest entered the room - scented and warm and impregnated with a blatant feminity: lacquered hair, linen freshened with pot-pourri, and the overwhelming presence of a soft vibrant young body. Even before his eyes became accustomed to the gloom he knew that everything was in its place. Pink flower-sprigged wallpaper, blue velvet curtains, a thick mustard coloured carpet, and on the chest of drawers, sole concession to her parents' sensibilities, a blue-and-white statue of the Blessed Virgin. This he knew would already have been placed on its back and covered with a handkerchief: a gesture of reverence which he entirely approved.

He undressed quickly, and folded his jacket and trousers neatly over a chair. He took off his Roman collar, but left on his shirt and socks. Then he felt in his jacket pocket for his wallet, took out the rubber with practised ease and turned to the bed.

His love-making was matter-of-fact, slightly brutal in its lack of tenderness. Never once had he kissed her lips; never had he made the slightest move to encourage those intimacies which she associated with the act of love. She longed to stroke and fondle his body, run her lips down his chest and belly and take him in her mouth, abandoning herself completely to that worship of the male which she confused with experience. She thought of herself as a woman of the world cherishing a particularly clumsy man because she happened to be at a loose end. He had come into her life at a time of emptiness. In the nature of things he could never be anything more than an interim lover; especially after Karl. Often during those brief bouts of sensuality with the priest she thought of her first lover.

She was eighteen when she met him in Dublin: tall, blond, handsome and forceful. The memory of that questing mouth and tongue had remained with her when much else had been forgotten; he had she imagined somehow revealed her to herself, in spite of all that

19

had happened later. Had he not delighted in his hard
turgid masculinity, and taught her to rejoice in her
worship of it?

For a while she had hoped to rediscover this with
the priest; a brief interlude of purely tactile pleasure
was how she thought of it. He was clumsy and stiff; and
no doubt thought of her as comparatively inexperienced.
She would alert him to her needs; they were no less
violent than his. But he had never given her the
opportunity; it had always been swift, direct and so far
as she was concerned often unsatisfactory. She put up
with it because his large well endowed body excited
her; a body perfectly fashioned for the intimacies
which stirred her imagination, filling her senses with
a primitive phallic longing. There was time enough even
in a half-hour for some degree of relaxation; but languor,
gentleness and the probing intuition of highly sensitive
natures were quite foreign to him. Once, greatly daring,
both of them had stayed in the same large hotel in
Dublin. He had spent most of the night in her room; and
nothing had been changed. He had proved his virility
over and over again, but little else. He had inherited
his masculinity from peasant forebears, to whom
nakedness was anathema and sexual experiments
unthinkable. In such a loveless embrace had he himself
been conceived.

But to-night she bore his rough burden gratefully;
and breaking all the rules of their unspoken agreement
would not release him after he had come. She cried
out softly, coiled her legs tightly about him and clasped
her hands about his shoulders. He made no movement
and for a moment she thought that he was about to
wrench himself free of her embrace. But something
frantic and abandoned in her excitement communicated
itself to him, and wordlessly he entered her again, no
less abrupt in his movement, but quickened now in his
hasty response. Had he but known she was making a
declaration of love; but it was not for him.

When it was over he disentangled himself from her
clinging body and was about to climb off the bed,
impregnated with the musky odour of their mingled
limbs; but at the last moment he stiffened, raised his

head and turned his head towards the door.

'Is that the door-bell?' he muttered.

Marie sat up and listened. The faint jingling sound came from downstairs.

'No,' she whispered, 'it's the telephone.' She slid off the bed, dressed hurriedly in the darkness, rolled up her stockings and slipped her feet into her shoes.

'Let it ring,' he commanded gruffly, reaching for his clothes.

'No, no,' she said excitedly, 'it might be about Daddy.'

Before he could restrain her she was out of the room and hurrying down the stairs. She reached the telephone just in time.

'Hullo.'

'Hallo. Is that Marie?' The male voice at the other end sounded impatient. 'I thought you were never going to answer. Aren't the old folks out at the Rosary?'

'Yes, they are.' With her breath recovered, her voice had regained its soft, slightly throaty tone. 'I was in the bathroom.'

'Oh, I see. Are you alone?'

'Yes, at the moment.'

'I'm in town, at the hotel. Can I see you to-night?'

Marie hesitated for a moment before replying, listening intently for the sound of footsteps on the stairs. But all was silent.

'When?'

'As soon as you're able. Would half-eight be OK?'

'All right.'

She put down the receiver, and turned to discover that Father Moran was standing in the inner hall, his face tense, his head thrust forward. How long had he been listening, she wondered?

'Who was that?' His voice was quiet and controlled. A phone call was innocuous enough; but it made him uneasy, in spite of the system Marie and he had worked out in case anyone called unexpectedly during their hurried love-making. Although the house had a cloak-room with a wash-hand basin off the hall, it had never occurred to the Fogartys to install a lavatory there. Mrs. Fogarty firmly believed that a downstairs lavatory was both unhygienic and unnecessary. In the event of anybody calling, Marie would answer the door and explain that the priest was 'washing his hands' upstairs. This would allow him to come down with a clean conscience. But so far no one had disturbed them; for the Fogartys entertained little, on the ground of needless extravagance; and casual callers were not encouraged. One never knew who would come to count the house and report their findings to the revenue commissioners, with which Pat waged an unrelenting battle.

'Oh, a fellow I met at a dance a few weeks ago,' replied Marie calmly, taking a comb from her pocket and running it through her long dark hair. Then she went into the outer hall and re-touched her lips with a stick she kept for this precise purpose on the reproduction Chippendale table that stood in highly polished splendour under a gilt mirror inside the front door.

'What did he want?'

'He wants to see me.'

'This evening?'

'Yes.'

The priest smiled and shook his head. Marie's boy-friends were a bit of a joke. Mostly they consisted of young men drawn from 'suitable' families picked by her mother and hopefully invited to tea for her daughter's inspection. But her interest soon waned; and they, feeling that they were getting nowhere, had been relieved when she gave an excuse which made it quite plain that she had no intention of seeing them again. Yet Mrs. Fogarty did not despair.

'Will I give you a lift?' he asked as he reached for his coat.

It was Marie's turn to smile; a curious, half-mocking grimace that he did not see. How very typical of him to use this latest turn of events as a cover-up. If it had been one of her mother's hopefuls she would have agreed at once, taking a certain cynical pleasure in the sheer casuistry of the arrangement. But not with Brian. He had nothing to do with the half-life she led in her parents' house.

'No, I think I'd better wait until they get back. They might wonder where we've gone.'

He nodded, completely convinced by this argument; and for a moment she felt a surge of sympathy for him: that playful tenderness which women sometimes display towards men they are about to ditch finally and without regret.

'All right.' He moved towards the door, in a hurry now to get away, as he always was before the Fogartys arrived back.

It was not only a sense of freedom which prompted her to call out a gay good-bye to the priest as he climbed into his car and drove off. She felt she owed him something for the sharing of an identical dilemma.

CHAPTER FOUR

At half-eight in the evening most provincial towns are
at their lowest ebb. The narrow, luridly painted houses
were smudged and formless against the row of clinical
street lights; vague blobs of colour against a foreground
of yellow-white path and roadway. A row of chimneys
reared along the sky-line, stiff fingers held up to the
moon. Brian thrust his hands into his pockets and gazed
up at them; a tall, yellow-haired young man, pensive
and watchful.

'Hullo. '

Marie was standing on the path looking up at him
enquiringly. He sprang to attention, pulled his hands
out of his pockets, and hurried down the steps.

'Where have you appeared from? Have you walked? '
He made as if to touch her arm but drew back, looked
about him and grinned.

'Lace curtains have eyes with lamps, ' he went on
looking across the street at the muted lights behind
half-drawn curtains in rooms above the shops.

'I have the car in the yard, ' she went on briskly,
opening her gloved hand and tossing the key in her
palm as if it were a coin.

'So have I. ' He jerked his head towards the hotel
entrance. 'I don't suppose you want to come in. '

'God no. ' She turned on her heel and walked back
towards the hotel yard. He hesitated for a moment,
glanced at the glowing windows, and started after her
with long loping strides. It was cold, but he had
forgotten about his coat. He caught up with her at the
entrance to the yard.

'Which shall we use? Yours or mine? '

'Yours, I think, if you can get it out. ' She slipped
the keys into the pocket of her suede coat, and looked
about the yard with cars as usual parked anyway. The

moon turned their tops to silver.

'You bet. ' He pointed to the red mini parked in the middle of the laneway, bonnet faced towards the gate. 'Where shall we go?'

'Anywhere. '

'Good. ' He ran across the yard, fumbling in his pocket for the keys, drove out and stopped at the gateway to pick her up. In a few minutes they had glided through the main street, and on past the long row of council houses that led to the Dublin road.

'What did you tell them?' he asked as he reached under the dashboard and took out a packet of cigarettes. His hand touched her knee as he handed them to her, and he patted it lightly; a gesture that mingled desire with sympathy and encouragement.

'I said I was going to post a letter. ' She took out two cigarettes, lit them and handed one to him. Her little finger brushed against his cheek and he leaned against it for a moment, rippling the muscles in his jaw.

'And?' He took one hand off the steering wheel and took the cigarette out of his lips. She rested her head against the back of the seat and blew smoke towards the roof. It coiled back, merged with his, and mingled with the scent of her suede coat, her fresh perfume; and the strong smell of hotel soap which came from his hands.

'I can always run into somebody. That's one thing about this town you can take advantage of. ' Her voice was light, amused; but he gripped the wheel fiercely and hunched his shoulders, as if he were driving at breakneck speed, instead of ambling along at thirty.

'Christ, it's brutal, ' he burst out. 'Somebody must have seen us to-night. And even if they haven't, they're bound to find out sooner or later. '

Marie smiled to herself in the darkness; sensing his indignation, his passion, and his carefully restrained sexual appetite. In every love-affair, especially at the beginning, there is always an element of play-acting. From the moment they first met, three weeks before, he had cast her in a certain role; and she in her turn had given him the cue to his. It was as if they were acting behind a dropped curtain which might be lifted

at any moment by someone in the audience beyond.
'Yes, of course they'll find out,' she murmured almost
to herself.

'And then?' he demanded in a light, uncertain voice.
'We'll see.'

He rolled down the window and threw his half-smoked
cigarette out of the window. It flashed back into the
darkness like a glow-worm.

'What does that mean?' He looked round, swerved
across the white line in the middle of the road, and
then straightened out and drew in near the grass margin.
He was driving very slowly now; and she knew that he
was looking for a quiet place to park. She sighed, looked
at the glowing end of her cigarette, and felt a soft quiver
of excitement as his knee touched hers.

'It means that I'm not going to give you up,' she said
flatly, tapping his thigh with her finger-tips and slowly
withdrawing her hand. He sucked in his breath, turned
on to a side road, and brought the car to a halt.

But instead of the embrace which she had been
expecting, he turned towards her, pressed his shoulders
against the door, and looked at her silently. For a
moment she felt a throb of apprehension and drew back,
immediately regretting the loss of contact with his body;
that hard, warm vitality to which she loved to attach
herself. She closed her eyes with pleasure and relief
as she felt him opening his legs and resting his calf
against hers; a steady, vibrant weight that restored her
to life.

'If we only had somewhere to go,' he said softly, in
a dull complaining voice. 'Would you -' he broke off and
reached out his hand appealingly. With a sudden swoop
she bent down and kissed the palm, hard and calloused
from driving without gloves.

'Yes, of course I would, Brian. I'd do anything.'

'Don't say that,' he muttered, clenching the hand she
had kissed and pressing it against his chest.

'But you wanted me to say it, didn't you? The first
time I met you I could see it in your eyes. You're not
telling me anything I don't know.'

'What are we going to do?' he muttered,
unembarrassed now by the hard swelling in his loins

and the violence of his desire.

It was true their attraction for each other was over-whelmingly physical. It had like so many instant infatuations been a chance encounter. Fogarty had stayed in bed nursing a cold; and Marie had been sitting at her father's desk checking the vanmen's dockets when one of the clerks came in to tell her that there was a traveller outside looking for the boss.

They had taken each other by surprise. Brian, new to that particular run, was expecting something plain, spinsterish and non-committal. Marie had anticipated the usual small, neat, insinuating salesman, with a loose mouth, a sharp line in small-talk, and an automatic deference towards the boss's daughter. But this casual stranger had been completely different and unexpected. The visual impact had been blurred, as it often is when the senses are suddenly and desperately aroused. Broad shoulders, narrow hips, close cut blond hair, a wide sensual mouth - that was all she could and would remember of him. Even now she could not precisely reassemble his features when she closed her eyes and thought of him; the sense of physical rapport was too strong. Her first reaction on seeing him had been possessive and arbitrary. Who owns him, she wondered, as he sat down and looked at her with a vaguely troubled expression.

They had not spoken much. He was a traveller for Galway Mineral Waters, had been in the job for a week, and was staying at the Kennedy Arms hotel. Both of them knew as he took his leave that they would meet again. It had been simple. Marie dropped into the hotel that evening. He was sitting in the lounge reading a newspaper. They had exchanged a few words, mentioned that they both had letters to post, walked to the post office, and came back to her car in the hotel yard.

'I don't know,' she replied, secure now in the knowledge that he belonged to her, grateful that on this night particularly there was no place where they could make love. 'Not here, not now.'

'No, no,' he agreed hurriedly, genuinely dismayed at the idea of coupling in the back seat of his tiny car.

He liked to think of her as a little remote, imprisoned and frustrated by an archaic family code which he detested. 'It's shocking the way they keep you bunched up in that house. You'll have to make a break someday.'

'Yes, of course. But it's not going to be easy. When they do hear about it, you're going to lose your order.'

'To hell with that. I only got it through you anyway.'

'No, you didn't. Daddy always gives a new thing a trial. If it sells he goes on ordering it. Yours has taken on, that's all.'

'You can't enjoy it in that office,' he went on pressing his image. 'Counting the money, and checking dockets. What are they trying to make out of you anyway?'

Marie rolled down the window and threw out her cigarette. Then she looked down at her hands, quietly folded on top on her gloves. The fact was that she rather enjoyed counting the money for the bank each morning.

'A business woman,' she said with a chuckle. 'And that applies to everything.'

'Even to this?' He stretched his arm along the back of the seat and drew her to him. Marie was hungry for kisses, hands that held her body gently but firmly, legs that did not imprison her with urgent anonymity. She lay back against the seat and opened her mouth, allowing his tongue to coil about her own. Starved as she was for the long delicate preliminaries of love, that tactile stimulation which causes a woman's body to blossom and swell like a flower in sunlight, his probing tongue seemed to her at that moment as deeply pleasurable as an orgasm and no less intimate. There is in every sensual woman a sort of infantile sensitivity that makes her entire body respond to the lightest caress. As she lay with this chosen man in her arms, insistent yet humbly restrained, Marie knew that the ultimate throb of a complete surrender could give her no greater satisfaction.

Brian, already intensely aware of the quivering excitement in his loins, drew back abruptly, pressed his shoulder against the door of the car and wiped the saliva from his mouth with the back of his hand. The slightest touch of her fingers would at that moment have

28

given him instant release. Agitated though he was he felt a certain pride in husbanding his potency; a triumph no woman can share.

Marie sighed and looked out of the window. The road on which they were parked topped a hill overlooking the town. A long line of amber lights stretched across the horizon like a chain of beads. The full moon lay in the middle of the river; and reigned triumphantly in the sky.

'Look,' she said, rolling down the window and pointing out. 'Over there, where the street lights end.' He peered over her shoulder and saw a tiny pin-prick of light swaying and flashing against the sky below the edge of the horizon. It seemed as though a small lamp was being hoisted up from the far end of the world. It steadied, flared up and slowly flattened out and moved on over the black land like an arc-light. He watched another light begin to flicker and mount up beyond the hard line which separated earth and sky in that great plain.

'I never saw it like that before,' he said in a voice awed as much by desire as the strangeness of the sight below them.

'That's what comes from living in Galway,' she laughed. 'All those mountains.'

'I wish to God they'd send me here,' he muttered fervently. 'A week is too long to wait.' Five days of living in hotels, drinking with other commercials in the same bars, looking at television, masturbating with loveless frenzy onto hotel towels.

'We'll manage somehow,' she said softly, sensing his mood, his rigid ardour, his romantic conception of their sudden passionate relationship. 'If you don't think of something, I will.'

'We've got to think of something,' he insisted. 'It can't go on like this.'

'I know, I know,' she said softly with the generosity of a woman secure of a deferred pleasure. 'Why can't I ring you? Wednesday is your day here. Where are you on the other days?'

Planning is a powerful tranquilliser. As he thought of this tenuous line of communication he became almost brisk and businesslike and his taut nerves relaxed a little.

'Good God, why didn't we think of that before!
Monday is no good because I'm in Galway, and I never
know what time I'll be anyplace, but I'm in Limerick
on Tuesday, Sligo on Thursday, and Castlebar on
Friday. The week-end is no good because we have no
phone at home. '

Calmly and carefully they made their arrangements.
He was always back to his hotels by seven in the
evening. Marie would ring while her parents were out
at Mass. She would contrive to meet him in the
hotel yard on Wednesday nights; and they would arrange
for him to be in some hotel in Galway at an appointed
time on Saturday or Sunday, if she wanted to get in
touch with him.

They giggled like children as they reflected on the
simplicity of it all; and their own stupidity in not
thinking of this before. It eased the tension between
them, and increased that understanding which they both
imagined had drawn them together with such compulsive force.

'I suppose, ' said Brian vaguely, 'I'd better bring
you back. No use in asking for trouble at the beginning.
But you'll ring me up in Sligo to-morrow, won't you?'

'Of course I will. ' She touched his arm lightly with
her finger-tips, and drew back with a little sigh of
regret. 'And don't worry. There's no turning back
now. '

'Was there ever a question of it?'

'No, Brian, never. Not for a moment. I didn't
really have any choice. ' She spoke with deliberation,
and actually believed what she said, giving no heed to
the fact that long ago in the knitted and twisted inter-
play of birth, upbringing and circumstances, that
particular choice had been made for her.

CHAPTER FIVE

Not once during tea had Mrs. Fogarty looked at Pat
or Marie; and it was entirely typical of her to wait three
days before confronting Marie with the news she had
heard after first Mass on Thursday morning.

Now she seated herself on the sofa, sighed, rubbed
her chilly hands together, and dilated her nostrils as
if she were suffering a bad smell. Pat wandered over
to the window and looked out at the darkening lawn;
while Marie sat down calmly in her chair and crossed
her legs.

'Marie.' Her mother's voice was low, almost sup-
plicating; and the girl felt her stomach contract as she
listened to the familiar self-pitying tone. 'Marie, how
could you. The whole town is talking about it.'

'Talking about what?'

Mrs. Fogarty took a deep breath and looked at the
clock. On Sundays Mass was half-an-hour later:
there was still plenty of time before Nelly came
knocking on the door.

'You know well what I mean. This young man you've
been seeing. You met him at the hotel on Wednesday,
and went off in the car with him, and didn't arrive back
here until after eleven.'

In the window embrasure Pat shifted his weight from
one foot to another and clasped his sweaty hands tighter
over his backside. He felt a nagging pain at the top of
his stomach and swallowed hard.

Behind him the two women glared angrily at each
other; something of their very real animosity coming
to the surface in their eyes, which glinted like tips of
icebergs with all the hidden bitter knowledge of flesh
and blood.

'I suppose some old cat ran to tell you first thing on
Thursday morning,' said Marie with cold scorn. 'Never

fear, there were plenty of them watching behind the windows.'

Mrs. Fogarty took a deep breath and clenched her bony fists. She wished she had a headache or something; but she rarely felt better in her life and could only suppose that God had given her special strength for this particular task.

'Going off like that,' she said, making a vague gesture as if she were blowing away smoke. 'Someone you never told us about. A nice thing to have dished up to me the way it was. If you had only told me I might have been prepared, but I was left without a word to say. It was as clear as a pikestaff that I didn't know what my own daughter was doing.' Her voice gained strength as she suffered once again the blow aimed at her pride and self-esteem by the kind neighbour who knew exactly where to strike. 'But you knew what you were doing, you always do. Going out the road with a common commercial traveller. You'd imagine you were a servant girl.'

Marie smiled and relaxed, feeling her breast brush against the arm of the chair as she sat back and raised her hand to pat her hair.

'Daddy was a commercial at the beginning,' she replied innocently, feeling a slow surge of excitement as she thought of Brian and the conversations she had had on the telephone every night since. She wondered why she was not taking this more seriously; and felt it was the strength that one draws from a satisfactory love-affair. She was as yet not aware of anything else.

'He was nothing of the sort,' snapped her mother. 'He was travelling for himself.'

'And before that he was working in Williams,' Marie looked round at her father with a conspiratorial smile.

'I have never denied it,' he said gravely, as if it were something debatable. But he was not angry. It was a subject he had brought up more than once to cool the fever of his wife's social aspirations. 'What your mother objects to in this young man is that, first of all, you didn't tell her about him, and secondly she expects you to do better than that for yourself. Well, naturally.' He puffed out his cheeks and blew through his inflated lips. It was a gesture which often eased his stomach a little.

Mrs. Fogarty squeezed her mouth impatiently. As usual she suspected her husband of playing down to the girl; of indulging her in short at his wife's expense. But there was nothing she could specifically criticise in Pat's remarks except that they were so aptly put. Taking the words out of her mouth again. She narrowed her eyes and peered at her daughter; and wondered not for the first time in her married life how in the name of God she had ever borne her.

'Nothing but a smart young whipper-snapper trying to get on by playing up to the boss's daughter,' she wailed, and then went on, not without some cunning: 'I wonder you didn't see through him at the very beginning.'

'Oh, but I did,' put in Marie quickly with a level smile.

'Before you got your name mixed up with him,' went on her mother, determined to complete her charge, although she had been somewhat knocked off-course by Marie's remark.

'I saw through him very well,' went on the girl looking into the fire with a sudden frown. Pat and his wife exchanged an anxious unrehearsed look. They were puzzled. 'So well that I intend to marry him.'

Mrs. Fogarty gasped and clutched her throat with her bird-like fingers, while Pat opened his mouth, thought better of speaking, and licked a drop of saliva from the corner of his lip. Then he clenched his jaws as he felt his false teeth loosen with nerves.

'But we know nothing about him,' wailed his wife. 'He might be anything. Nowadays you can't tell who's who or anything - ' her voice trailed away and she watched her daughter with dull complaining eyes.

Pat coughed and lowered himself gently into the chair opposite Marie who continued to stare into the fire with set brows.

'Well, that's not quite true,' he said in a light breathless voice. 'I've made some enquiries, and he comes from a perfectly respectable family in Galway.

True, they've come down a bit. His father used to have a pub of his own, but he died when the family was young and it had to be sold. His mother kept boarders for a while, but this young fellow went out to work early, and the others got on very well. His brother won a University scholarship and is in his last year in medicine, and there's one sister a nun and another a chemist.'

'Why didn't you tell me all this before?' demanded Mrs. Fogarty in a voice full of perfectly genuine resentment. It was a feeling she never had to dissemble.

'Well, I had to find out, Aggie. Besides you were in no mood to listen to anything good about the fellow.'

'I've never heard nothing good about him so far, family or no family. I'm glad to hear he has a sister a nun. How does he come to have a name like that? There must be some Protestant blood somewhere. Langley is not a Catholic name.' She looked at her husband with a quick enquiring glance which Marie intercepted; and which immediately made her relax. So deep were the differences between her parents that even a put-up job could be made to appear perfectly genuine. Now that she had got the message Marie rubbed her forefinger along her upper lip and smiled thinly behind her hand.

'His grand-father was Church of Ireland, but turned when he married,' said Pat, reeling off his information slowly as if it were an effort. From the way his colour deepened Marie was sure that he was aware of her scrutiny; but he did not allow himself to glance in her direction. And after all in his own way she was sure that the part he was playing was giving him some satisfaction.

Her mother's official acceptance came quicker than Marie expected. With her abnormally quick intuition she must have been aware that it would be dangerous to allow this discussion to go on too long. She looked down at her hands twisted in a blue-veined knot on her lap, and sucked her teeth. Father and daughter carefully avoided looking at each other. Marie felt her blood rising with excitement and was glad that she had never suffered from blushing. She remained calm and outwardly collected while her heart beat wildly with triumph. For once the circumstances of her life had conspired to protect her. Brian was safe; even if her parents regarded him for the moment as little more than a convenient foil.

Presently Mrs. Fogarty raised her head, cleared her throat and made a speech in a low hurt voice, her eyes wet with tears of self-pity, her mouth twisted with embarrassment. She had done her best to give Marie the best of both worlds; nothing in her opinion was too good for her; and no marriage, even with the highest in the land, could be considered as beyond the range of the product of such a home. And so on and so on.

It was a speech Marie had heard often enough before in many another context. By now it had a soothing ritualistic quality, like listening to the litany of the Sacred Heart while ones thoughts were pleasantly far away. It lasted about four minutes during which Pat sat with lowered eyes and puckered lips; his hands quietly folded on his knees: his church sermon position.

At the end of it Marie raised her eyes and looked fixedly at a point somewhere between her parent's shoulders. Her expression was suitably restrained and respectful; and her mother and father might with justice have congratulated themselves on having brought off a carefully planned coup with complete success, a success all the more gratifying, since the real purpose of the exercise had not once been mentioned by them in the 'little talk' they had had that afternoon.

Marie sat up in her chair and allowed herself a rueful little smile, - instead of the loud guffaw which she would have liked to give. Her expensive education had not after all been wasted on her. She was carefully jubilant.

'I suppose,' she said slowly, looking from one pair of guarded eyes to another with an expression of abashed innocence, 'I should have told you sooner, but -' She shrugged her shoulders and held out the palms of her hands towards them.

Mrs. Fogarty rose and looked at the clock intently. She knew that her daughter was mocking her, and was anxious to escape before she lost her temper.

'All I ask is that you don't bring him into this house without telling me beforehand,' she said acidly, her head half-cocked as she listened for the creaking board that announced Nelly's progress from the kitchen to her room to tidy up for Mass.

Pat flashed a look of warning at his daughter as he lumbered to his feet, and wiped the sweat from his upper lip with the back of his hand.

But Marie was laughing gaily; hardly bothering to conceal her contempt.

'Don't worry,' she said. 'I won't.'

Mrs. Fogarty rustled from the room, making a sign to her husband to follow her. He knew her too well to attempt to contact his daughter with a smile of under-standing; for just as he anticipated she would Aggie turned round at the door, glanced at him sharply and stood waiting for him.

Marie got up, sighed deeply, leaned her elbows on the mantelpiece and stared at her reflection in the mirror. Marie stood back from the fire, smoothing her dress over her hips and listened for the sounds that would leave her alone and free in the house. At last merciful silence; for her the only real benediction.

She waited for a few moments savouring the moment before rushing out into the hall and picking up the telephone. Thank God for a direct dialling system to Galway. On Friday evening, speaking to Brian at the hotel in Castlebar she had arranged to ring him at half-seven on Saturday and a little later on Sunday at the Railway Hotel. She got through, asked to have him paged in the bar and waited with a sort of sick longing that made her limbs tremble and her eyes to blur.

'Marie?' The voice was so close that she felt her ear tingle with delight.

'Brian,' she exclaimed, 'I have news for you -'

'I have news for you.' His voice rushed on, as if he had made up a prepared speech and was determined

to deliver it correctly. 'I met a fellow this morning
on the links who has a chalet on the lake and he's given
me the key. Why should I stay in the hotel he said
when I could keep this warm for him one night a week,
he only uses it in the summer for a month for the kids
when Galway is crowded and he does the Shannon in a
boat, and he can hardly ever get away in the winter-
time, Marie isn't it wonderful?'

What lake? she almost asked stupidly, until the
implications rather than the sense of it struck her and
she laughed with relief.

'Oh, Brian and I was just about to tell you that
Mummy has heard about us, and has invited you here,
to the house.' Although she was not aware of it there
was a certain note of condescension in her voice. Her
mother's house meant more to her than she knew.
There was a pause, during which she felt her heart
jump and her bowels contract.

'Brian - '

'Yes, I heard. Was there a row?' His voice was
suddenly guarded.

'No, no, of course not. It's just that everything is
OK.'

'Oh.' Another pause, during which the pips sounded.
'But the chalet. Does this mean - '

'It's a wonderful idea, Brian, just what we want. Oh,
I can't wait to see it.'

'I mean the house wouldn't be the same at all.'

'God no. Where is it?'

'Well, I was thinking about that. You know the
Lake Hotel? Go there and walk round the foreshore,
you know it?'

'Of course, the path by the golf-links. I know the
chalets too, at the point. Which one is it?'

'The very first one. None of them are occupied at
this time of year, thank God.'

'Oh, Brian.' Her voice sounded breathy and affected;
yet her emotion was genuine, and she was too excited
to hear herself. 'What time?'

'Eight, I suppose.' He paused and added: 'On
Wednesday.'

She frowned at the wall, remembering another

phone call she would have to make in the morning.

'Marie.' His voice was gentle, now that his plan was unfolded. 'Will it be OK?'

'Of course it will, Brian. I'll be there at ten to eight. Oh God, three more nights to go and I can't call you tomorrow night. You said - '

'I'll make it here at half-seven somehow, and then we'll arrange for Tuesday in Limerick.'

She cradled the telephone in her two hands as if it were a live thing; as indeed it was: a six-day life-line.

'Oh, good, good,' she said firmly but vaguely, not daring to say all the things she really wanted to say. The life-line was a sort of guardian too; and she was at the end of substitutes. 'Oh, Brian, I don't know how I'm going to get through the next two days. No, no, I'm all right. I didn't mean that. It's just that I've just discovered that I'm no good on the telephone except taking orders and things like that.'

'This is an order.' His voice was theatrically firm, with the upward inflection that signified that he too had come to the end of his resources. 'Go on thinking of me.' His voice trailed off, embarrassed; and she felt an opening void of pure happiness within her; a sensation of weightlessness.

'I will,' she whispered and left down the receiver. And now the evening stretched before her, as free and empty as she could wish it when he was not there. A long hot bath; a session with her hair, the lustrous abundance of which she carefully tended; and then bed with that new book about Mayerling, her favourite period in history. Happy doomed romantics who could pull down their own glittering world about them.

CHAPTER SIX

Father Moran took up his breviary and began to read
his office. He opened the prayer-book, settled his
marker and began to pace the carpet, adapting his long
strides to an indoor confinement. Three steps to the
brick fireplace and three back again to the book-case
inside the door. To and fro with soft muffled tread,
the breviary resting in the crook of his thumbs.
Occasionally he paused and looked at the window down
which the rain was dripping. The small low-ceilinged
room was as close and airless as a cell; the silence
broken only by the fat ticking of the clock on the
mantelpiece, and the spluttering of the coal fire as a
few raindrops fell from the chimney. He glanced at
the clock, his lips moving mechanically in prayer.
Eleven o'clock.

At length he sighed, blessed himself, closed his
breviary and ran a finger along his jaw which was a bit
bristly, as he had over-slept that morning and had had
to shave in a hurry. He put his prayer-book down on
the arm of a leather chair, buried his hands in his
pockets and hunched his heavy shoulders.

'Bloody rain, ' he muttered to himself, frowning at
the misty window and thrusting out his lower lip.
'Will it ever stop. ' He took up the 'Independent' and
looked at the picture of a nun who had just celebrated
her golden jubilee. The bland, ageless face stared up
at his impassively. He crumpled the paper and threw
it on the table. It made the same soft purling sound as
his own soutane: damp got into everything here. Paper.
He looked about the room; at the books heaped on the
table and piled up on the floor; at the jumble of letters
and documents on his desk; at his breviary with its fine
rice paper stuffed with memorial cards, and the fading
souvenir of his own ordination. Paper: smooth and

unwrinkled as a child's face when new; so yellow and
brittle and scribbled upon at the moment of dissolution.
In its own way a more complete image of man than
his reflection in a mirror. He rubbed his eyes wearily
and smiled to himself. Wet days were apt to bring
forth a stream of such useless thoughts.

And then just as he was about to go into the kitchen
for a cup of coffee, the telephone rang in the hall. He
reached it a split second before Miss Price, who
conceded defeat with a sniff and a half-smile and
retired to her kitchen to continue her perusal of the
deaths column in yesterday's 'Independent', her
favourite reading.

'Hullo.' His voice was low and guarded. There is
something about a telephone which brings out the
confessional side of a priest's nature.

'Hullo. It's me.' Marie's voice was equally
muted. She never used her name on the rare occasions
when she rang him up. She did not need to; he always
knew.

'Daddy's gone home, not feeling well. Listen,
could you come on Tuesday or Thursday instead of
Wednesday? Something's turned up.'

He thought quickly. Tuesday he had a meeting of
the parish council in the school, Thursday he had
planned to visit his sister in Roscommon. Nothing
serious, a routine call. She would have to wait.

'The latter,' he said shortly.

'Thursday?'

'Yes.'

'Right. So long.'

'Good-bye, and thank you.' They never wasted
time on trivialities. A pause, a half-tone was signal
enough on the telephone with Miss Price all ears in
the kitchen. It was a technique which he had perfected
over the years on all matters public and private since
he had been able to enjoy the dubious luxury of a housekeeper. He put down the receiver and went into the
kitchen to fetch his coffee. Miss Price looked round
with that 'who-was-it' expression in her beady eyes.
Poor avid spinster, she would never learn how inflexible
was the mask Rome fastened on the features of its

40

anointed sons.

Since Father Moran knew he would not escape without some small talk, he went into a long harangue about the weather, a favourite subject when he wanted to keep off more intimate matters. They both agreed that the rain was terrible, and that the flood would drive the rats swarming over the town. The priest disengaged himself before Miss Price could develop this agreeable topic, drank his coffee quickly and went back to his study to write a few letters in his clear formal hand to relatives in England of a few infirm and illiterate parishoners. This was a task which he fulfilled every week; picking up the news on his sick calls and setting it down carefully and meticulously, well aware that every word would be weighted and spelled out in drab lodgings in Liverpool, Nottingham and Camden Town.

The chore completed he stood up, stretched his shoulders, lit a cigarette and walked over to the window. The spire of the church was visible through the withering leaves of the chestnut tree inside his garden gate. On a clear day the roofs and spires of the town could be seen pricking the sky across four miles of flat midland country; but to-day the veils of rain were down. He could just make out the giant turbines of the state-owned factory which had saved his small half-parish from withering away like so many others in rural Ireland. The factory processed compressed peat and employed many of the farmers' sons in the district, thus saving him and his parish priest Father Melody from penury. He looked at the gleaming flat-topped towers with affection. In the grey light they looked like Aztec temples rearing up against a humid jungle sky; curiously incongruous and altogether fascinating in that great sodden plain.

Then as he turned away and put out his cigarette he thought idly of Marie in the detached fashion which was second nature to him, especially in his own house, where he sometimes felt even his thoughts were analysed by the watchful eyes that surrounded him. He had grown used to this and no longer resented it, as he had so fiercely in his youth when he had nothing to conceal.

What was she up to now, he wondered, thinking of Marie's message? Some silly woman's business, no doubt. An intensely masculine man, imbued from his earliest years with a truly Roman suspicion of femininity, Tom Moran did not hold the opposite sex in high esteem. Women in his opinion were fit only for bed and breeding; and Marie having a smattering of education was more tiresome than most on any other level. Instinctively, all of them, literate or not, turned everything to their own advantage with their shameless self-pity, their sentimental glorification of their own emotions. Pretty, elemental creatures, how sly they were, how clever at getting their own way, how completely lacking in any sort of scruples. Poor Marie, he thought as his mind wandered idly along this pleasant but cloying terrain so full of slimy hollows and treacherous quicksands.

Presently he shook his massive head, glanced at his watch and checked it with the clock on the mantelpiece. There was still time before lunch to pay a call on old Mrs. Kelly in the cottage by the church.

He hurried into the hall, put on his waterproof, took up his umbrella and strode out briskly into the rain, humming softly to himself.

CHAPTER SEVEN

Marie looked up at the crescent moon shining in the
blue-green sky; and throwing a spoor of light across
the swollen lake. A ghostly mist rose from the shore
and coiled about the twining branches over her head.
Out in the bay the little folly on an islet - a Victorian-
Gothic tower - glimmered in the cold filmy moonlight;
a backdrop for fairies, ballet-dancers and haunted
lovers. At the point of the headland which swept out
in an arc into the great lake with its flat undulating
shores, she thought she saw a glimmer behind a window
in one of the chalets. She clutched the collar of her
coat about her neck and hurried on peering down at
the winding track to avoid the black blobs of cow-dung
which littered it.

She was the only wandering soul about. The chink
of light behind the window grew harder and more
incisive as she drew nearer. He was there. But just
before she came to the door the streak went out and
she stopped and gasped, until the door opened and she
saw him standing there in the moonlight; tall,
mysterious, almost frightening in his passive silence.

'Marie?'

'Yes.'

'Come in.'

She hurried past him into the darkness; and
immediately his arms were about her, his lips
pressed against her ear; his body moulding itself
against hers. Even through his thick lamb-lined coat
she could feel his excitement.

'Oh, Brian.'

'Don't move.'

'I'm not late, am I?'

'Yes. No, no. Are you cold?'

'No.' She shivered as she felt his hands moving

down her back and his thighs pressed against hers, forcing her back into the middle of the room.

'It's cold in here. But I have been able to get the heaters working. The pump is out of order or something. There isn't any water. But the light is working. I switched it off when I heard you coming. '

'Put it on again. '

'No. '

'I love you. '

'Oh, Christ. ' His voice was so tense it sounded sulky. She was excited but a little frightened by the passion in his body. Woman-like she contrived to smell his breath before she allowed him to kiss her. No, he had not been drinking. She relaxed and opened her mouth; and the warm coiling tongue invaded her being. She shivered with pleasure; but her mind was alert. It was he who drew back first; trembling and confused by his own recklessness.

'What is it?' she whispered reaching out in the darkness and touching his arm.

'I'm sorry, ' he mumbled. 'I'm not very good at this. I mean I can't play it cool. All this waiting, a whole week in hotels. I'm all strung up. '

She smiled to herself and licked her lips, relishing the taste of his mouth on hers. It was a delicious sensation, a prelude to what might develop into an ardent and, handled properly, deeply satisfying act of love. But already she had sensed in him the dangerous quality of romantic sensuality; and this she knew would have to be tamed, even if to keep him she had to go along with it until it was too late for him to draw back in some adolescent sulk, and accuse her of all the things he precisely wanted in his own imagination.

'Yes, I know, ' she said gently, stroking his arm tenderly. 'But it's only the beginning, Brian. We'll think of something. '

He pulled away from her roughly, breathing hoarsely through his mouth.

'How can we, with me travelling about all week?'

She sighed, and stepped back, holding herself alert and ready. In his present state she knew that he would soon be coming seeking blindly the warmth and reassurance always demanded by a guilty conscience.

'You won't always be travelling about, I hope.'

'The Wandering Jew.' His tone was suddenly but not surprisingly facetious. Even in the darkness which surrounded them he felt naked: lost and at the mercy of his own longings, heightened by a week of solitude. But already he felt his ardour turning into something deeper, steadier and more protective.

Suddenly he blinked and held his hands up before his eyes. Marie, reaching out in the darkness had found a switch and pressed it. Light flooded the small living-room, with its rope flooring, utility chairs and tables, electric storage heater, and gaudy red bawneen curtains. He made immediately for the window and pulled the curtains together with a swift furtive twitch.

He looked at her with a slight frown; and felt helpless. How calm, beautiful and remotely desirable she was! How could he tell this golden girl of that alter ego which existed in his mind; yielding, abandoned, avid for all the total intimacies of pleasure with which he had invested her? He felt himself reddening; and half-longed for a rebuke.

'I like Jews,' she said with a smile, looking about the place with a casual but counting eye. These chalets she knew were let at fifty pounds a month in the season; and she knew a good thing when she saw it. She wondered what rent the man from Galway was paying to keep it all the year round.

'Oh.' He bit his lip and looked at her out of the corner of his eye; anxious now and frankly curious. 'Have you known any of them well?'

'A few.' She shrugged and smiled teasingly.

'Great lovers, I hear,' he went on sullenly, feeling that he was making a fool of himself.

'I've only known them in business,' she laughed, reading his thoughts exactly. 'They're a lot more reliable and honest than we are.'

'That wouldn't be hard,' he said automatically. He was not thinking clearly. Talk was coming for the sake of a desperate communication.

'Speak for yourself,' she said tartly. She threw back her head and sniffed. The room had a curious

smell that reminded her of damp washing being
ironed. Then she remembered that it had been
unoccupied since the autumn and must have been
wringing damp until he turned up the heaters full blast.
She was reminded incongruously of the old-fashioned
laundry which the nuns used to run in the town: hot
hand-irons, big steam washing vats, and groaning
rollers through which shirts disappeared like card-
board men: a place of wonder as a child. Well, she
had come a long way from that; and yet across the
years the scrubbed face of the friendly old nun who
managed the place rose up and filled her mind. She
closed her eyes and looked away. Immediately he was
at her side, staring down at her with troubled eyes.

'It's not much, but it's the best I can do, Marie.'

Caution slipped, and passivity invaded her as she
looked up at the tense handsome face. Somehow she
had to make this man her own. She longed for a
complete and mindless equality of pleasure; but knew
that her power over him lay in her being a 'good' girl
who would only give herself out of love. How tiresome
all those conventions were; and yet she knew most of
them had been invented by women for their own
protection. But she could not resist the temptation of
putting her hands on his shoulder and drawing down
his mouth on hers again.

And now something stirred in both of them; something lazy, indolent and insidious, from far-back in
their blood. As they kissed they came to a kind of
rhythmic understanding; physically close with the
knowledge that each represented an ideal for the other.

He was the first to break away, heavy-eyed and
sullen. He looked at the door which led to one of the
bed-rooms and tugged her gently by the hand. Marie
allowed herself to be led across the lighted space; and
paused only when they had crossed the darkened
threshold. The laundry smell was even stronger here;
and now she knew that she would remember it all her
life. Boiling shirts, an old nun's face, and a strong
vibrant body, rigid with clumsy passion.

'It's terrible in here,' he whispered, keeping his
hand on her breast to give him courage. When he

46

touched her he no longer wanted to think, either of himself or of her; but only of both of them.

'There are no sheets, only blankets. Oh, Marie.'

She caught her breath and clutched the trembling hand at her breast.

'Brian, there's something I ought to tell you.' She was not entirely in control of her voice, and she sounded too loud and assertive. But he hardly heard her.

'Not now.' He fumbled with the collar of her coat; but she caught his fingers in a surprisingly firm grip and held them away.

'What is it?'

'I don't know how much you know, but you're not the first,' she blurted out in the same hard, aggressive voice.

'Oh.' She heard him sucking in his breath, and drawing away felt the edge of the bed against the backs of her knees. She was surprised to discover that her legs were trembling; and she would not forget that either in the future.

'How many?'

'Only one. I was eighteen. It was in Dublin. I didn't know anything.' She spoke rapidly like a woman in confession hurrying over her sins. And so far as it went it was the truth. Karl, handsome, promiscuous, charming, with a beautiful wife and four children. Marie had been a little in love with him; until she discovered that he liked only virgins, of which Dublin surprisingly enough, provided an unending procession. But it was he who had delivered her to Brian.

Now she felt his arms tightening about her and his mouth close to her ear.

'I could kill him, I could kill him, I'd kill anybody who touched you.' It was like an incantatory recitation of some primitive religion as he repeated his words over and over again. It frightened and excited her; but she had not yet yielded up her right to choose. Over his shoulders as she stood mute and passive while he undressed her with trembling hands she could see out through an opening in the curtains. The moon floated pale and serene over the black lake and the grey-green tower on the island; under that shimmering radiance everything was cold, still and virginal.

Did he mean it, she thought as she lay back on the bed and arched her body to receive his weight? No, no he's only using it as an excuse to cover his haste and urgency. She felt his lips on her breast and sobbed with pleasure; she had no wish now to restrain him. But even when she knew that it was too late, some residue of feminine caution in the depths of her being, forced her to cry out 'no, no' when the questing mouth moved down from her breasts and her secret lips were parted by his. She wanted this flowering magic that he was working on her and yet with her fading consciousness she knew that it was he who must be made to appear the aggressor, she the victim. No, no. And then the waters of pleasure washed over her like a torrid wave from some tawny shore, and she sank prayerless into the depths.

CHAPTER EIGHT

Agnes Fogarty looked at the bed-side clock under the
pink shaded lamp on her night-table. Half-eleven.
She looked at the book resting against her drawn-up
knees, and wished she could concentrate on Agatha
Christie her favourite reading, next to the Catholic
Truth Society pamphlets which she kept stacked on top
of the chest of drawers beside the statue of St. Martin,
the lovely black martyr. She bent forward, listening
intently for a few moments, while the book fell back
against her flat chest.

She leaned back against her piled pillows and
clutched the cross and the miraculous medal pinned
to her nightdress. There was no mistaking the source
of the sighing groans in the next room. Carefully,
murmuring an aspiration - 'come, Holy Ghost, fill
the hearts of Thy faithful, and enkindle in them the
fire of Thy love' - she reached out and switched off
the bed-side lamp. Gradually as her eyes became
accustomed to the darkness she was able to make out
the thin sliver of light under the locked door that
connected with her husband's room. Although she had
put him to sleep with a tablet over an hour ago, it was
clear that he was awake again.

A curious expression passed over Mrs. Fogarty's
face, which if she had been looking into a glass she
would not even have permitted herself to contemplate.
It was a mixture of loathing and eagerness; and there
was no mistaking the triumphant gleam in her eyes.
It was however but a flicker; and immediately replaced
by her habitual mask of tense awareness. She patted
the net that enclosed her sparse curls, sighed,
murmured another aspiration - 'Angle of God, my
Guardian dear, to Whom His love commits me hear,
ever this day be at my side, to light and guard, to

rule and guide'. She reflected bitterly that this little prayer was once good for a hundred days' indulgence each time, but now all that was changed. What had happened, she wondered, to all the indulgences of seven years and seven quarantines, not to mention the innumerable plenary ones that she had gained in her time, especially during that period when she was having all the trouble with the sick man in the next room? Ah, well, she thought, as she got slowly and carefully out of bed and reached for her dressing-gown, God is good.

She padded silently across the room, pulled back the curtain on the front window and peeped out. The light was still on outside the door. Marie was not back yet. Not that she expected her home early on that particular night.

She opened her door softly and went out onto the landing. A hoarse breathless voice replied to her chaste knock. She opened Pat's door and put her head into the room.

'Are you all right?' she whispered.

He did not look it. He was sitting up in bed with a blue shawl thrown over his shoulders looking at her with an expression at once half-drugged and painfully wakeful. He was purple in the face; but she knew how suddenly he could grow pale. The room smelled strongly of medicine and sweaty feet. Pat's feet had always been overpowering even in his healthy days; and she often wondered how she had stuck him as long as she did, with his lewd mind and his constant demands.

'I woke up,' he said in a whining voice. 'I don't suppose I'll sleep much again to-night. I'll have to change the tablets, they're wearing off.'

'Would you like a little something?' she enquired in what she thought was a gentle voice, but which merely sounded conspiratorial. 'I'll go down and get it for you.'

'Oh, Aggie, I'm a terrible nuisance,' he sighed, shaking his head, but unable to conceal a little quiver of pleasurable anticipation at the sagging corners of his mouth.

'I'll get it for you.' She began to back out; but he held her with a loud whisper.

'Is Marie back yet?'

'The light is still on.'

For a moment they looked at each other with complete understanding; but the moment passed; as so many others had faded in their long uneasy relationship.

She closed the door and crept slowly down the stairs, noiseless as a cat, for she knew the exact position of every creaking board. Nelly slept on the other side of the stairs from the kitchen. She was a light sleeper, especially when anybody was out. The light outside the front door cast long uncertain shadows in the back hall which seemed to move, vaguely and sluggishly, like obscure objects, half-fish, half-weed, at the bottom of a pool. Agnes had never been afraid of the dark, not being burdened with a numinous imagination; but she was always perpetually afraid of being found out in something - she hardly knew what - night and day. She therefore glided along with something of the incorporeal lightness of the ghosts she did not believe in.

She wafted into the kitchen, found the switch and put on the light, closing the door noiselessly behind her. Then she set to work quickly, like an artistic and experienced thief. The glass of milk, the slices of rich fruit cake, the butter, the wing of chicken out of the fridge, the pile of brown bread.

Now, balancing the tray and putting off the light with the edge of her shoulder, she went back upstairs with the light firm carriage of long experience; no tinkle of delft, no rattle of spoons, not a foot misplaced as she reached the landing a little out of breath. She tapped on the door; and Pat opened it himself, standing aside with a greedy glance at the tray as she slid past him and put it down on the table in front of the window. It was a very small room, which in the old days had been used as a dressing-room. She pressed herself against the wall as her husband waddled over, drew up a chair, and sat down in front of the tray.

'I shouldn't do this,' he muttered as he took up the wing of chicken in his fingers and held it in front of his nose.

'No, you should not. But it might help you to sleep.
I won't be responsible for giving you another sleeping-
pill. You know well how dangerous they are. And
habit-forming too. I dread them.'

He bit into the chicken, his fat shoulders heaving
with gluttony; and she watched him for a moment with
unconcealed distaste. But it was nothing to the
loathing with which she looked at the chest-of-drawers
inside the door. There, not so many years ago, she
had discovered proof of his utter depravity. It was
her habit to inspect the bed-room during Nelly's day-
off to search for signs of careless dusting. She had
long been avidly curious about the top left-hand
drawer of the chest which for some time Pat had kept
locked. And then one day he had forgotten to lock it.
She closed her eyes and shivered with disgust as she
remembered that awful discovery: the pile of filthy
photographs of naked women in the most abandoned
and obscene poses; most of them alone but many of
them with male partners in positions which she did
not think were possible even for animals. She shuddered
again and opened her eyes wide to fix her gaze on the
oleograph of the Sacred Heart which hung on the wall
facing the bed. How could he gloat over such things
with such a countenance gazing down upon him. It was
madness, madness, pure insanity; and yet she knew
she would never get him committed on such a plea,
even if she could bring herself to reveal the shame of
it. Men were like that, the filthy creatures!

That moment of forgetfulness had indicated the
beginning of his illness; and also the proof of her
justification. If she had ever needed evidence of his
rotteness she had it then. Could any greater vindi-
cation of her decision to banish him from her bed have
been found? She closed her eyes again, shutting out
the Sacred Heart, as her memory recalled the first
terrible years of their marriage when, a frigid woman,
she had discovered with horror the insatiable appetite
of her husband. He was little better than an animal;
worse in fact since animals did not have souls, and
could not be held responsible for their filth. But that
a good Catholic, coming from a decent respectable

family, could have possessed such instincts was beyond her comprehension. There must be something depraved in him which she did not know about. That awful slobbering mouth, that hot sweaty self-indulgent body, the searing pain that he had caused her: it had been a nightmare.

She opened her eyes again and gazed at the oleograph fixedly as she banished these thoughts from her mind. She was conscious of her husband guzzling the food; and tried to think of him, under that benign gaze, with some element of pity. She could not. There were some things that flesh and blood could not stand. Her embittered mind wound back relentlessly in an inflexible coil, like a lost soul condemned to revisit forever the scene of its fall. Supposing Nelly knew? It was a thought which tortured her. Had she, when she was making his bed that morning, also inspected the unlocked drawer? If so she had given no sign; but Agnes knew how false, and hidden people of that class were. Oh, Sacred Heart of Jesus, have pity on all suffering souls!

She was wringing her thin cold hands, pressing the gold band of her wedding-ring into the flesh until she could stand the pain no longer. She thought of Marie; the spit and image of her father. What was she doing now? Agnes held her hand to her damp forehead. She was spared nothing. Suddenly she could not bear to stay in the room any longer: the closeness, the heavy smell, the sound of clamping jaws were too much for her.

'Go back to bed at once when you're finished,' she said as she moved to the door. Pat hardly heard her; he was too busy with the fruit cake on which he had plastered a thick layer of butter, compulsively catering to a sick body which cried out for some sort - any sort - of gratification. And besides Aggie never did stay very long on these mid-night visits. Afraid he'd make a pass at her perhaps. God, why had he not known more about women before he married; but the cake was good. He knew he'd suffer for it; but he no longer cared.

Outside on the landing Agnes paused and looked in the direction of Marie's room. She felt an impulse to go into it; but restrained herself. She had suffered enough. And in her heart she was afraid of her daughter; terrified also of the dark mystery which surrounded her; and of which it was not proper even to think. She crept back to her room; to her aspirations, to Agatha Christie, and to wait for the sound of Marie's return.

CHAPTER NINE

Miss Nelly Fall and Miss Margaret Price were
ensconced in their favourite meeting place, the stile
at the end of the cemetery in Father Moran's half-
parish. They were neighbours, born in the same town-
land within sound of the church bells; and here,
sheltered by a few yew trees, which the ladies called
palms, their parents and relatives lay cosily awaiting
the last trump.

'Very quiet here lately,' said Miss Price, looking
about her sadly.

'Terrible', sighed Nelly, shaking her head. And
indeed it had been a terrible month for funerals in the
half-parish - not one since the thirtieth of September,
and it was now the twentieth of October. Mission
Sunday.

'Ah, well,' said Miss Price, recalling the last
funeral fondly, 'it was a great day for the parish when
you had your funeral. Didn't he go awful quick, poor
Mickey Joe?'

On the last day of September Nelly had buried her
third cousin-in-law. Miss Price opened her capacious
shopping bag, took out the little trowel and fork which
she kept for her Sunday work, looked at them fondly,
and put them back again.

Nelly drew herself up and pressed her own shopping
bag against her stomach. She too had a trowel and
fork snug within; but while she was proud of her cousin's
demise, which had drawn a gratifying crowd, she
nursed a grievance about the procedure.

'That old bitch, Sarah Jane Murray, the so-called
nurse, and she not even a reputable handy-woman,
didn't send me word until he was half coffined. And
didn't I put the pennies on his brother's eyes, as well
as help his sister, God be good to her, to wash him

and lay him out proper? I told you about that before.
I never saw anything like the size of what he had, and
he a fusty old bachelor and all. If you ask me Sarah
Jane had her own reason for keeping Mickey Joe to
herself. '

'Don't talk to me about nurses and handy-women, '
shrilled Miss Price. 'If you ask me, they do have
hells bells with the corpses. ' Then she lowered her
voice and added piously: 'The Lord preserve us from
all harm, the dirty sluts. '

'Much good may it do her, ' said Nelly moodily,
her eyes ranging over the headstones. 'Mickey John
is crumbling now. '

'Cremation will come in too, ' said Miss Price, who
by reason of her position was an authority on Church
matters. 'Everything is changing. '

'It won't be the same, ' sighed Nelly sadly, 'burying
a handful of ashes. ' She looked glum for a few moments
and then brightened up. 'However I hear there's a
hellish blaze in them ovens. '

They fell silent, allowing their imaginations to
dwell on this revolutionary development. Ashes or no
ashes they'd still have to bury them somewhere, and
people would still have to go through the motions of
dying, always a delicious sight. Both of them, mind-
ful of the sights nurses and handy-women were
privileged to behold with male cadavers, wondered if
it was necessary to wash and stuff corpses destined
for the ovens; and looked affectionately out over the
old familiar headstones, among which a few old
women in black were picking their way, peering and
pecking at the crosses, like superannuated birds of
prey. A comforting sight.

'Well?' said the priest's housekeeper. Then she
took off one glove, blew into it hard and replaced it
quickly. It was as cold as hell in that graveyard.

'Well, you, ' retorted Nelly sharply, stretching
her bust and allowing her chin to melt into her neck.

'How are things at your end?' Miss Price's voice
lightened and took on a curve which anybody more
sensitive than her friend might have recognised as
insinuating. She took off her other glove and blew

into that also.

Nelly too felt her fingers cold even in her thick fur-lined gloves; but she had long ago laid it down that her friend had bad circulation, whereas her own was above reproach; and for this reason would go home stiff from the graveyard on one of those bleak autumn days, when an icy east wind cut across the plain, rather than admit it. And as for blowing into her gloves like a snotty school-girl, that in her opinion was not in keeping with the dignity of a priest's housekeeper.

'Bad,' she burst out suddenly, with a wild look at her companion. 'As bad as they can be. There's an awful reckoning in store for some that I could name.' She puffed out her lips and closed her eyes solemnly.

Miss Price's nose twitched, and she leaned forward eagerly and jabbed her friend's arm with her elbow; a go-ahead signal to which she was addicted.

'Mother of God, do you tell me that now?'

Nelly squared her shoulders and swelled her neck.

'What time did your man get back on Thursday night?' she asked slowly, flicking her blue nose with the tip of her gloved finger.

'The usual time.' Miss Price's voice was restrained; and her eyes glazed over with caution.

'After the usual business, I suppose. She changed him from Wednesday because she's meeting this other fellow on Wednesday nights now. Where exactly I haven't heard yet. But don't worry, I will. She didn't get back until nearly one o'clock, and if you were to see the sight of her next morning. Purring like a cat that got the cream. God Almighty, what a slut for your man to get himself mixed up with.'

'My man is not mixed up with her, or anybody else,' retorted Miss Price acidly. It was her habit to listen to every bit of gossip from Nelly, and then deny every-thing that related to her employer. It would have lowered her dignity and self-respect to be in the pay of an irregular curate. Privately she believed every word that Nelly told her; but officially she continued to deny it: thus clasping to her bosom the best of both worlds.

'All right, all right,' said Nelly patiently. She knew

the form and accepted it for what it was in an imperfect world; but that did not prevent her from deriving a peculiar delight in her friend's discomfiture. 'But we and the world and the crows know that he wouldn't be the first to be pulled down by a shameless hussy that doesn't care what man she gets, so long as he's a man.'

'A common commercial traveller,' said Miss Price coldly. 'I know the sort Marie is. After all she didn't pick it up off the ground with that father of hers. Will you ever forget those photographs of his that you found? All the same, you'd imagine she'd find something better to amuse herself with, and all the money they spent on her education, the eejits.'

'The same thing happened to the King of Italy's daughter,' replied Nelly grandly. 'They nearly had to lock her up, as I suppose you know.'

'Do you think she might marry him?'

'Could be.' Nelly pressed her cold hands against her knees and repressed a shiver. It was getting unbearably cold; and a granite cross was glittering as a ray of frosty sun played over it. Behind her a bitter wind blew up from the flooded meadows by the river: and it picked up a spiteful lick as it travelled across the sodden land. 'As it is this Langley is a fine front for all of them, the poor sap.'

'In that case my Father Tom's name would be cleared,' declared Miss Price triumphantly.

Nelly gave her a pitying look. Really Peg Price was too true to be good. Had she not told her in explicit detail of the whole affair, down to the statue of the Blessed Virgin she had found in Marie's bedroom covered with a handkerchief, when she came home early to turn down the beds only the week before last? Had she not, suspecting something from the very beginning, slipped out of the church one evening and returned to the house to watch? From the lawn she had seen the empty drawing-room; crept round to the back and let herself in on the cellar door, from which a stone stair led to a door opening onto the hall. There, reckless with excitement she had heard the priest come downstairs, followed in a few minutes by Marie; had overheard their conversation which in the early days of their connection had been somewhat freer than it afterwards became from necessity and increasing wariness. It was the biggest coup of Nelly's life; and one which she had shared to the full with the officially reluctant but privately eager Miss Price.

The priest's housekeeper interpreted the glance unfavourably and felt the need once more to defend her position.

'It's disgusting the way young sluts like that will go to any lengths to tempt an honest man. The holier they are the more it stirs up the devil in ones like Marie Fogarty that don't know the meaning of shame. That she may fester for flaunting herself in front of a decent, god-fearing man like Father Tom, that does nothing but work himself to the bone for the ungrateful people of this parish. May the Lord protect him.'

'Amen,' said Nelly tartly.

'Are you suggesting,' said Miss Price agressively, but with a prurient glint in her eye, 'that she's carrying on with both of them, the Lord between us and all harm?'

Nelly gave her another pitying look; and Miss Price could do nothing but look away and give a silent assent. That's the way the world was. Did they not know it all?

'If I were you I'd drop his reverence a hint,' said Nelly grimly, 'before he makes a complete ass of himself. I have nothing against him myself, and I know it's all her fault, one hundred per cent. If you can't work up enough courage to tell him to his face drop him a line in your left hand. If you don't, some-one else will.'

Although Miss Price had already thought of this course of action, she had no intention of revealing it to her friend. So she adroitly changed the conversation.

'How's the old couple?' she enquired politely.

'The same. He's guzzling himself to death, and she's helping him. Good nature, moryah. She's poisoning him into an early grave with big feeds in the middle of the night, and his blood pressure is half-way to heaven already. I can't say much for the dirty old clown myself, many's the time he tried to interfere with me, _me_, himself; but God knows any man would go queer married to an old faggot like Aggie Fogarty. I only stay with her so that the house will have one person in it that prays direct to God for mercy.'

Miss Price gave her a side-long look and repressed a smile. She stayed because Mrs. Fogarty paid the best wages in town.

But now it had become impossibly cold. They climbed off the stile slowly and straightened up on the gravel path. A black wind blew through the huddled trees. Already the sun was sinking towards the mauve rim of the horizon and the headstones were throwing their shadows east. Time to depart.

'Do what I tell you now,' snapped Nelly crossly, hoping for the hundredth time that she had not got piles on that stone. 'Because I have a feeling in my bones that there's going to be a blow-up. Remember that if your man loses his name your job is up the spout.' Suddenly she grew rigid, threw back her shoulders and stood like an avenging fury with a scowl on her face; as she thought of all the rottenness which flourished in the world of successful people. 'It's enough to make you - ' she broke off and sucked in her cheeks as she gathered spittle between her teeth.

And the two friends, the corporal works of mercy completed for that week, went off arm in arm through the leaning crosses in search of tea and buttered toast in Father Moran's kitchen, while the wind coiled like a whip over the holy ground behind them.

CHAPTER TEN

October is not one of those months that melt into their
successors like wax under the flame of a candle,
betraying little difference except a shorter light.
November in spite of Government decree is winter
unalloyed; and comes heralded by its own peculiar
rites. The half-pagan feast of Hallow-een, with its
strange ambiguous symbols from the earth-bound past,
is followed by the joyous commemoration of All Saints.
Any lingering roses of autumn are committed to the
black soil on the next day, the commemoration of all
the faithful departed, when the church militant is
encouraged to remember that it is a holy and whole-
some thought to pray for the dead, that they may be
loosed from their sins. The long night of winter is
officially proclaimed.

On the great plain it set in with a mild but lowering
breath. The mornings were dark and children and
workers found themselves setting out to schools and
factories in pitch black at nine; while the sky which
brooded over the place with such familiarity seemed
to have descended and settled upon the very roof-tops.
The horizon was vague and shadowy; the swollen river
purple as if arrayed in mourning for its shimmering
summer self. The moisture which rose from the mist-
haunted ground penetrated every door, window and
crack, writing odd patterns on weeping walls; an
indefinable but triumphant presence.

Father Moran came back from his three masses on
All Souls' Day in a thoughtful mood. He had his breakfast, and then went into his study to sit by the fire for
a while and warm himself after the cold damp church.
He thought of Marie and smiled a little sadly to himself. It was clear to him that this particular liaison
was dying a natural death; and he found himself heaving

a sigh of relief. It had gone on too long; and ought, of course, never to have progressed beyond that first fumbling encounter, when he had admittedly lost his head, and allowed things to get out of control. Whose fault was it, he wondered? His, he supposed, since he had been aware that the girl's interest in him was much more than mere friendship; insofar as a man and woman could ever really be friends, which he rather doubted.

He stirred in his chair and lit a cigarette, inhaling slowly and expelling smoke through his nose as he leaned his head against the leather chair. He thought of his ordination; and the first bright years after his solemn vows. It is easy enough for enthusiastic young men to keep their vows of celibacy: the whole force of their personality is directed towards an ideal and on the whole impossible goal. Even in Maynooth he had been taught that complete celibacy was not possible. He knew from experience what that involved; unconscious pleasure when the body obeys its nature in the mindlessness of sleep. That and the inevitable conscious acts of self-gratification; followed by nagging guilt and quick confession. But the shining ideals of youth are very easily eroded by the long day-to-day struggle with mediocrity. He had accepted in youth a system and a way of life for which few men are fitted by nature; it was not surprising that he had fallen from time to time; and he did not particularly regret these lapses. The Church was still for him the greatest of all mothers; the true Rock of Peter; the one Holy, Catholic and Apostolic refuge. His faith, like that of his fathers, was simple and strong; and he felt that he knew the answers to most of the world's problems, including his own.

If Tom Moran had been one of those priests who suffered from intellectual doubts he would very likely have gone through a greater agony than anything he was capable of feeling as a result of his sexual lapse. Sins of the intellect were anathema to him; while for the sins of the flesh he knew he possessed any time he wished to avail of it a saving remedy. Priests who leave the church to marry and face the world on their own are nearly always those who have evolved convenient arguments for their actions. Tom Moran had none. He knew he was in mortal sin; and so accustomed had he become to dealing with it in and out of confession, it no longer held any great attraction for him. It was he knew, drab, ordinary, and given the right occasion and a firm purpose of amendment, easily put to rights. He had allowed himself to drift, to fall greviously from grace in the full knowledge that an imperfect vessel can still dispense the sacraments; and at the back of his mind was the knowledge that the affair would never be more than an interlude; a weakness which he would one day have to overcome and atone for; but something which in the last analysis would not cut him off eternally from the hope of salvation.

He did not reason thus, as he sat smoking in his chair; but that was the way he felt. A guilty episode was drawing to a close just when both parties were beginning to tire of it. He could perhaps look back upon it with a certain nostalgia; something for which he would have to account to a higher judge; but something which he felt sure that judge would understand.

These not unpleasing reflections were interrupted by the ringing of the doorbell. He threw his cigarette into the fire and jumped to his feet to make for the hall. But half-way across the room he realised that Miss Price would get there before him; so he picked up his breviary, opened it and stood on the hearth-rug with his back to the fire. A full five minutes passed before she knocked - this meant that she had been interrogating the caller.

'A message for you from Fr. Melody,' she said, looking at him with a curious half-smiling expression, as if they shared a secret. But then Miss Price's expressions were all curious. He privately suspected the poor thing of being half-mad.

The parish priest did not have a telephone, which he regarded as an invention of the devil, and was in the habit of sending communications by hand when he could not get over himself.

Father Moran stepped back and tore the envelope open. He took out the piece of ruled paper torn out of a note-book which the old man used for writing-paper and read: I should be obliged if you would remember my sister Ellen in one of your masses. I have just received word that she died in New York yesterday.

Well, that was that. Father Moran looked at the note again. It was entirely characteristic of the parish priest that he should write such a clear graceful hand on such shoddy paper; just as his ugly face and shabby clothes gave no indication at first sight of the strength of character, the subtle mind and the calm irony of the man. Perhaps he was as holy as people said he was. Father Moran did not know. But he stood in considerable awe of him; without ever realising that Father Melody was precisely the sort of priest he would like to be himself.

He sat down and looked at the note again; and immediately felt a strange heaviness in his limbs; a langour which he had rarely experienced, and then only very recently. The parish priest's writing was a reminder of something peaceful and serene in life, which he had often glimpsed, but had never attained. And as he gazed at the beautiful letters, formed in resignation and sadness, he was attacked by one of those onslaughts of the body which often overwhelm those who have resolved to deny themselves a physical pleasure to which they have become accustomed. A quiver of lust ran through him like an electric shock, taking him almost completely by surprise. Scenes of the past year suddenly flooded his mind; and he yielded to them completely and without a struggle. Indeed it seemed hardly worth while to resist, now that the end was so near at hand. He lay back in his chair and pressed his back against the cushion; his eyes closed, his mouth half-open. At that moment, his mind and body heavy and sullen with desire, he attributed it to his decision to make his next meeting with Marie, his last. He did not realise that he was at the beginning of a long pilgrimage.

CHAPTER ELEVEN

'Oh, that one, a hot number. I'd know by looking at her, even if I hadn't heard it straight from the horse's mouth.'

'Who?'

'The boss's son, the younger one, Bud. Bud the stud.'

'Did I see his picture in the paper? Would it be at the races?'

'You did. He hunts too with the Meaths. If the girls didn't like it so much he'd iron out the Yankee accent too if he could. He wants to be an Irish gentleman.'

'Jasus.'

'Yeah, I know. But he's not a bad sort all the same. Gave me a few good numbers in Dublin, and when he heard the old man had put me on the midland circuit, he tipped me off about this jane too. Best blow job he ever had, he said.'

'Old Fogarty's daughter. Well, well. Pity I never met her.'

'I'll say. She'd like you. Tall, blond and brutal. That's the way she likes them, so Bud told me. He had a run-around with her in Dublin for a few months. Wouldn't have minded making it more permanent too, he says, but she dropped him like a hot potato. Next time he saw her was in a hotel lounge with some hefty-looking priest type. She didn't pretend to see him, so he put two and two together.'

'A priest. Jasus.'

'Don't tell me you believe those boys cut it off. Listen, I could tell you - '

'I know, I know, I know all about that. It's only that I have a brother a priest myself.'

'No offence meant.'

'Aw, cut it out. I mean - stop grinning - I didn't mean that. Go on about this Fogarty jane. I might be transferred down that way myself, and I like it for free. She's got lolly, hasn't she? Might settle a little present on a guy that tickled her fancy.'

'Wait a minute, wise guy. I'm down there myself two days a week. If there's any leavings, you can have them, but first, oh, boy - '

The recollection of the conversation at the next table during lunch at the Sligo hotel made Brian Langley at first feverish with anger and then cold with fear.

He finished his lunch hurriedly; paid his bill and checked out of the hotel. At four he had finished with his business in Sligo and was on the way back to the town where he had spent part of the previous night in the lake-side chalet with Marie. Their second meeting there, it had been altogether more successful than the first. The process of discovery was only beginning; and yet he felt that already there was little left for either of them to know about each other. Their first passionate encounter had left him dazed, singingly happy, and yet a little guilty. Had he forced her to do things which she would neither forgive nor forget? The first phone-call on the following night to the very hotel in Sligo which he had just left had not left him entirely happy. She seemed brusque, in a hurry, almost eager to get it over with. Careful, too, almost as if somebody was listening. Suspicion feeds upon suspicion, and as he drove through the lowering November landscape his imagination involved Marie in a dozen lurid betrayals. The mist was thick on the Curlew mountains and he had to crawl with dimmed headlamps through the haunted slopes, across which weird wraith-like figures floated and dissolved in the foggy darkness; a stark, disturbing place even in summer with its great prehistoric columns and memories of ancient battles. The long slope into Boyle, past the hotel by the bridge over the rushing waters, scene of many a merry evening among the friendliest people in Ireland. Out onto the plains, so wide and green and lush in the summer; now blank and silent and seemingly uninhabited; through Tulsk of the kings and the legends, and into Roscommon. He felt very much like having a drink but pushed on doggedly in the knowledge that he had only another twenty miles to go.

And all the time the loose bantering words that he had overheard kept coiling and uncoiling in his mind like maggots. How often had he engaged in just such a conversation himself; partly through boredom, partly because one had to be one of the boys, partly because alone and without a woman it could sometimes be exciting. But he had never enjoyed it; and now the memory of it made him want to vomit. Another half-hour and he would be there. He gripped the steering wheel; and was not surprised to feel salt tears prickling his eye-lids. It was a long time now since he had wept; but he was no stranger to uncontrolled emotion. The bitch, oh the false, cunning whore.

From the ridge over-looking the town the lights glimmered eerily through the mist; and he thought of the night they had sat in his car and watched them strung out against the sky, with the head-lamps moving up from under the horizon. And then, half out of fear and half out of hope, it occurred to him that there may have been nothing truthful behind the conversation he had overheard. Bud the stud, whoever he was, might very well be one of those compulsive talkers, essentially timid men, who like to give the impression that they have slept with every woman who smiles at them, especially if she is attractive. Brian knew from experience how inaccurate the prattle of commercial travellers usually was. It could have been nothing more than wishful thinking on everybody's part.

This made him feel a little better as he parked his car in the square and went into one of the pubs. It had taken him almost three hours to travel the seventy odd miles from Sligo: it was now almost seven. He would have time to have a drink before he went out to the house. This was something that could not be discussed over the telephone; and besides he had to see her in her own setting if he was to banish that awful conversation from his mind. He ordered a hot whisky with sugar and sat down in a corner away from the usual local bores.

Marie would explain, he thought, as he lit a cigarette and settled back against the slippery leather seat. But he had to make sure.

CHAPTER TWELVE

Father Moran took a long hot bath; dried himself carefully and dusted some talcum powder on his body.
With a towel wrapped round his flat stomach he looked at himself in the mirror with admiring care. Not bad for close on forty. He hummed to himself as he put on fresh underwear and a new shirt. His best suit was getting a little shiny; and he made a resolve to visit Clerys to order a new one if he had the money in hand after the Christmas collection. There were the instalments on the car, the rates and the usual cash present to his sister to take into account; but he was not in the mood to think of these things now. Somehow he'd manage a new suit; and the thought lightened his spirits still further.

He let himself out, shook his head at the heavy mist, and observed the curtain twitch in Miss Price's kitchen. The old bitch. Tomorrow he'd really be free of her prying eyes. There was nothing more vulnerable he knew than a man with a secret.

The fog was heavy by the river and he made the house just in time to see the Fogarty's off to Mass. They were as usual, making no comment on why he had changed his day from Wednesday to Thursday. That was Marie's business; and this new young man was after all a good front. No point in dwelling on that either. The old man was failing rapidly; he looked as if he might drop dead from apoplexy any minute. Father Moran had seen that drawn staring look too often on sick calls; like all priests he was a good diagnostician. What would happen to Marie when the inevitable happened?

She was waiting in the drawing-room, a book open on her lap, staring into the fire. She did not look up as he came in.

'A penny for them,' he said with a grin, boyish, frank, indicative of a certain slightly heavy charm; and all the more potent since he had never 'worked' on it.

'Would you like me to tell you what they were?' She looked up at him with a serious expression.

'I don't think so,' he said carefully, sitting down on the chair opposite her and covering his knees with his hands. He was surprised to find that they were trembling a little and decided against lighting a cigarette.

'All the same I intend to tell you.' She closed the book and leaned back, patting the nape of her neck with her fingers. He noticed that her eyes had an added sparkle; her skin an extra glow; and that her movements, which could be abrupt and jerky when she was in a difficult mood, were slow, graceful and lazily confident. 'I was wondering if you'd turn up this evening.' She had in fact been thinking of Brian; but feeling as she did, sleek, sated and triumphantly possessive, she felt she could afford to humour the sad-looking man opposite. Last week she had definitely felt that he was deliberately beginning to withdraw from her; now she was sure. And she was glad since it would have given her no pleasure at all to show him the door. Perhaps after all he was more sensitive than she had imagined.

'Well, you see I have,' he said with an effortful smile. He looked down at his hands for a few moments; then raised his head and looked beyond her shoulder to where beyond the window the neon lights of the town lit up the horizon with a soft rosy glow, like a false dawn. 'I haven't injured you in any way, have I?' he asked anxiously.

She chuckled; more than willing to give him the reassurances he needed. Besides it sounded very much like the beginning of a farewell speech; and she wanted to play that gracefully.

'Lord, no,' she said merrily. 'You'd disapprove if I told you how I had been injured. But that was long before I met you. No, I'm not going to develop a thing about priests, either for or against, if that's what you mean.' She was silent for a moment, and then added meaningly: 'And I've always been careful. No real need for the precautions you always took.'

He shifted uncomfortably in his chair, already feeling the sweat gathering in his arm-pits and on his upper lip. The central heating seemed to be hotter than ever to-night. The furniture must be as brittle as old bones, he thought aimlessly, unwilling to pursue the subject she had so casually broached.

'You don't really have any religious feeling, do you?' he said heavily, looking her straight in the eyes. She smiled back and rubbed her nose with her forefinger doubtfully.

'No, I don't think I have. I mean I don't suffer from a load of guilt, if that's what you mean.'

'Well, no it isn't,' he said earnestly, more convinced than ever that women like Marie did not know what remorse means, except where their own vanity was concerned; and clearly he had not abused that. A good thing she had never imagined herself to be in love with him. 'It's just that I wouldn't like you to think that everything in life is a bit of a humbug. It's easy sometimes to jump to that conclusion.' He felt a fool preaching like this; but there was something which he wanted to explain, and didn't quite know what it was.

'I have no reason to feel like that,' she said lightly, standing up and leaning her elbow on the mantelpiece. 'Expecially now.'

'This other man?' he enquired softly, as if he were proceeding with a delicate confession and a difficult penitent. Not that he had many of them. All the same he rather fancied himself as a confessor; firm but understanding. Nobody lives up to the rules all the time; but that was no reason for changing them.

'Yes,' she murmured, staring happily at her reflection, the slim graceful line of her body seeming to trail away from her supporting arms. He felt the first stirrings of desire.

'I'm glad,' he responded, anxious to assure her that he was not jealous.

'I rather thought you would be.' She smiled at him in the mirror, and slowly turned round, holding out her

hands on either side palms turned back to the fire; a
curiously elderly gesture, completely at odds with
her glowing youthfulness. She was well aware of his
glance; and felt instinctively that he was not thinking
of Brian just then; but of himself and her.

'I suppose you're wondering how it all happened,
between us I mean,' she said inclining her head gracefully towards him.

He looked at her with a slightly frightened expression
before rubbing his forehead wearily with his fingers.

'I'm sorry,' he mumbled.

'You don't have to be. Nobody got hurt. You
haven't turned me into a sex maniac or anything. The
real question is: what damage have I done to you?'

He was not expecting this and snatched his hand
away from his brow as if he had heard a sudden noise.

'What?' he asked dazedly, wishing to God he could
beat down the tide of lust that was rising in him; and
yet allowing himself to be carried along by it.

'It was one of those muddled things. Of course I
knew you were interested for a long time. After all
there's nothing unusual in that. It would really be
serious if you weren't - I mean not interested in
women generally, not just me. But I was bored and
lonely, and I encouraged you. Oh, there are a hundred
ways a woman can do that, and I'm not going to tell
you how. And that first night, do you remember?

'Yes,' he said uncomfortably, 'I remember.' He
had deliberately suppressed all thought of that first
fumbling, confused encounter; but now it came flooding
back so vividly that he had a sense of time contracting
and tightening inside his head like a steel band.

'You wouldn't have gone on if I hadn't encouraged
you,' she said meaning to be helpful, and glad that
she could be truthful at the same time; an unusual
conjugation. 'We were both lonely, but make no
mistake about it, I wanted it to happen.'

'You don't think - ' he began awkwardly.

'No, of course you wouldn't have seduced me if I
hadn't wanted it. You're not that sort of man at all.'
She smiled down at him and he looked up gaping. She
had never been more lovely, never kinder, never

more understanding. He was fortunately not subtle
enough to attribute it to the passionate love-making of
another man. All he knew was that he was very much
moved.

'The big mistake of course was in letting it slide.
We should have called it a day, left it at that and
forgotten it.'

It was like a cold shower after a hot run; and he
blinked with the shock of it. Her voice and manner so
cool and collected that she might have been a marriage
counsellor.

'It's easy to talk now,' he said in a voice that
sounded a lot angrier than he felt. Unconsciously he
had fallen back on his professional manner. This was
the way women had to be handled; especially one as
frankly disturbing as Marie Fogarty. What a fool he
had been; and happy to be so. What did this magical
feminine lure consist of? No wonder it had been dis-
trusted in all ages by men anxious to save their souls.
That was how he thought; but his feelings were very
different.

'Yes, it is,' she said softly. 'But I have no regrets.
I suppose you will have in time, but please don't think
that you have ever harmed me. I shall always be
grateful to you. You see I was so miserable.' She
said this simply and without a shade of self-conscious-
ness; so that he was again reduced to staring at her
with a sort of child-like wonder that such balm could
be applied with so diffident and generous an air.

She looked at him and shook her head. Then with
a sudden brisk graceful movement she was standing
over him, bending down and kissing the top of his
head. She did not seem surprised when his arms went
about her hips and he buried his head in her waist.

Marie felt a warm glow of tenderness as she held
him. There had been no great tension between them;
nothing hurtful or really ugly, as she remembered it.
She felt all a woman's compassion for the baffled and
childish male; and something also of the pity which
well-off people sometimes feel for those who have to
count every penny. She had noticed his brave turn-
out; but she also knew that his suit was well worn in

73

spite of its pressing and cleaning, and that his shirts
were often frayed. She could smell the heavy
brilliantine in his hair; and the talc with which he so
ingenuously powdered himself. He was not a bad sort,
she thought, with something like real affection.

'Come,' she whispered softly, putting her hands on
his shoulders, which she was moved to discover were
trembling.

But for a few moments he clung to her; overcome
by the only real temptation he had suffered since he
met her. It was he knew the moment of farewell to
many things: to youth, and physical love, and the
exultant content of the body which only a submissive
woman can bring to a man of his type. He clung to her
like a little boy about to be sent away from home. The
future was dark and almost certainly lonely; and he
knew in his bones that he would never have another
affair like this.

But she gently disengaged herself, took his hands
in hers and raised him to his feet. The over-heated,
over-furnished room was a blur of blue and gold; and
he was conscious only of the throbbing nerve at the
base of her throat; and the sharp fresh scent which
she wore.

'Come,' she said again with a smile. 'We haven't
much time.'

She walked quickly from the room; and dazedly he
followed her.

CHAPTER THIRTEEN

Marie opened the door and gasped with fright when she saw who the mysterious visitor was. At once her hand went to her throat, the other to her hair. Thank God it was not mussed up.

'Brian, what are you doing here?' Her voice broke and she stared at his white set face with wide glassy eyes. Her only thought now was to get him out of the house. If she could, Father Moran would cope with her parents. But she was at a disadvantage; she had kept him waiting for at least five minutes.

'You don't seem very pleased to see me,' he said, narrowing his eyes and looking her up and down.

'It's just that it's such a surprise,' she said, playing for time. 'Is anything wrong?' Feebly she clutched at this straw. Perhaps he had lost his job or something.

'That's what I'd like to ask you,' he said grimly, stepping into the hall and stuffing his gloves into the pocket of his suede jacket. She could smell the whiskey on his breath; but she knew he was not drunk. It was something much worse; and she cursed the weakness that had led her to indulge a grown-up lonely boy just once too often.

'Where have you been, I thought you'd never open the door?'

'I went down in the cellar,' she burst out wildly. 'I was turning up the heater, it's so cold.'

His nostrils quivered as he looked about the stuffy hall.

'The cellar,' he said harshly, snorting through his nose. 'The house is roasting already.'

'Yes, the cellar,' she stammered. 'And it isn't roasting. Daddy feels the cold - '

'And Daddy is out.' Daddy was certainly out; and

the cellar had not been a very good excuse.

'Whose car is that outside?' he demanded, watching her carefully with darkened eyes. She felt that he was undressing her and shifted awkwardly from one foot to another.

'Somebody who called,' she faltered, feeling her bones turning soft. If only she had had time to think, to make up a real excuse; but this interrogation under his angry sullen eyes was terrible. He had never appeared so attractive with his set lips and clenched jaw. If she wanted proof of his involvement she had it now and it destroyed her.

'Where are they?' He raised his voice and looked into the hall. 'There was no one in the front room. I looked before I rang. What are you up to Marie? You'd better tell me or there'll be real trouble, I promise you that.'

'There's no one here,' she began shrilly; but he cut in, brushing her explanation aside as if he already had proof of her weakness.

'Not even the Reverend Thomas Moran,' he spat out at her.

'How did you know that?' she gasped, stepping back and looking over his shoulder into the night. If only her parents would come back. But no, what would she do with the man upstairs? She was trapped.

'I looked in the car when I saw the room empty and found his licence, his driving licence. I suppose he has one from Maynooth, too, a special dispensation.' The sarcasm was flat-footed; but he was now very angry.

Suddenly she was angry too. How dare he come snooping round the house like that, and treat her like a criminal!

'You missed your vocation,' she spat back at him. 'You should have been a policeman.'

'Are you sure you haven't missed yours too?' he said hoarsely. She raised her hand, but he grasped her wrist with a quick violent gesture. She gasped with pain; and did not attempt to control the tears that sprang to her eyes.

'Take your hands off me.' She did not know that her

voice was pleading; she could think of nothing but the
pain in her arm, and for a wild moment thought that
he was going to beat her on the head. With her free
hand she covered the side of her face and felt the tears
on her cheeks. Now cold fury came to her rescue, and
with it some degree of artifice.

'Take me out of here, Brian,' she whispered.
'Please. I can't tell you here, not like this with
Mummy and Daddy due back any minute. It's nothing,
I promise you.'

For a moment he wavered; and she felt a quick
flush of hope. But even as he released her he narrowed
his eyes and peered into the back hall and his face
hardened again. Oh God, she prayed, make him blind,
deaf and dumb, now this minute.

'Where is he?' he said in a cold level voice, a great
deal more frightening than his blustering tone.

'Brian, please - '

'He's in the house, isn't he?'

She could think of nothing that would explain the car
outside, and remained silent, staring at him with
bright trusting eyes; the frank expression of a woman
who has decided not to defend herself.

'So it's true what I heard about you,' he said slowly,
staring back at her with a look of contempt. If he had
not taken his pleasure of her with such complete
abondonment he could not have achieved so completely
withering an expression. He was consumed with self-
loathing as well as wounded pride.

'So you listen to gossip,' she fired back at him,
hitting lower than she knew.

'It seems it's true.'

'How can you be sure since you won't let me talk?'

'All right, talk.'

'Not here. I'm going out with you. You're not in
your right mind.' She made as if to leave the hall, but
he grasped her arm again. This time more roughly
than the last. She gave a little scream; but made no
effort to disentangle herself. She knew from the
expression on his face that passivity was safer.

'You're very anxious to get me out of the house.
Where is he? I'm not going until you tell me, and if

you don't I'll search the place myself.'

'All right,' she said wearily, not altogether aware that she was saying exactly the right thing. She was playing it from instinct now; a woman's strongest line of defence. He hesitated for a moment too long, looking past her into the dim hall, and she was quick to seize the advantage. 'Go on,' she murmured spitefully, 'use your warrant.'

There was nothing left for him to do except carry out his threat or withdraw. When he realised his mistake his anger grew vicious; and he tightened his grip on her arm, unaware of his strength. She whimpered and cried out; and turned her head away from him as if she were warding off a blow. And then out of the corner of her eye she saw something move in the shadows at the bottom of the stairs, and stiffened with terror. Brian stared at her vacantly as if she were a stranger.

'Bud too,' he muttered as his anger drained away in confusion; and fear again invaded his body like the first shivering onslaught of a fever. 'Do you still have him too?'

'Oh, God, Brian, stop it and go. Please.'

The confusion grew as he too became aware, without actually seeing it, of the presence of a third party. He was like a man who smells a fear greater than his own and is blinded by it. In hot blood he would never have struck her, but now almost without knowing what he was doing he raised his hand and drew back.

'That's enough.' The voice was cold, hard and crackling, as the priest moved quickly out of the shadows and into the yellow light of the hall. His face was pale and stern: a professional mask all the more intimidating since it covered a very real menace. Father Moran was a strong man in good condition; and his forebears had not been noted for their willingness to turn the other cheek. 'There is no occasion ever to do that. Pick someone your own size, and sex.' Brian's anger flared again but it was a last licking flame in a fire that was already damped down with conflicting emotion: shame, heart-sickness, and baffled guilt. He turned to face the other man with a slightly over-done swagger of defiance: the gesture of a man already defeated. This black-clad figure, with the clenched fist and the tensed shoulders might have been steeped in all the vices of Sodom and Gomorrah; but he was still a priest, and atavistic attitudes of superstitious awe do not wither easily in the hidden depths of the soul. The man confronting him was a rival and certainly his own size; but he represented in his cloth a terrible antique power, mute and mysterious; the long, lingering shadow of Rome.

'So you are Father Moran,' he said with an attempt at scorn which deceived himself; but did not entirely succeed with either Marie or her priest lover. They knew they had won a battle, even if in the long term they had lost a war.

'Yes,' the answer was curt. 'I think you'd better leave now.'

'We'll leave together,' snapped Brian quickly. 'There are a few things I'd like to ask you.'

'As you wish,' said the priest calmly, turning to the stand where he had hung his hat and coat.

'No,' burst out Marie, holding out her hands appealingly, and looking at Brian with wide moist eyes. 'Stay a few minutes, Brian. I want to talk to you. The is all so ridiculous - '

'Is it? It looks pretty obvious to me.'

'Oh, for God's sake, Brian, we can discuss this calmly if only you'll give me time.'

'I'm sure you could discuss it like that, after all you're more used to this sort of thing than I am.'

'I wouldn't altogether say that,' she retorted, stung by his words. Something in her eyes seemed to reflect exactly his own thoughts: the dark, passionate fantasies which he had translated into reality in the chalet by the lake, he cursed the age-old power of women to turn their own pleasure into a potent weapon of guilt. How much of all that had she really wanted? How much had she risked to please him? Or was she simply a whore? Slowly but surely he felt the tide beginning to flow against him.

'I wouldn't expect you to,' he said lamely.

'Well, you'd better make up your mind quickly,'

said Father Moran, stepping forward and holding up his hand. 'I think I hear the car.'

They all turned towards the window which looked out on the avenue. Already the head-lights were sweeping the lawn as the car glided slowly round the corner of the avenue. The gravel crunched under it like sea-pebble in a sucking tide. Then Marie gasped; and the priest took command again.

'There is no need to draw the old people into whatever quarrel you imagine you have,' he said quietly to Brian, who looked pale and panic-stricken; suddenly rendered lost and vulnerable in a situation which was no longer of his own making.

'All right, I'll go but you'll hear from me again,' said Brian moving to the half-open door, and then turning, his mouth twisted with impotent bitterness. 'Fuck you,' he spat out in a low hoarse voice before running down the steps and hurrying past the Fogarty's car. They heard his footsteps quickening until he had broken into a run as he made for the gate outside which he had parked his own car.

Father Moran had watched the rout of his antagonist with hostile eyes which did not change their expression as he looked coldly at Marie. He did not feel any compassion for anybody involved in this sordid episode, including himself. Marie rubbing her throbbing arm, and desperately attempting to control herself experienced a moment of pure, passionless hatred for all men. In the last resort these two would, she knew, settle their own differences in their own way. Men never really fight over women; but only in defence of their own vanity and self-interest.

'He was a stranger,' said the priest quickly, giving his orders calmly and decisively as if he were the captain of a sinking ship and she one of the passengers. 'Unless I'm mistaken your mother doesn't know him to see, and your father - ' he shrugged slightly and turned to the door to meet the two old people who had hesitated at the foot of the steps, staring down the avenue at the retreating figure. There was nothing for Marie but to take his instructions: he was right.

'Who on earth was that?' enquired Mrs. Fogarty

coming in the door and looking from her daughter to
to the priest with frightened eyes. Her instinct had
told her at once who the mysterious stranger was; but
she had never actually met him.

'Some stranger,' replied Marie in a dull voice.
'Come to the wrong house.'

She saw her mother relaxing; and knew that the
moment was saved. But for what? Her father had met
Brian in the office and must have recognised him. She
looked questioningly at him and was shocked at the
effect the encounter had had on him. His face was
livid; and his hand shook so violently that his hat slipped
out of his grasp as he took it from his head, and fell on
to the carpet at his feet. Marie bent down with a swift
movement and picked it up.

'Father Moran was just going,' she explained as she
hung the hat on the stand. 'I think the man was looking
for Craigs opposite. Probably one of those dealers,
you know how they're always buying and selling furniture, the Craigs, I mean.' Something in her father's
dough-like face caused her to project her interest to
him.

'Daddy,' she said softly, 'you look as if you've
caught a chill. Will I make you a glass of punch before
you go to bed?'

It was a perfect get-away for the stricken man; and
he nodded vaguely, making a hideous attempt to smile.
He looked like a bloated corpse.

'He's not supposed to,' put in his wife swiftly with
a shrewd glance at her daughter. 'But he has a bad
cold all right. I've been telling him about it all day.
Yes, dear, you make the punch, but be sparing with
the whiskey.'

'Well, I think I'd better be off,' said Father Moran
shortly. For all he knew the idiotic bastard was
waiting for him outside the gate; but it was something
which would have to be handled swiftly and surely.
Better perhaps to see him now than let him sleep on it.
And he couldn't stay here all evening, hiding behind
these people. Not that I have not been doing it for some
time, he thought grimly.

'Oh, must you, Father?' said Mrs. Fogarty brightly,

taking off her grey suede gloves, and placing them together carefully finger to finger in the attitude of prayer to which they were long accustomed.

'I'm afraid so. I'm late already. Good night, now, and take care of yourself, Pat.'

And he was gone with that swift bird-like movement of which priests, even of heavy build, seem to have the sole secret. The family were left alone; but Mrs. Fogarty did not let the occasion get her down. This was no time, her instinct told her, to show the white flag. Attack was now the best means of defence.

'Marie,' she said gently, as she took off her expensive flat hat, 'a little bird told me that you've been seen out at that Lake Hotel. Now, you know I never listen to gossip, but you must know the name that place has for drinking. I'm just telling you now, mind. I know you hardly drink at all, but you know the way people talk. Two cocktails at the wrong time and they have you an alcoholic. It's a great wonder the priests don't preach more about that.'

CHAPTER FOURTEEN

The following Sunday Father Moran received a visit
from his oldest clerical friend, after an appointment
made on the telephone on Friday. It was not a visit to
which he attached any particular significance; and he
did not think much about it on the two days that followed.
On Saturday he was busy with confessions; and on
Sunday he had to say two masses because his parish
priest was in bed with one of his periodic attacks of
imagination. He delivered two perfunctory sermons on
the gospel of the day, the twenty-third Sunday after
Pentecost. There was little that one could say about
that without falling into clichés and Father Moran, his
mind tired and fretful, made no attempt to avoid them.
The healing of the woman with the issue of blood; and
the bringing back to life of the ruler's daughter. Had
she really been dead? Theological subtlety of that
kind did not interest him any more than it did his con-
gregations. He told them to have faith; and left it at
that. They would have been very much surprised if he
had said anything else. Father Melody occasionally
confused and annoyed them with his sharp lectures on
dishonesty and hypocrisy; but the curate was a solid
man: they knew exactly where they stood with him.

When he got home Miss Price was in a flutter, as
she always was when the bishop's secretary came to
call. The meat was more than usually tough, and the
pudding tasted of cement; for the housekeeper's mind
was preoccupied with the lavish high tea which she
intended to lay before the guest. Father William
Conway was a favourite of hers, a real gentleman as
she was in the habit of saying loudly and often to annoy
her employer. A likely candidate for the bishop's
place too; but this thrilling thought she kept to herself.
His visit meant that she would have to cut short her

gossip in the graveyard with Nelly; but who cared?
Her friend did not entertain a prospective bishop, and
was never likely to do so. It was in little matters of
this kind that she Margaret Price was set apart and
above from her more menial friend.

After his lunch Father Moran went to his room to
put on his good soutane and his best pair of shoes to
welcome his old class-mate. Bill usually came on
Sunday so that they could have at least an hour to themselves while Miss Price was performing her weekly
stint among the headstones. And promptly at four
o'clock he arrived.

Father Moran went to greet him at the door, standing
on the step while Bill extricated himself with typical
sinuosity from his typically humble little Volkswagen.
He was a tall, well-fleshed man who moved with light
but careful steps, carrying his slightly bloated body
as if he were aware of the burden of the flesh and
determined to make the most of it without false
modesty. His face was large, pale and blank, except
for the expression of professional benignity which had
become second nature to him; and which was all the
more effective since it was not entirely affected.
Bill could be benign, patient and kindly - when it
suited him. He could also be completely ruthless, as
his colleagues had good reason to know. There was
no clerical trick with which he was not acquainted; no
backstairs with which he was unfamiliar; and no
avenue of power closed to him by reason of his unswerving dedication to the status quo.

When he saw his friend waiting for him outside the
door he gave his quick flashing 'boyish' grin: which
took ten years off his age and had been known to wreck
havoc at meetings of the womens' sodality.

'Hallo, Tom,' he said extending a soft white hand,
and patting the curate's muscular arm with the other.

'Dead on time as usual, Bill.'

'How is Miss Price?' asked Bill as he got out of
his coat in the hall, hung it up and placed his gloves
and hat on the chair beside it. This was his way of
enquiring if the old busy-body was safely out of the
house. Should she be listening behind the kitchen door

she would merely have heard a polite enquiry.

'Over in the cemetery, as usual,' replied Father Moran, supplying the required information.

'Poor old thing.' Bill nodded his head sagely, but allowed a twinkle to pass over his usually opaque eye. 'She doesn't get much out of life, does she?'

'How is the old man?' Tom opened the door of his sittingroom-study and stood back politely to allow his guest to enter. Habits of deference die hard and Bill hesitated a moment before sailing into the room like a billowing yacht on smooth waters.

'Fine.' This was the secretary's way of saying that the old bishop was acting predictably, and leaving most of the day-to-day business in his own capable hands.

He sank back in one of the arm-chairs, puffed out his waxen cheeks and unbuttoned his jacket comfortably.

'Do you know Tom,' he said archly, 'I could do with a drop of brandy, so get out your key and unlock that cupboard.' As the other man fumbled in his pocket and opened the hidden cache Bill narrowed his baby-blue eyes and studied his profile closely. He doesn't know, he thought. That's just as well, since it probably means that he thinks no one else knows either. Always easier to fix these things if they think it can be done quietly. All the same, something has happened. He looks paler than usual; and those circles under his eyes are new. He passed his plump hand over his own eyes and when he took it away and held it out to accept the glass which Tom was holding out, his expression was mild, bland and affable as usual.

'Are you all right, Tom?' he enquired gently, raising his glass in a silent toast.

'Why?' said Tom, bluntly standing on the hearth-rug with his legs planted wide apart, his glass held against his chest, his body thrust back, looking down at his friend with a sudden aggressive stare. 'Do I look as if I had been hitting the bottle or something?'

'No, I know you don't do that.' Bill spoke in a voice which clearly implied that all the secrets of his world were by the nature of things revealed to him. 'It's just that I got a letter about you.' His honest eyes

85

stared back into the other's face, steady and clear. Bill never beat about the bush. He was too subtle for that amateur technique. He came straight to the point always, having carefully prepared his own position beforehand. He was a born administrator; and those who thought of him merely as an intriguer were nearly always convinced against their will that he was in fact a formidable man.

'Oh.' Tom sat down slowly in the opposite chair and put his glass down on the table beside him where it gleamed in a ray of wintry sun that also played over his breviary and the little silver box in which he kept his stole. 'From whom?'

'It was anonymous,' said Bill with a shrug. 'These things usually are.' He sipped his brandy, cradling the glass in his warm palms, and looking into the fire.

'Could I see it?'

'No. I burned it. I usually do that.' Bill looked across at the window beyond which the sun was sinking in a tangle of wintry boughs behind the chestnut tree. He could just make out the slated roof of the church. His eyes glazed and he seemed to have fallen into a kind of trance as he went on: 'Cheap ruled paper, a woman's hand, I should say, uneducated, although spelling mistakes are sometimes deliberately made in these communications. However, there's no point in being too subtle.'

Father Moran looked down thoughtfully at the hollow his soutane made in his lap. One of the buttons was loose. He had not been particularly surprised to find that Brian had gone as he drove out the Fogarty's gate on Thursday night. He had half expected a visit from him during the last few days; but on reflection he decided that this was not likely. The young man did not strike him as the type who would cold-bloodedly pursue a rival to the bitter end; nor did he look like the sort who wrote anonymous letters.

'When did you get it?' he asked quietly, surprised that he was not more disturbed; but then in a strange way he had always felt completely at ease with Bill; and there was no denying the fact that he had taken an unprecedented risk with the thought at the back of his

mind that the bishop no longer read letters, and that
his old friend could be relied upon to look after his
interest. A thought not worked out; but contained.

'On Thursday morning.' Bill stroked his short
fleshy nose and crossed his legs, his plump thighs
straining against the black cloth.

So it was not Brian. Somebody else who had prior
knowledge.

'Miss Price?' probed Bill gently, and then as the
other frowned and shook her head, went on: 'It very
often is, as you know. But I never thought she was
in love with you. Have you any ideas yourself?'

'Some busy-body in the town I suppose.' He stopped
short, suddenly aware of his slip.

'In the town.' Bill looked down at his glass and
pursed his lips. He felt a curious nagging sense of
personal injury. Widely regarded as a man with little
or no heart; dedicated to the pursuit of ambition; self-
reliant to the point of inhumanity; and absolutely incapable of a single spontaneous action, he had, like
many another man of his type, one weakness. He
needed a friend on whom he felt he could rely. Social
life meant nothing to him; but like any other man he
could not operate in a void. Tom Moran had been his
chosen disciple since their first term in Maynooth;
someone whose discretion could be counted upon; a
solid fellow of no particular brilliance who had from
the beginning accepted his natural inferiority in
intellectual matters, and never questioned the right of
his clever friend to lay down the law on any subject
that might be under discussion. Indeed Tom was not
interested in argument; and had never been anything
other than a pass-pupil in any subject. But he had his
own justification; for it very soon became apparent to
him that Bill, who was not popular with his class-
mates, relied on him a great deal more than he liked
to admit. Behind the confidence and the subtle working
of an essentially lonely mind Tom sensed the need for
uncritical approbation, and unswerving loyalty. In a
sense Bill was a great deal more reliant on him than
he had ever been on his single-minded friend. Until
now.

So it's true, thought Bill bleakly. He had been half-hoping that the letter was simply another communication from the lunatic fringe.

'Are you thinking of marrying her?' he said in the soft voice he used when he was really upset.

'Good God, no!' Tom opened his eyes and gave him a hostile stare. Bill felt a little better. This man was well known to be his closest friend. Any scandal that he was involved in would reflect upon himself. At all costs this affair must be hushed up: there were enough stupid scandals in the Church already. He hoped they could settle this in a civilised manner.

'The letter gave names, dates and the place,' went on Bill slowly. 'I'm sorry in a way I didn't keep it for you, because it would appear to have been written by somebody who knows the family well. I don't imagine they'd want any publicity of that kind. That is of course if the letter is true.'

'I don't want to see it.' There was a note of suppressed passion in the other man's voice which Bill Conway did not like. 'Anyway there's nothing in it.' He rubbed his mouth with his hand, muffling his speech. 'It's all over.'

'Any complication?'

Tom shook his head and frowned.

'I mean, does anybody else know?' went on Bill, probing gently.

Father Moran stood up suddenly, and clenched his big fists like a boy. Bill waited patiently, hoping that the truth would not be worse than he suspected. There were some things even he was incapable of fixing. It was now almost dark and he could not see his friend's face clearly; yet neither of them thought of putting on the light.

'All right, all right I blotted my copy-book,' the deep voice was harsh and defiant. 'She knew what she was doing and so did I. It's over now and I've got the rest of my life to think about it. That's my business. What are you going to do about it, Bill?'

'Nothing, of course. The old man knows nothing, and he won't if I can help it. Do you think there's any possibility of anybody else trying to tell him? The letter was addressed to him, of course. Has anybody any real proof?' The voice was calm and business-like. These were waters in which Bill was at home; even if this particular rock-pool made him a bit sick. Would he ever be able to trust Tom again? The thought made him feel desolate, and he gripped the arms of his chair until his knuckles shone in the fading light.

'No. No one has any proof.'

The ivory knuckles relaxed; and the soft hands were crossed gently over his stomach.

Father Moran strode over to the switch and put on the light. It would never do for Miss Price to come back and find them sitting in the dark. He could not bring himself to tell Bill about Brian. That was something on which he would have to take a chance. And if that young man decided to make trouble there was nothing any of them could do about it. But he reckoned without Bill's extraordinary intuition, which often struck home without knowing exactly what he was nailing. It was one of his most formidable gifts.

'Is there any other man in the case?' He began in an idle almost aimless tone, but before he had finished the sentence he knew by the darkening of the other's face that he had hit a sensitive nerve. Father Moran stood in the centre of the stuffy little room, with its hideous brown carpet covered with dusty cabbage roses, and looked about to cover his confusion. At the heavy repp curtain the colour of dried blood; the leather arm-chairs with the horse-hair stuffing visible through the tears in the cushions; the lowering book-case and the untidy desk which he had bought cheap at a parish priest's auction; the reproduction of Titian's 'Assumption' on the wall inside the door facing the portrait of highland cattle on the opposite wall. A decent room for a country curate. It all seemed very useless now; this room which had so impressed his relatives. Was it for this that they had scrimped and saved to send him to Maynooth?

'Yes, Bill, there is, a young fellow by the name of Langley who works for the Galway Mineral Company. I think he wants to marry her.'

Bill made a mental note of the name. He knew the

owners of that company. It might come in useful.

'And will he?' Bill flicked a speck of ash from his knee with his thumb and middle finger.

'I don't know.'

'You mean you think he has certain suspicions?'

'Well, yes.' Tom Moran slumped down in his chair again and covered his face with his hand. 'I don't want to leave, Bill. I wouldn't know what to do. It's the only life I know.'

'Then you'll have to tell me exactly what the position is.'

Tom looked at his friend with haggard eyes. He could not bring himself to confess the happenings of last Thursday night. It was something he wanted to forget, to banish forever from his mind.

'I've told you everything,' he muttered sullenly.

'No, you haven't,' retorted Bill sharply. 'Did he find you together, come on any letters? You haven't been crazy enough to write any letters, have you?'

'No, no.' There was no mistaking the sincerity of that denial. 'He came to the house last Thursday when I was there.'

'My God!' Bill half raised himself on his wrists and then sank back into his chair again. 'What kind of fool are you. Did he find you together?'

'Not in that way. He came to the door, she opened it, I overheard what they said in the hall. Apparently he had heard some gossip about her.'

'Concerning you?'

'Well, yes, but there was some other man mentioned too, Bud something or other.'

'Oh, I see.' Bill did not breathe a sigh of relief, but he felt a little easier. There is always some safety in numbers. 'Did you speak to him?'

Tom looked up with some of his old spirit.

'Yes,' he said grimly. 'I showed him the door.'

'Good.' Bill nodded his head sagely. 'And you haven't heard from him since?'

'No.'

Bill stretched out one of his shining toes and smoothed out a wrinkle in the hearth-rug. He hated untidiness.

'It's very possible that you may not. If he does - '

he threw out his hands and shrugged. 'But in the meantime it's clear somebody knows.'

'Nobody knows,' the other replied firmly. 'They
couldn't. It's all conjecture. I'm absolutely sure of
that. No one has any definite proof.'

'What about the parents?'

Tom looked at his friend sharply, as if for the first
time in his life he had found him lacking in subtlety.
Bill took the unspoken point; and felt easier still. A
certain pattern was emerging in his mind; but it was
still too early to commit himself. For the time being
he would continue to see that no anonymous letters
reached the bishop; but beyond that he could not go.
Tom looking into his friend's face for some sign of
encouragement knew that he was alone.

'You'll stay to tea?' he asked humbly. 'Miss Price
will be very upset if you don't.'

And so will you, thought Bill. He paused a moment
before he answered. Twenty years of friendship was
at stake; but so was his career, and the fabric of the
institution to which he had dedicated his life. But it
was early days yet. Nothing might happen; and if he
left now it would only provide the housekeeper with a
question mark. He decided to make the best of it, and
hold his fire.

'I'll have time for that,' he replied. His way of
saying that the old cosy evening sessions of friendly
gossip were for the moment at any rate at an end.

'Good.' Father Moran reached out and took up his
glass of brandy again. He would have time to polish
that off before the old witch came back. They both
stared silently into the fire, each absorbed in his own
thoughts. It did not occur to either of them to discuss
or even think of Marie's position. To Bill she was a
faceless female whom he did not want to talk about. To
Tom she was already an uneasy memory. They were
not concerned with the idle romantic question of who
hurt whom; but with an ancient and far more realistic
business: survival. At this game they were both in
their different ways experts. They knew that an
intimate acquaintance with human failings does not
necessarily soften the heart. Sin was their profession,

and they had long since accepted it for the dreary thing it was. In the meantime a certain course had to be steered; a certain clearly defined destination somehow attained; and this was never achieved by lowering the sails and allowing the ship to toss and flounder at the mercy of every stormy wave. The map was clear and the compass set. Somehow one had to abide by them.

CHAPTER FIFTEEN

For the next week they all waited for something to happen. A deceptive calm settled upon their lives like the first snow of winter muffling field and garden under which root and bulb and seed lie dormant, until the time comes for them to thrust blindly upwards and proclaim themselves.

The Fogartys fell back on the reassuring rhythm of bourgeois life. An overheated house, drawn curtains, thick carpets, heavy meals and hot-water bottles in the beds at night. Nothing was said. Pat complaining of the cold stayed away from his office more and more, lying in bed most of the morning, coming down for lunch, and going up for a long nap afterwards. Marie drove her mother to the church in the evenings, and to nine o'clock Mass in the mornings on her way into the office. She was now running the business single-handed, with the help of Pat's old foreman and Miss Rafferty, his grim but competent secretary. She found that she was enjoying the work; and was glad to see that sales had not dropped off since her father's illness.

A united family. A mother devoting most of her time to ministering to her ailing husband; snatching time off to attend to her usual devotions; and bearing herself with quiet, stiff-lipped fortitude. A daughter who was proving herself an excellent business-woman, with a clear head and a flair for organisation. Even her worst enemies who had listened to the recurrent waves of gossip about her had to admit that she was her father's daughter. Attendance at the church and a quiet god-fearing life were virtues to be treasured and commended; but money in the bank has its own inexorable morality, the first law of which is: don't rock the boat.

But underneath the snow the earth was stirring.

Pat struggled up into a sitting position, his mouth open as he gasped for breath, a thin line of saliva dribbling down his chin like the trail of a slug. For some time past he had slept with the small pink-shaded bed-side lamp burning all night; for he often awoke in pain, or fumbled his way back to reality through the coils of some fleshly many-headed nightmare.

The tray on which Aggie had brought him up his usual snack lay on the dressing-table. In the morning while Nelly was at Mass she would bring it down, wash the plates and cup, and put everything back in its place. After a few minutes he began to breathe a little easier; but his stomach was sour as always when he woke after sleeping, and required something sweet. He edged himself to the side of the bed, opened the locker of the night-table and took out a bar of chocolate, unwrapped it carefully, broke it silently and stuffed two blocks into his mouth. After he had swallowed it he felt better; and knew this improvement would continue for ten minutes or so until the burning in his stomach started again. He lifted himself on his fists and farted softly; then plopped down again into the mattress to cover the smell.

Then he became aware that his head was hurting him. It had merely been muzzy when he had woken up; but now a heavy burning pain throbbed behind his temples and stiffened the back of his neck. With a groan he reached out and opened the box of pills beside the lamp and swallowed two of them. They did not seem to take much effect lately; but he knew that he must continue to believe in them. When that faith was gone nothing remained.

He looked around the room, holding his head in his hands. There was something he wanted to do; knew he must do; but had been putting off because it too denoted something final and irrevocable. Without turning his head he put out one hand and groped for the switch of the lamp, turned it off and kept one hand over his eyes to help him grow accustomed to the darkness. Then he leaned forward and looked at the locked door leading to his wife's room. The light was not on there.

He switched on his own lamp again and began to edge out of bed slowly and carefully. Lucky he did not have a creaking mattress. Aggie could not think of everything. But there was a loose floor-board which he avoided as he put on his dressing-gown. He found his hands were trembling as they often did lately as he fumbled in his trouser pockets for his keys. He could not help making a slight scraping noise as he opened the top drawer of the chest inside the door; and stopped, stiff with fright, listening intently. He could hear nothing except for the drumming in his own ears, and closed his eyes as his sight began to swim. When he opened them there was no sound, and the sense of relief made him feel better. Gently he opened the drawer, and put his hand down under the pile of socks and ties which formed a protective layer above his treasures. It was some time since he had looked at the photographs, and although he knew every one of them and remembered their details vividly, he had not realised they made such a thick bundle. It would take quite an effort to burn this bunch.

Fortunately the fireplace was at the other side of the room, away from Aggie's wall. He got out the lighter from his jacket pocket and sat down on the bed to rest himself. His vision was still a bit cloudy, so he took another pill to help him through his ordeal. It made him feel curiously weightless; and he glanced down at the bundle in his lap to make sure they had not slipped to the floor. He should not look at them, he knew. It was a mortal sin. But it was for the last time. What pleasure they had given him in his time, those billowing breasts and voluptuous thighs. It was so easy to identify oneself with those handsome young men with their huge and seemingly tireless organs upon which the women fed so avidly. Lazy-eyed pashas with their seductive hand-maidens - these poses were his favourites; although there were moods when he saw himself hard-jawed and frowning as he subjected a mass of quivering flesh beneath his ruthless body. A shiver of impotent desire ran through his flaccid thighs, followed immediately by a feeling of guilty nausea. These creatures with their twining limbs and voracious organs were sinful, forbidden, depraved. There was only one thing to do with them before it was too late.

He knelt down before the fireplace, clutching a chair to support himself, and flicked the lighter. The flame bit into the paper and engulfed a naked rump, coiled round a monstrous breast and enveloped a heavy face, its mouth open in the agony of pleasure. They burned silently, these monuments to a dumb lust; arms, legs, penises and gaping feminine slits dissolved under the flames and disappeared in a small mound of ashes; as their owners would one day, Pat felt sure, burn in hell.

After it was over he felt exhausted, his body covered with sweat, his limbs slack and his head whirling, as if he had awakened from a drunken orgy. When he tried to lift himself to his feet he could not find the strength and sank back on his haunches, panting and clasping his hands before his chest in an attitude of supplication. An old prayer from his childhood flashed across his darkening mind. Hail, Holy Queen, Mother of mercy, Hail, our life, our sweetness and our hope. To thee do we cry, poor banished children of Eve, To Thee do we sigh, mourning and weeping in this valley of tears.

And then, like a cloud of black smoke the darkness descended upon him.

In her room Agnes Fogarty opened her eyes and saw the light go off and then on in her husband's room; listened intently to the tiny sounds that followed. What was he up to? An instinct told her that it was something furtive. Was that the rattle of a bunch of keys? Those photographs. Oh, mother of God, the dirty hound, and he with one foot in the grave. She clasped her hands across her breasts and closed her eyes. I must not think of that, she prayed. If he wants me he'll call. But he did not call; and she slowly drifted into a light blameless sleep again.

Marie, sleeping on her back, awoke to find a hand on her left breast. She sighed and moved her legs contentedly. The hand moved and she felt a tingle of pleasure which grew and awakened an urgent response as the fingers stroked the sensitive nipple. She stirred, opened her eyes, and felt the familiar sensation of titillation in her knees. Awoke fully to find her whole body shivering with anticipation at the touch of her own hand on her breast. She kneaded the breast gently and felt the warm weight of the bed-clothes pressing upon her nakedness; and remembered that she must crumple her pyjamas in the morning to give the impression that she had slept with them on. A figure appeared in her imagination, the only figure that now appeared in her dreams, tall and fair-haired, his face sullen with desire, his body swollen to minister to her pleasure. She pressed her back against the mattress and ran her hands down the soft silken length of her body. The figure melted into her, and release came in a slow throbbing shudder under the frantic caress of her own hand.

Downstairs Nelly slept the sleep of the righteous, with her rosary twined about her neck, and the crucifix - blessed with a plenary indulgence for the hour of death - clutched in her big red fist.

In the morning Agnes Fogarty found her husband huddled on the carpet in front of the fire-place, with his mouth hanging askew and the lid of one eye loose and hanging. She bent over him, felt his fluttering heart, and ran downstairs to phone the doctor.

And in his presbytery Father Moran got up heavy and dark-eyed after a night in which he had unsuccessfully struggled with a nervous system which had become accustomed to a certain definite and entirely natural ritual of the flesh. Pulling back the curtains and looking out of the window he saw that the first snow of winter had fallen during his night of darkness.

CHAPTER SIXTEEN

'Well, what have I done now?' The woman's voice
was appealing, but it still held that undertone of
tolerant amusement which had attracted him in the bar
a few hours ago.

'Nothing,' said Brian gruffly, frowning as he caught
sight of his own limp, pendulent nakedness in the
mirror. He picked up his shirt, sat down on a chair
by the wall and covered his lap.

The woman raised herself on one elbow and regarded
him with an indulgent smile.

'You look like a sulking school-boy who's been caught
doing something he shouldn't,' she murmured in her
low, slightly hoarse voice. 'Come over here and relax.
Nobody is going to beat you.'

He shook his head, and for want of something better
to do looked about the dimly lighted room. It was
exactly the same as his own, a few doors down the
corridor. Functional and impersonally comfortable in
the modern quasi-American style, he had begun to
stay in this hotel a few weeks before because all the
rooms had telephones. It was more than he could
afford; but he could wait in comfort here for that
evening call to which only a few weeks ago he had
looked forward to with such eagerness. He should
never have come back here again. He plucked at his
thin nylon shirt; and the woman leaned forward, pulled
the sheet over her waist, and looked up at the coloured
photograph of the Treaty Stone which hung over the
bed. She sighed and began again.

'In the bar you seemed so gay.' She pulled the sheet
up and held it against her naked breasts. 'I'm sorry.'

'You don't have to be,' said Brian, wondering how
in hell he was going to get out of this blasted room
without hurting her feelings. She was a nice woman

and he had been glad of her company in the bar after
that telephone call from Galway. He had been paged
just as he got back to the hotel at six o'clock. After
that there didn't seem to be anything to do except get
drunk. He looked at his watch surreptitiously. Nine.
They had been together three hours; two-and-a-half of
them in the bar, where he had drunk a great deal less
than he had intended after he got into conversation
with this pleasant woman who like himself was drinking
alone, and had that aura of solitude which always
attracted him without his ever attempting to analyse
the reason why. She was perhaps thirty-five or forty;
high-browed and handsome in a rather boyish way;
well-dressed, with humorous, kindly eyes; and an air
of quiet self-confidence. It had seemed a good idea at
the time; and now he felt exactly as he used to feel
with those other pick-ups he had had. Most of them
seemed to promise what he wanted; and some of them
actually provided it. But he had never really enjoyed
himself. There was only one person who had made
him feel that the whole thing was natural and inevitable.
Would he ever get the bitch out of his mind? What was
behind the telephone call from his boss?

'Perhaps it's you who are sorry,' the woman was
saying, as she lifted a glass of water from the night-
table and held it before her lips.

Brian felt like standing up; but realised that he
would have to clutch his shirt about his middle: an
undignified procedure. So he remained sitting.
Waiting: for what?

'I suppose I've been a disappointment,' he said,
making an attempt to be civil. After all the woman
was a good sort. Why should he feel contemptuous of
someone who had so off-handedly divined his taste and
had so skilfully ministered to them? Had he not encouraged those experienced hands, that warm receptive
mouth? But he could not bring his sullen rebellious
body to perform the rite of response which he knew .
she had every claim to expect. He had used her; and
the thought made him uneasier still.

'Not at all,' she said politely.

'I'm afraid it was a bit one-sided,' he went on with

99

a shy attempt to make amends.

'It very often is.' She gave a little laugh, almost a gurgle; but he thought he detected a note of bitterness in her voice. Or was it pain?

'I don't think it was me you were thinking about,' she went on softly. 'Was it?'

He gave her her answer by standing up abruptly, forgetting that his shirt slid to the carpet at his feet. She looked at him with a kind of ironic regret: a woman who knew too much about men, and sometimes hated herself for doing so. But he did not notice: he was bending down to pick up his shirt. Then he sat down again ashamed of his confusion.

'You mustn't worry too much about it,' she said, hoping that the effect his splendid body made on her did not show in her voice. 'These things happen.'

He wanted to turn his head and stare her in the face; but with an effort forced himself to look ahead. What did she know? What sort of life had she led? A husband, a lover, a succession of them? Where did she come from, and where was she going? The thoughts flitted lightly through his mind. He did not really care. She was just a woman one had picked up in a bar; a rather better type than most of them, and therefore more interesting. But he did not want to be involved.

'What things?' he muttered, playing for time. He could feel the first faint stirring of renewed activity; and he wanted to get out before it began to show. She was like all the rest of them; pretending to read his mind; delaying until she got him going again. Did the bitches ever think of anything except their own pleasure? And how cleverly they used the hit-and-miss method of their famous intuition. Because he had not given her her release it must be somebody else's fault. He stood up, picked up his shorts and stepped into them.

'Who is it?' she said, feeling she had the right to tease him a bit. 'A girl, or a boy?'

She heard him suck in his breath and stop fumbling with his clothes. This was not the time to look at him. What can they ever know of us anyway, she thought.

'No boys,' he replied in a voice which was neither too angry nor too embarrassed. So it was not that.

Her instinct had been right at the beginning. She wondered idly what sort of girl she was. Lucky young woman, if she played her cards carefully. With the blessing of God and society he would make a marvellous lover; she had rarely encountered such a reserve of latent sensuality.

'Good.' She inhaled slowly and watched the smoke drift towards the ceiling. 'If it was your fault, try to forgive yourself. If it was hers, remember that women are often the victims of circumstances.'

'Is that so?' he said, putting on his tie and tugging it viciously. But he was to remember what she said later.

'Yes,' she went on in a low voice, almost as if she were talking to herself. 'Most of us will settle for one man, if we get the chance. But the man sometimes doesn't know, and sometimes, which is even worse, he does. But mostly, it's a failure of communication. If we could make ourselves understood over all the misunderstandings a lot of things could be salvaged. But men won't listen. They're too busy with the moral law.'

'That's a good one,' he scoffed as he put on his jacket. 'I didn't think I was much of an advertisement for that.'

'Oh, but you are,' she replied with a chuckle. 'Why am I telling you all this?'

'I don't know.' And he genuinely did not. He could think of nothing except how to get out of the room; and ponder the implications of the telephone call. Was he caught in a spider's web? An easy lay in a strange hotel did not count.

'No, of course not,' she said, and now the note of bitterness was plain. 'I'm just a ship that passes in the night.'

'No,' he said politely as he made for the door, 'not just that.'

'Thank you,' she murmured, putting out her cigarette. 'And good luck.'

CHAPTER SEVENTEEN

'How is your father this morning, Miss Fogarty?'

Miss Rafferty looked up anxiously from her desk as Marie came into the office. The young woman took off her coat and threw it over her arm. Her face was pale and her eyes strained from lack of sleep. She looked frail and vulnerable and a great deal less self-assured than usual. The secretary, who did not relish the idea of working for a woman - they were so much meaner and more niggling than men in small matters - found herself regarding this girl with something like sympathy. Perhaps all the talk about women in business was just male propaganda after all. Behind her frosty exterior Miss Rafferty preserved a small residue of feminist zeal, as well as a romantic heart. Long years of pounding on her typewriter and looking after her invalid mother had not entirely smothered the maternal instinct within her. Red-nosed, gimlet-eyed, taking a fierce pride in her integrity, she had to admit that Marie had proved herself calm and business like; and was taking over in an entirely proper manner without any theatrical flourishes of new brooms.

But Miss Rafferty was convinced that she had a secret sorrow, as she put it to herself; and wished she had a little more romance in her life. What had happened to that nice, good-looking young man who travelled for Galway Minerals, and who was supposed to have been seen about with Marie. He had always been most polite and civil to Miss Rafferty; not forward and leering like some commercials she could name. But last week he had rung up for his order. Something must have gone wrong.

'Not too bad,' said Marie wearily. 'He can speak fairly well, but his side is still affected. He told me to ask for you before I left this morning.'

Miss Rafferty flushed with pleasure; and felt the tears burning her eyes. This would never do. She took out her hankerchief, cleared her throat and blew her nose.

'Ah, sure that's the way it is,' she said plaintively. 'Look at my own poor mother, ten years now since she had her stroke, and still alive, thanks be to God.'

Marie shivered and turned away. She had not slept much the previous night and felt cold and chilly. But the thought of old Mrs. Rafferty, moribund and bed-ridden all those years, almost made her lose her control. If Daddy doesn't get better than that, he'd be far better dead, she thought bleakly.

'Any letters this morning?' she asked shortly to cover her panic.

'The usual invoices I'd say by the look of them,' said Miss Rafferty briskly, automatically returning to her professional manner, although she would dearly like to have had a cosy chat about the awful things that can happen to you with high blood pressure. It was all very well for the Fogartys, they could afford a nurse; but how would Marie like it if she and her mother had to put the old man on a bed-pan twice a day; and feed him out of a spoon; and give him a wash every week? And yet she did not want to lose her poor mother: the thought of the empty little house and all the lonely years ahead terrified her.

'It's the will of God,' she ventured helpfully as Marie looked about the tiny office blankly. A desk, a filing-cabinet, a plug for the kettle, and ten calendars ranged about the walls in every conceivable style from reproductions of expressionist paintings that looked like strips of linoleum, to rosy-tinted pictures of the Christmas crib. Time was not only money in Miss Rafferty's office; it was an obsession, for every one of the calendars was religiously crossed off every morning with a red pencil. A whole series of scarlet kisses covering the dead days.

'Oh, by the way,' said Marie, pausing with her hand on the handle of the door which led to the corridor and to the big private office on the other side, 'you know that traveller from Galway Minerals?'

103

Miss Rafferty looked round eagerly, her eyes sparkling behind her flashing spectacles; but Marie was studiously looking over her head at one of the calendars. The Holy Family in technicolour.

'Mr. Langley? Yes, of course. He rang up last week and I gave him the same order. I suppose that was right?' Miss Rafferty trembled with anticipation.

'If he rings up to-day, will you ask him to call.' Marie felt the door-knob moving beneath her damp palm; and gripped it tighter. 'You might tell him that my father wants to see him here.'

'Your - ' Miss Rafferty bit back the word and opened her eyes. Marie turned her head jerkily as if she had a stiff neck and looked at her. She had to take somebody into her confidence; and she had often heard her father say that old Rafferty was as discreet as a dead bank-manager. 'You see, Mr. Langley and I had a misunderstanding, something about, well, some books I asked him to buy for me at an auction in Galway.' Marie drew a long breath and went on feeling more confident as the tissue of lies thickened. 'They weren't the right books, and I said something - I forget what it was now - but he thought I was accusing him of dishonesty. So that's why he's been ringing up. I thought it might be a good idea if you told him that my father wanted to see him. Actually I wanted to apologise. It wasn't his fault, of course.'

Miss Rafferty scented a lovers' quarrel.

'Of course not,' she murmured diplomatically. 'Those auctioneers are awful. It's well known that you couldn't trust them as far as you'd throw a taxi-cab.'

'Awful,' agreed Marie warmly. 'I was most em-barrassed.'

She opened the door and went out, while Miss Rafferty returned happily to her typing with spring in her heart. Those rumours she had heard of Marie's friendship with poor Father Moran. The usual exaggeration of course. It was terrible the way a girl couldn't talk to a priest on the street in this country without somebody putting a construction on it. It was shocking the way people talked about priests. Nothing but sex, sex, sex all the time. Disgusting.

At eleven o'clock, as she was partaking of her second cup of mid-morning tea, the telephone rang.

'Fogarty's wholesale,' she sang out. 'The office.'

'Langley here,' answered the deep voice with its Galway lilt. 'Galway Minerals.'

'Oh, good morning, Mr. Langley.' Miss Rafferty was all atwitter; but long years of experience stood her in good stead. She sounded as welcoming as a bird of prey. 'And how are you this merry morning?' It was her usual salutation to commercials; but somehow it did not sound right in the present case.

'All right,' he answered curtly. 'Will I take the same order, Miss Rafferty?'

A good head for names, thought Rafferty. That young man will go places.

'Well, I'm not quite sure, Mr. Langley.'

'I see.' He sounded as if he was about to slam down the telephone.

'It's not that, Mr. Langley. It's just that Mr. Fogarty told me that he wanted to see you if you called.'

'Mr. Fogarty!' The voice rose with amazement. 'But I heard last night that he was very ill. My own boss rang me in Limerick and told me.'

'Did he?' Miss Rafferty's voice was dead-pan, but she was enjoying herself hugely. Wheels within wheels. This was a moment of high diplomacy; and she was not going to fail. 'Well, of course I can't speak for him. All I know is that I was told to ask you to call and see Mr. Fogarty.'

'Who told you?'

Miss Rafferty paused significantly to give the weight of silence to her amazement.

'Are you suggesting Mr. Langley that I am making this up?' she enquired haughtily.

'No, I'm not.' He sounded nonplussed. 'But if he's as ill as my boss says -'

'And who, may I ask, told your boss that?' snapped Miss Rafferty icily; comfortably aware that she was keeping well inside the confines of truth.

There was a long pause at the other end; but the sound of his breathing told her that he was still there.

It was a long time since Miss Rafferty had had such an exciting conversation.

'Oh, all right, I'll call,' he said at last. 'There are a few things I want to ask him too.'

'Indeed?' Miss Rafferty sounded suitably surprised. 'Well, thank you very much.'

'Thank you,' he answered lamely, sounding thoroughly confused. 'In about half-an-hour. Will that be all right?'

'I suppose so,' she said graciously, 'provided you don't mean an hour.'

'Good morning, Miss Rafferty.'

'Good morning, Mr. Langley.'

She let down the receiver gently and took up her tea. Should she tell Marie that he was on his way? After mature consideration she decided against it, unless specifically asked. The element of surprise is very important in these matters, as she knew from her reading of romances. Expecting somebody is an awful wear on the nerves. Far better just to show him in; and let the pair of them work out whatever was between them their own way.

CHAPTER EIGHTEEN

Money. The frosty sun shone through the window; a
blue-white light neatly striped by the venetian blind so
that it played over the desk at which Marie was counting
the morning's cash in long horizontal bars, flickering
with silvered dust, moving gently but inexorably across
the leather-topped surface as the morning wore on.
The office was well heated, and the strips of weak sun
emphasised the comfort of the large carpeted sanctum
compared with the cold functional glare of the yard
outside.

Pat Fogarty had cut off a sizeable section of the
huge store for his own private use. The corridor
which separated his office from Miss Rafferty's cubby-
hole led to a frosted glass door opening on to the main
store itself with its loading bays for the vans, and its
business-like divisions of dried goods: all the stock-
in-trade of the family grocers and general merchants
who were his main customers. Since the rise of the
super-markets he had also instituted a cash-and-carry
service with a ten per cent discount on all goods bought
for cash. This was much used unofficially by many
housewives who found that they could do their bulk
buying at Fogartys cheaper than at the super-market;
thus ensuring that Pat enjoyed the best of both worlds.
It meant taking on three extra clerks; but it had been
worth it. Many of his old customers had had their
business divided in two by competition from the new
retail giants; but their wives and many of their friends
continued to get their supplies wholesale from the old
firm, while Pat buying in bulk from the suppliers, and
officially closed to retail business, was able to offer
as good a bargain as the markets under the intriguing
label of 'wholesale'.

When she first came into the business Marie was

given the task of counting the money and preparing it for the bank whence it was taken in a large canvas bag by Miss Fogarty.

Marie found that this hack-work, far from breaking her back and making her dizzy was in fact much to her liking. She enjoyed the little piles of silver neatly counted into their paper bags; the cheques marked on the back with the number of each van-man in case any of them should bounce; and the crisp piles of notes and dollar bills from American exiles which were placed carefully on top of one another with their numbers all faced the same way for the convenience of the bank-teller.

Money. Marie surveyed her morning's work with satisfaction. Eight hundred and seventy nine pounds and eight pence. Not bad for a Tuesday's takings. She had been so engrossed in her counting that she had almost forgotten the interview which she told Miss Rafferty to arrange for her. Money, the only God whose existence had not been questioned since the rise of civilisation; the only power which still reigned supreme over all the people of the world. The idol before which the most rampant atheist bowed his head; the ruler alike of tory, socialist, communist and priest; the great leveller in whose presence all are equal for no one knows the day nor the hour that the god may favour the humblest with his favour. Grace from heaven is but imperfectly understood by even the holiest. The blessings that flow from the unseen god of gold are manifest to all. As Marie counted her takings every morning she experienced a curious sense of reflected power, as in ancient times a courtier might feel near the person of the sovereign. The kings had departed, their divine right a joke; but this more ancient religion was still triumphant; and before it men prostrated themselves as they had never done before the throne of the mightiest emperor.

Marie did not formulate such thoughts in her mind; and would have been the first to accuse anyone who did of cynicism. She, like most other people, was content to worship a god she did not understand.

She took up the bank docket and began to write in

the entry. Half way through there was a knock at the door.

'Come in,' she said in a low voice.

Miss Rafferty opened the door and put her head in. Her face was more than usually flushed; and she spoke in a whisper.

'Will I show Mr. Langley in?'

Marie nodded and looked around the large rather splendid office. Curiously enough she felt no need to pat her hair or steal a glance at her face in a hand-mirror. Her surroundings gave her courage.

Brian opened the door and stood looking down at her with a puzzled expression. He looked more hurt than angry. And as always his presence affected her physically; a quickening of the pulse, a heaviness in the limbs, a dryness in the throat.

'Won't you come in?' she said politely.

'I thought your father wanted to see me.' His voice was toneless and he kept his eyes on the pile of money on the desk.

'No,' she said simply, 'he's sick. I did.' Her instinct told her that a brisk business-like approach would be most effective at the beginning. But she was not sure that she wanted him to adopt the same tone, and was a little taken aback when he did.

'I see,' he said dryly, as if she had been explaining the price of imported fruit. She felt faintly disturbed. If he was one of those people who cut others out of his life, then the game was lost from the beginning. But that was something she had to find out. What a lot of hotel soap he must have used on himself this morning. She could get the faint acrid tang of it from where he stood across the expanse of soft-piled carpet.

'I wanted to see you,' she began in an uncertain tone, staring at his large well polished shoes.

'I can't see why. I've got my order from Miss Rafferty.' There was a suggestion of animosity in his voice. Just a hint; but enough.

'Did you?' She was genuinely surprised.

'I thought that would come up,' he said with a little chuckle which restored the balance in his favour.

'What would come up?'

'The order. I didn't get it, and you know it.' He made a sudden gesture outlining the pile of money with his hand. 'I suppose all this is calculated to drive the point home.'

She looked up and stared him in the eye.

'I don't know what you're talking about,' she said flatly.

'Your father is sick.' His right hand was uncovered; now he put his glove back on it. 'I heard all that last night. I was told that he had had a stroke on Sunday.' He put his gloved hands in the pocket of his jacket with the thumbs out gripping the hip bones.

'So he had.' The memory of that awful discovery on Monday morning made her blanch; and her pallor was instantly misinterpreted. He smiled grimly as he went on:

'My boss told me about it last night. He rung me up in Limerick to tell me. I was a bit surprised when your secretary told me he wanted to see me this morning. Now of course I can see why.'

'I don't see what your boss has got to do with it,' she said sharply, annoyed that the conversation had taken a turning which she could not follow. 'I suppose he heard about it, and passed it on to you in the way of business. It was known in the office here on Monday morning. He could easily have heard it that day. News like that travels fast. Anyone could have told him.'

One foot took a step forward, the thumbs were jabbed viciously into the hips and the voice was hard, angry with a snarl in it which made her look up at him in pained surprise. This was a tone she had heard a few times before from men surrounded by union officials defending their jobs. It was a sound which she associated with the under-dog, the traditional enemy, out for all he could get from a hard-pressed employer. She did not realise that she could very easily find the same voice if somebody threatened the pile of money in front of her. But now she was startled. Was it possible that he had simply been making use of her all along?

'Did they also tell him that I was making a nuisance of myself here, that I was partly responsible for your father's stroke, and that if I didn't lay off I could get out?'

'I don't know what you're talking about,' she stammered, frightened by the angry set of his mouth, and the blazing animosity in his eyes.

'Oh, don't you? I think you know very well. You're trying to blackmail me into keeping my mouth shut. Your father couldn't have done it because he's sick. Although I suppose it's the kind of thing he'd do. A few words on the phone from one boss to another, and I'm out. And in my job I don't have a union behind me. You knew that too.'

'You think I told him to tell you that?' All her plans were thrown into confusion and she stared at him stiff with astonishment and genuine bewilderment. Something in the blurred outline of her mouth, in the haggard weariness of her eyes conveyed her feeling to him. Either she was a superb actress or she was not aware of what had been going on.

'What else can I think? Or maybe your father dropped the hint before he got sick.'

'Oh, Brian.' Her face sagged and her eyes filled with tears. Behind the pile of money, surrounded by all the appurtenances of solid bourgeois prosperity she looked lost and vulnerable. Then he remembered the skilful use she had made of him as a front; and his resolve hardened. Misunderstanding and wounded pride rose between them like a train in the night cutting off two people on either side of a track.

'It figures, doesn't it?' he went on relentlessly, deriving a pleasure altogether sensual from her discomfiture. 'You're all afraid I might tell tales. What a mess that would be. Well, I won't, if that's any comfort to you. I don't care that much any more. But I have my living to make. I don't just count money, I earn it. You've done enough harm as it is. The least you might do is get on to my boss and tell him that the whole thing has been a mistake, a very big mistake - on everybody's part.'

'But I can't do that,' she wailed, jumping to her feet and pressing her knuckles against the top of the desk. 'I don't know the man. I've never spoken to him in my life on the telephone or anywhere else. What's his name?'

'Donovan, ' he rapped out, thinking quickly on his feet and watching her closely. No glimmer of suspicion crossed her face. He was impressed against his will. She really was a superb actress.

'What can I do to prove that I didn't do this?' she went on earnestly. 'Could I ring Mr. Donovan up while you're here and ask him?'

'That would make a nice little comedy. Do you really imagine he wouldn't get the message the moment he realised it was you? You don't expect a man like that to give any kind of game away over the phone?' He took one hand out of his pocket and pointed at the telephone. Outside the window a hoarse male voice rose and splintered in the clear frosty air. 'Aw, go fuck yourself.' Neither of them really heard it. At another time Marie would have taken up the house phone and rung up the foreman.

'We won't know unless we try. Besides I'd like to find out more about this myself.' She picked up the telephone. 'Galway Minerals will get him, I suppose. What's the number?'

He gave it to her while she looked up the Galway code number in the directory; and began dialling. He watched her set, intent face; and wondered if she could really be serious about this little farce.

'Hullo, could I speak to Mr. Donovan, please?' There was a pause at the other end and then the crackle of a voice. Marie looked up with a frown, her eyes perplexed. 'Yes, Mr. Donovan, the proprietor.' Again the crackling. Marie put a hand over the mouth of the phone. 'There is no Mr. Donovan there. What does all this mean?'

Brian decided that the matter had gone far enough. After all she might be telling the truth; and if she did get on to the boss it might make things worse. God only knows how he would interpret a complaint of this nature from the Fogartys. One thing he felt sure of: he would be at the losing end.

'Forget it, ' he said, waving his hand impatiently. 'There is no Mr. Donovan.'

'I see.' She put down the telephone gently and looked

112

at him enquiringly. 'I'd still like to find out. Do you really think it likely I'd do a thing like that, unless I wanted to get rid of you for good and all? Why should I bother to make up this story in order to see you today, if I had done that? I know you better than to think that you'd come back after a threat, even if I wanted anyone on terms like that. I thought I'd be able to explain things to you, and now - '

'It would take some explaining,' he said roughly, narrowing his eyes and looking over her shoulder at the slatted window. The sun had moved and the thin pale bars of gold were now flickering across the surface of the blue carpet.

'On both sides.' Her voice was cold, her manner distant. But there is a telepathy in deep attraction; a language of the body which is a truer means of communication than words. They were separated by many things; not least their confusion; but the binding power to hurt was still theirs. The words they exchanged were like sparks flashing against a night sky over a blazing pyre.

'What do you mean by that?' Against his will he was singed.

'Listening to gossip about me, and believing it.' If she had been asked to swear an oath to her innocence she would have done so with a clear conscience, so completely did she feel herself bound to him by her own sense of the inevitable. It was a passion which had its own logic.

'Seeing is believing,' he retorted, his mouth twisted with distaste.

'You saw what you wanted to see. Who told you?' She knew then that she would never let him go, no matter what lengths she had to go to keep him.

'It doesn't matter,' he said sullenly, 'I heard it.'

'I would have told you myself, in time, and given the chance.' She saw no obstacles now; only the blind need to cling to him until she had warmed his body with her own conviction.

'Yes, you made one admission,' he replied, his face burning as he remembered their first night by the lake. Would he never be able to make love like that

with anybody again? 'To cover yourself in case I - '
he broke off, like a small boy who realises that a word
he has picked up in the streets means something shame-
ful.

'I did not ask the same of you,' she went on relentlessly, watching his flushed face with a kind of
smouldering defiance.

He thought of the woman in the hotel the night before;
and of the other casual pick-ups he had had, and made
his first false move.

'But a priest,' he burst out wildly. 'All the time
you were seeing me you were - Christ, it's disgusting!
I was a perfect front wasn't I?'

'If I needed that I could have found one quite easily.'
She was calm now; icily sure of her justification. 'And
if I wanted that it would mean that I was in love, which
I never have been until I met you. Since then I've
known that nothing else matters. There is no one else.
If there was I wouldn't be talking to you like this.'

'But a priest - ' he went on doggedly.

'A priest is like any other man,' she insisted,
allowing herself to smile for the first time.

'But he doesn't like it to be known,' he replied
floundering; not knowing what to think. 'And some
people will go to any lengths to cover him up.'

She bit her lip and looked down at the pile of money
which now seemed so irrelevant. She could not buy
her way out of this; and yet the god hovered in the
background. His job; Father Moran's way of life, for
he could not live on prayers: her own self-confidence.
Would Brian have been interested in her without it?

'Which is the more important,' she asked, 'this
mysterious phone-call from the man in Galway, or
the fact that I've known more than one man before I
met you?'

'How many?' he blurted out, giving her the answer
she wanted. To her at that moment it seemed silly;
but men were so old-fashioned.

'Several,' she replied with a shrug, looking down
at the shifting bars of light on the carpet. 'They mean
nothing now.'

'Perhaps no man means anything to you,' he said

114

uncomfortably, aware that she was invoking a dangerous and subtle truth; something that cut through the tangle of pride, anger and wounded affection in which they found themselves.

She raised her eyes and looked at him steadily.

'There is only one way of finding out,' she said softly.

At first he did not grasp her meaning; and then as the full weight of it sank in he felt his body relaxing, and a quick flame of excitement licking his chest.

'I told my parents I was going to marry you,' she went on steadily, aware instantly of his response.

'I haven't asked you,' he retorted, feeling a fool.

'No, but you would have, I think,' she said, smiling now into his baffled eyes. 'You don't think we could go on the way we were indefinitely, do you?' If so you must think I'm just another woman, fun to be with for a while, and then good-bye. That's not the way I think of you.' She sat down and slowly and carefully began to collect the bags of silver into a canvas bag. She went on with her task mechanically as he crossed the office and stood before the desk looking down at her.

'I haven't much of that,' he murmured. 'Do you think you can buy me?'

She looked up and shook her head. His closeness disturbed her calm, and she could feel her hands beginning to tremble.

'We'll have to get over that too. Hardly anything seems to be working for us, except - ' she covered the heavy bag with her hands and looked up at him with a little smile - 'neither of us will ever be satisfied with anybody else.'

He did not realise that his lips were trembling; but he knew that it was no good: there was still too much to find out, and he had nothing to lose. If she was a whore it would soon become apparent. If not, they were only at the beginning of a mutual discovery.

'To-night,' he said brusquely, turning from the desk and hurrying out of the office. Marie went on filling the bag slowly and methodically.

CHAPTER NINETEEN

After she had dispatched the money with a discreetly poker-faced Miss Rafferty, just it time to catch the bank before it closed at twelve-thirty, Marie put through another call to Galway, made a note, carried the secretary's typewriter into her office and wrote a letter. This she folded, put in her bag, and went home to lunch through streets already heavily hung with Christmas decorations.

The snow had turned to rain and slush, and motor-cars and lorries moved through the narrow streets with soft sucking sounds, like seals wading ashore on damp sand. When she got home she was glad to discover that the nurse, a tiresomely cosy woman with blonde curls like washed-gold bracelets and a false smile, was already taking lunch with her mother, with whom she had struck up an intimately casual friendship based on the gossip of the town, most of whose affluent alcoholics she had at one time or another nursed through the horrors.

Marie put her head around the dining-room door, greeted them warmly - there was no other way to deal with Miss Potter - and told them that she would be with them in a few minutes.

'Your daddy is a little better this morning,' said the nurse stretching her monstrous breasts beneath their starched armour. She fluttered her little claws and simpered at the girl, who had wondered more than once how such a roly-poly creature could have such steel-like talons. 'Mind you don't tire him now. It all comes back on poor me.'

'I won't,' replied Marie shortly, making her escape and running up the stairs to her father's room.

He was lying propped up with pillows, his face turned to the door, his glassy eyes strained with expectation. The room was heavy with mingled scents of disinfectant, starched linen, and the aftermath of injections, which did not hide the sickly odour of stagnant human flesh.

'Mmm.' he grunted, greeting his daughter by raising his right hand from the eiderdown and holding it out for her to grasp. She sat down on the edge of the bed and held his fingers.

'How are we?' she asked softly, stroking his forehead with a cool gentle hand. He closed one eye and pulled up the right corner of his mouth in a grotesque attempt to smile.

'Alive,' he mumbled. Although his speech was thick he could still make himself understood. Since his illness his affection for his daughter had shown itself more openly. She it was who interpreting his anguished glance had insisted against her mother's wishes that he should be kept in the house and nursed there. All Agnes' appeals to heaven and the nuns had gone unregarded.

'Well enough to sign a letter,' she said, coming straight to the matter in hand. 'I hate to ask you to do this, Daddy, but we haven't much time. You know what Potter is like.'

He nodded, staring fixedly into her face, all his old sly guardedness of expression obliterated by a belated surrender to this living extension of his own personality. Quickly in a low voice Marie told him of the threat Brian had received from his employer. Pat listened attentively, saliva oozing from the corner of his mouth. She took out her hankerchief and wiped it away.

'You didn't do it, Daddy, did you?' She put her hand on his good arm and leaned over him, staring into his glaucous eyes.

He shook his head. At one time he would have prevaricated; but now he abdicated, handed over control; and longed only for peace.

'I didn't think you did,' she said with a smile. 'You would have trusted me to handle matters better than that in my own way.' She paused, and he nodded and attempted to smile again. 'However,' she went on,

'Brian doesn't see it like that. He suspects all of us, which is why I wrote this letter. It simply says that Mr. Langley has apologised to you for any annoyance he may have caused you, but that you are at a loss to understand what that might be. That he has always behaved with perfect propriety towards you, and that furthermore he is engaged to be married to your daughter. Finally, that you would be obliged if Mr. Farrell - that's his name, the man who owns Galway Minerals - would convey this to Mr. Langley and apologise to him for any inconvenience caused him in the matter.' She took the letter out of her pocket, opened it and spread it out on the eiderdown in front of her father, who looked at it stupidly. He did not like this; but sick as he was he knew Marie well enough to realise that he must do it.

'You will do this for me, Daddy, won't you?' she pleaded. 'It's very important to me. Someone has tried to make trouble, and we must hit it on the head at the beginning. You do understand that, don't you?'

The old man nodded and sighed. His eyes had moistened, but Marie could not allow the genuine pity and sympathy she had for her father to prevent her from making this last desperate appeal to him.

'If I help you, will you make an effort to sign it?'

Pat raised his right hand and moved his fingers slowly; his other arm lay flat and paralysed under the eiderdown. Marie opened her bag again and took out her fountain pen. She took down a book from the top of the chest of drawers, Miss Potter's copy of 'The Shoes of the Fisherman', and put it on her father's knees with the letter on top of it. Then she sat down by the old man's side at the top of the bed, and put her arm over his shoulder. Something of the determination of both of them went into his slowly written signature: a bit shaky, but legible enough.

'Oh, thank you, Daddy,' cried Marie, kissing him on top of the head. Suddenly she felt him stiffen and swallow painfully.

'What are you doing?' The voice at the door was not Nurse Potter's but Mrs. Fogarty's; very pale, with wringing hands and twitching mouth she came

into the room and pointed her nose at the letter.
Marie took it up swiftly and folded it, while her father
sank back against the pillows, his mouth open, his
eyes staring fixedly at his wife.

'What are you getting him to sign?' demanded Agnes,
unclasping her hands with a cracking of knuckles and
pointing at the book on Pat's knee. Marie picked it up
and looked at her mother coldly.

'Just a letter.'

'What kind of a letter?'

'A business letter,' replied Marie taking up her bag.

'To whom?' snapped Mrs. Fogarty shrilly. Marie
looked at her mother with raised eyebrows. She had
never seen her so angry before; her mouth was twisted
with rage and her whole body was trembling uncon-
trollably.

'Mummy, why don't you mind your own business?'
Marie's voice was dangerously soft. It infuriated her
mother still more.

'How dare you speak to your mother like that, you
brazen slut! Give me that document at once, give it
to me I say. How do I know that you're not forcing
your father to sign over something to you? I wouldn't
put it past you, or him either.'

Marie was interrupted by a gasp from her father.
She looked round. Her father was shrinking back
against the pillows with an expression of horror on his
twisted features.

'Get the nurse,' she cried over her shoulder as she
leaned over him. He was trembling and moaning
incoherently.

'I will not,' she heard her mother retort in a
creaking voice. 'If you want to kill your father - '

'Oh, shut up, will you?' shouted Marie taking her
father's hand and pressing her hand over his forehead.
'Go and get the nurse I tell you.'

'Not until you tell me what you were getting him to
sign,' shrilled her mother. 'Your father is not in his
right mind, remember I'm here to witness that. You
forced him, you forced him, you want to see me left
out on the road. You're a nice pair, plotting and
planning behind my back. Pat, as God is my judge,

I'll never forgive you in this life or the next if you don't tell me.' Agnes had come to the end of the bed and was leaning forward, clutching the wooden post with her yellow hands and staring at her husband with burning eyes; wild, fanatical and haggard with rage and lack of sleep. 'And don't think the nurse will come up either. She won't come until I call her.'

'In that case I'd better call her myself. It might do her good to see you now.' Marie turned to the door, but her mother was too quick for her. She darted across the room and slammed the door, standing in front of it with her skinny shoulders flattened against it. She was weeping now, the tears rolling down her paper-pale face.

'Oh, no, you won't. You won't leave this room until you give me that letter,' she panted. 'Are you trying to get him to sign a will or something? Give it to me, give it to me,' she wailed.

Pat moaned and turned his head away, pressing it into the pillows and clutching the sheet with his active hand.

'In that case,' said Marie, contemptuously, 'I will.' She took the letter out of her bag and slowly read it out. When she was finished her mother came away from the door and held out her hand whimpering.

'Show it to me,' she whispered.

Marie held it out; but her mother did not take it. Suddenly she dropped on her knees and clasped her hands to her breast. 'Oh, Sacred Heart of Jesus,' she cried over and over again. 'Oh, Sacred Heart of Jesus.'

CHAPTER TWENTY

That afternoon Father Moran had two visitors. Just before he sat down to his lunch a messenger arrived from the parish priest and handed in a note which was brought into the dining-room by Miss Price.

'I hope everything is all right, Father,' she said, wiping her hands nervously on her overall. Of late the priest fancied that she looked at him in an oddly tentative manner, as if she had something to say and did not quite know how to say it. He opened the envelope and read the short note inside. 'I should be obliged if you would call over to see me this evening, about eight if convenient'. He looked up and found Miss Price still standing inside the door, watching him closely. He put the letter into his pocket and sat down at the table, unaware that his features betrayed any emotion.

Alone, slumped in his chair, he stared at the wall in front of him, his wide mouth slack and discontented, his nostrils dilated, his cheeks flushed, the dark shadows under his heavy eyes indicating not only sleepless nights, but a certain furtive sensuality.

'Jesus,' he muttered to himself, 'Jesus, Jesus,' the sacred name affording as ever a sort of animal relief to those who are bound to it forever; and drag it with them into the depths. A perverse litany, it afforded the most exquisite titillation of all; and beyond it there loomed only silence and satiety.

Brian finished his business early that day, and at five o'clock was asking a talkative publican where Father Moran lived.

After taking two wrong turns, for there was nobody in sight at any cross-roads, he arrived at Father

Moran's house a little after half-five. Cold trees, a church tower, leaning head-stones above the low wall of the cemetery across the road.

Miss Price received him ungraciously, looked him up and down, and asked his name.

'Father Moran will know me,' he told her sharply.

The housekeeper prepared for an argument. She did not know Brian by sight; but her instinct told her that he was in some way connected with the curious change she had noticed in the priest's behaviour lately.

'How will he know you if you don't tell me your name?' she insisted.

'I haven't come to see you,' replied Brian tartly. 'Please go and tell him that a traveller wants to see him.'

'A traveller!' Miss Price opened her eyes and stepped back, clutching her flat bosom with alarm. Could this big sullen looking young man be the famous new lover-boy she had heard so much about from Nelly? God in heaven, he looked dangerous. Suppose he was going to attack her Father Tom? She would be the laughing stock of the parish. 'He's not in,' she quivered, and instantly knew that she was once again on the sideline watching two people who were quite unconscious of her presence, for the priest, hearing their voices, had come out of his room, and Brian was staring over her shoulder into the hall beyond.

'Come in,' said Father Moran, standing aside and pointing to the door of his study. Brian strode past the woman and disappeared into the room. Father Moran looked at his housekeeper with a frown and beckoned her to close the front door.

'I'll tell you when I want tea,' he said, following his visitor and closing the door firmly behind him. Miss Price crept back to her kitchen, her nerves ajangle, and turned on the radio to divert her mind. She did not want to hear what went on in the next room for all the Nellys in the world.

In the study the priest looked the young man in the eye and took the offensive.

'Have you come to make trouble?' he asked frankly, planting his feet wide apart and folding his arms across his broad chest.

'Not unless you want to make it,' replied the young man with a sudden almost ingratiating smile which deepened the priest's suspicion. His eyes darkened and he raised his chin threateningly. He would have dearly loved to take the fellow by the scruff of the neck and kick him out of the house; but his training, his position, the memory of the whole unsavoury mess, prevented him; although the thought was clearly revealed in his hard aggressive eyes.

'Well, what do you want?'

The clock struck half-five. It was always slow. And from the kitchen they could hear the faint resonance of John McCormack singing 'I Hear you Calling me'. Miss Price was soothing herself with the most soulful tenor in the business.

Father Moran's dominant attitude had not called forth a similar response from Brian. He took off his gloves and tucked them in the pocket of his suede jacket; his large sinuous hands patting his hips gently; a curiously self-indulgent, almost feminine gesture. The priest looked at him with distaste; and Brian catching his glance straightened himself up and shifted his loose-limbed bulk from one foot to another, adopting a stance very similar to the other man, but with his hands hanging clenched by his sides.

'I've been talking to Marie this morning,' he began, looking down at the priest's big shining boots. 'Someone has got onto my boss in Galway and told him I was making a nuisance of myself round here, and if I didn't apologise I could get out. Would you know anything about that?' A ray of light from the setting sun flashed across the young man's face, polishing his cheekbones and glinting on his fair hair.

Father Moran unclasped his arms, studied one taut white fist and frowned. In the darkening room his tilted face looked older, the loose flesh gathering in a little pad under his chin.

'It wasn't me,' he said slowly. 'If that's what you mean. I know where you work, but I don't know your employer.' He looked at the chair beside which Brian was standing, and remembered its late occupant. He had told Bill where Langley worked. He looked at Brian questioningly, suddenly seeing him in a new light: a young man with a job to hold down, caught up in a net of intrigue which he could not understand.

'Who told you where I worked?'

'I heard it in Fogartys.' Father Moran sighed, shrugged his shoulders and walked over to his chair. He sat down and motioned to the other to do the same. Brian hesitated for a moment and then accepted, hitching up his shoulders so as not to 'seat' his jacket.

'Who told you, Marie?' He pressed his back against the leather and gripped the arms, his long thumbs sticking out rigidly from his hands.

Father Moran nodded and looked into the fire.

'Listen - ' began Brian, and then stopped as the priest held up his hand and silenced him.

'I don't think it was her,' he said quietly, 'and clearly you don't either.'

Brian looked down at his outstretched thumbs and flattened them back against the arm of the chair. He smelled whiskey and wondered if the other man had been drinking much that afternoon. At the moment he could do with another drink himself; but this was not an affair that could be settled over a shot of Jameson.

'Have you any idea who it might be?' he said watching the priest's dark face closely. The man knew something; of that he was sure.

'Yes,' said Father Moran simply, 'I have.' He held out one hand to the fire; and the flames lit up the black hairs on his wrist. 'Is your employer a religious sort of man?'

Brian gave a short hard laugh; but the priest did not seem to hear. He bent and unbent his fingers in the heat slowly, his eyes blank and secretive.

'He belongs to every known religious organisation in the city. More catholic than the Pope.'

'I see.' Father Moran sighed again and looked across at his visitor quizzically. 'As I say I know nothing about it, although I have my suspicions. However there's no point in telling you that either, since we just don't know. Has any harm been done? I mean you haven't been fired or anything, have you?'

'No.' The room was stuffy and Brian unbuttoned the top of his jacket.

'Take it off if you like.'

Brian stiffened and shook his head. The man was either very clever, or rather sadly honest.

'In that case there doesn't seem much point in discussing it. It's one of those things we'll never find out. I'm pretty sure of that. I can give no proof of course, except that it would be a damn silly thing for me to do. But then, that's not what really brought you here to-day, is it?' Tom Moran, his manner stripped of all priestly overtones, looked across at his rival with a faint smile. The young man looked away and bit his lip. He had thought he would hold the initiative in this interview; and was puzzled that he now seemed not to particularly want it anymore.

'You can go ahead and get married if you want to, Mr. Langley. Marie has not deceived you. How much do you know about her?' The tone was conversational, almost casual; and Brian, feeling his resolve weaken under the placid masculinity of the priest, fought back wildly.

'Everything.'

'If you do,' chuckled the other, 'you'll be the first man that ever got that far with a woman.' He shifted in his chair and darted a quick side-long glance at the young man. 'Who told you about us?' he said quietly, as if he really wanted information.

Brian felt himself getting red; and began to unbutton his jacket unthinkingly; his fingers coiling nervously about the buttons as he frowned into the fire.

'No one you know,' he replied defiantly.

'I see.' Father Moran ran his fingers through his thick hair and smiled with one corner of his mouth. 'Priests get married nowadays, you know,' he went on evenly. 'It's not the impossibility it used to be. So we're not arguing from quite the same positions as we might have at one time.'

'You don't mean to say - ' burst out Brian, opening his mouth and staring. The priest saw the glazed fear in his eyes; and realised that the young man was at a disadvantage: he was deeply in love, and anxious for a confirmation of it.

'No, no,' he said brusquely, waving his hand impatiently. 'I have no intention of marrying anyone, but it's as well to remember that it's no longer impossible.'

Brian tried to collect himself in the face of this new development. He felt his advantage slipping away from him, and shifted his attack.

'Anyway, you couldn't live round here,' he replied in a dry forced voice. 'It wouldn't be very convenient for you, would it?'

'No, not convenient.' Father Moran paused and pulled his soutane up at the knees: it was worn and shiny: his everyday outfit. Then he suddenly leaned forward and tapped Brian sharply on the knee, causing him to twitch. 'But if we were in love, as you two seem to be, we'd manage. People often do in more difficult circumstances, I don't think in the long run Marie's father would see her wanting. And I could get a job.' His voice warmed and grew freer as he spoke of this possibility, forgetful that he had told Bill Conway that he was unfitted for anything but the vocation in which he had been trained. Like most priests he liked to think at times that he could take his place in the world of ordinary men; prove himself capable of making a life outside the framework of a vast established institution.

'In that case why did you do it? I mean if you had no intention of getting out?' Brian pressed his knees together, and felt a curious fleeting tingle at the base of his spine.

Tom Moran smiled sadly and rubbed his blueish chin with his long thick fingers, making a sound like emery-paper drawn lightly over soft wood.

'Why does anybody do anything? It happened, and it's over.'

'But why did it happen in the first place?'

'You mean she makes a habit of it, is that it?' said the priest quickly, looking out from under his black eyebrows.

Brian blinked, and gathered his forces to combat the lassitude which had been growing on him; a physical languor which he could not explain, even though his mind was alert and excited. He longed for a real clash with this forceful man; and equally for a defeat, the exact nature of which he did not comprehend. But Father Moran had already sensed this latent passivity in the other; and felt he knew now why Marie had chosen him.

'Well, does she?' said Brian bluntly, but with an appealing glance; half coquettish in its sullen helplessness.

'I think she was pretty confused and a bit defiant before she met you. She felt that people did not approve of her, and that always leads to foolish impulses. What has she told you herself?'

'That there were other men.' Brian crossed his legs and clasped his knee; a gesture at odds with his strained expression. He was no longer altogether in control of his reflexes. 'At first I thought it was you, and then I thought there were dozens; and that I was just another one.'

'What you really want to know is, did she deceive you after she met you?'

The young man nodded helplessly.

Father Moran stood up, went to his cabinet and took out the bottle of whisky. He poured out two glasses and left one on the table beside Brian's chair.

'Have that if you feel like it.' Then he stood with his back to the fire, looked about the darkening room, strode over to the door, switched on the light, came back and sat down in his chair again.

'No,' he said levelly, 'I don't think she did. Things are rarely black and white in this world. I think she was caught in a difficult situation. Shall we say that she eased me out gradually?' He sipped his drink and sucked in his lips. 'I don't suppose she really knew what to do. Nobody ever does in a situation like that. It's never logical, and I don't see why we should expect it to be. I was wrong, she was wrong, no doubt, but we sort of drifted into it out of loneliness and weakness, and on my part no doubt the desire to have one last fling.' He paused and tapped the glass with his nail. 'We feel that too just like other men, you

know. Forget the collar for a minute, will you, and
think of it like that. It was wrong, yes, I know that,
but - ' Father Moran broke off and for the first time
showed signs of weakness. His heavy under-lip
trembled, and he drew it back over his teeth with a
quick intake of breath. In the light he looked paler,
more worn and drawn than Brian had remembered
him. But he could not stop now, especially since
they had achieved a certain natural balance of communication: two men talking about a woman.

'And that night I called?' he enquired, looking at
his glass of whisky, which he had carefully refrained
from touching. The clock struck six. Ten minutes
slow. And in the kitchen John McCormack had given
way to a pop group. Miss Price had evidently tuned
into another station in her quest for distraction.

'Yes,' said the other shortly, 'but it was the last
time, she made that quite clear. And after all I knew
very little about you. I was confused too, and I suppose
sorry for myself.' He swallowed hard and twirled his
glass in his big hands. 'I knew it was over, and I
wanted, well, what does one want when there isn't love
and no hope for the future?' He leaned forward, rested
his elbows on his thighs and stared into the fire with
knotted eyebrows. 'No, she didn't deceive you, not in
the real sense.' He looked up and raised his voice.
'So now the two of you will have to make the best of it.
Is there anything else you want to know?' The question
was unexpected; but Brian was grateful for it.

'Was it you, or her, at the beginning, I mean?' he
said awkwardly.

The man in the shiny black cassock made his last
move. It was the only untruth he had deliberately
formulated that evening: a kind of crooked salute to the
honour of manhood.

'Me, I suppose,' he said slowly. 'After all I'm a
great deal older and I should have known better. It
was just something I couldn't control at the time, and
Marie was at a dead end, bored, and beginning to
wonder if anything would happen to her. I took advantage
of the situation as they say.' He looked into Brian's
eyes and smiled ruefully, a last glimmer of boyishness

flickering across his heavy face. 'You're very old fashioned in some ways, aren't you?'

'No one likes to be made use of,' retorted Brian, slightly evading the issue.

'No, of course not,' Tom Moran agreed. 'But you weren't used in any deliberate sense, if that's what you're worried about. I give you my word on that. As far as her other - ' he paused and cleared his throat - 'experiences are concerned, I don't see why you should hold them against her. After all I don't suppose you're exactly inexperienced yourself.'

Again Brian felt that tingle in his loins as the other man's eyes searched his face with a hard examining stare and ran down the length of his taut body. Had he not read that some women felt undressed when they were looked at like that? A vision of his compulsive intimacies flashed through his mind; and he felt his face reddening. Instinctively he reached out and picked up his glass; then looked at it guiltily as if he had betrayed himself.

'Tell me,' he said in a gruff voice, his nostrils quivering as he inhaled the tang of the whisky, 'would you marry her, if you could?'

'No.' The voice was clear and decisive. 'I would not. But then I was never in love with her. I was one of the people who used her. That's why she has turned to you. You'll have to make up for all that. Do you think you'll be able to?'

Brian sipped his drink and moved his shoulders slowly and voluptuously, as if he were exercising a sleepy muscle.

'In one way, yes.'

'I'm sure you'll be able to satisfy her, and that's very important for both of you.' Unknown to himself Father Moran was unable to suppress a vicarious pleasure in encouraging these young people; a pleasure which priests as marriage counsellors experience more often than they care to admit. 'Yes, I think that will be all right.'

'I know it will,' said Brian in a low voice, not altogether devoid of smugness.

'I see.' The priest realised that he was in no

position to pass judgement on that. Privately he could not help thinking that from the masculine point of view Marie was a slut; and this thought comforted him somewhat, as it always does when a man has taken his pleasure of a woman, and tired of her. 'There is however, a great deal more to it than that,' he went on with a hint of his professional manner.

'Yes, I know.' Brian tilted back his head and looked up at the ceiling, his firm jaw straining against his skin. 'I'm meeting her to-night. At eight.'

Father Moran looked at the clock, unwilling yet to let the young man go, representing as he did all the legal aspects of a relationship which he himself would never know. Guilty they might both be at the moment, according to the book, but society had a compendious cloak to wrap around two young people who settle their affairs according to the rules. What went on behind the marriage front Father Moran well knew was often a great deal more guilty than the acts of passion and weakness that were transacted outside it. But he had no rights now as a priest to indulge in platitudes about sacred obligations and the dignity of the home. Nevertheless he felt he could prepare this young fellow a little for what he had to face; the sort of problems he imagined would confront himself in a similar situation.

'Why don't you stay and have some tea?' he said with a hint of pleading in his voice. 'I have to go out before eight too. We'll have time.'

'All right,' said Brian, warmed by the whisky, and convinced now that in his turn he had won a battle if not a war. Father Moran stood up and went out of the room to tell Miss Price; and his guest also got to his feet, took off his jacket which was smothering him, and folded it over the back of his chair. The priest came back silently and closed the door softly behind him.

'Tell me,' he said in a light toneless voice, 'just what do you know about women?'

CHAPTER TWENTY-ONE

The parish priest's house was bigger than his curate's, but a great deal more dilapidated. Ivy covered most of the front and hung down over some of the windows not in use on the first floor. The door was unpainted and the short avenue rutted and patched with moss. It looked thoroughly run down; a fitting abode for an elderly, absent-minded, eccentric clergyman. At night with a dim light burning in one of the windows; and as so often happened in the winter-time, a foggy mist from the river coiling about the walls, it had a ghostly, even slightly sinister appearance: silence, broken only by the dripping of bare and slimy trees or the distant barking of a dog, lay heavy about it, and was rarely broken in the evenings by the arrival of company; for Father Melody was a solitary man with few friends among his colleagues in the diocese.

That night he opened the door himself, having heard the squelching of the tyres on the sodden drive. As Father Moran stepped into the dank hall lighted by a single electric bulb of low wattage, he could hear vague muffled sounds of pistol shots and galloping hooves at the end of the passage. Miss Scally, the housekeeper, a grim silent woman who unlike Margaret Price, never gossiped and seemed to have even less friends than her employer, was at this hour always glued to the television set which Father Melody had installed for her in the kitchen.

He led his visitor silently into the big front room which Father Moran had always vaguely envied; but which in the evenings had a mysterious, almost forbidding aspect, with its rows of books, its white skull-like busts of Shakespeare and Dante glimmering in the corners on either side of the fireplace, its dark Spanish religious paintings dimly lit by the green-

shaded reading lamp which the old man kept by his
chair. It threw a beam of light carefully directed onto
the spot where he held his book, and left the rest of
the room blurred in its outlines and full of wavering
shadows.

'Sit down,' said Father Melody, indicating the other
chair on the opposite side of the big fireplace in which
a few beech logs smouldered drowsily.

Father Melody was a small stocky man with an egg-
bald head, bright sunken blue eyes, a flat nose, and
big ears, pointed at the top and thickening out into a
fleshy triangle. This gave him a sharp faun-like
appearance, which his quick light movements and airy
step did nothing to dispel. He was nearly seventy, but
looked much younger: a spry leprechaun.

He perched himself on the edge of his chair,
adjusted the lamp so that it beamed on the white hearth-
rug - a pool of yellow light between their two pairs of
shoes: the old man's small, shining and elastic-sided,
Father Moran's large, square and splashed with mud,
for he had had no time to polish them before seeing
Brian off at a quarter to eight.

'Well, Tom,' said the parish priest with a shy
smile which made his elfin face seem even younger,
'how are you keeping?'

'Oh, all right,' said the younger priest heavily.
His talk with Brian over tea had not been calculated to
sooth. So many women so freely available: there was
nothing new in that, but coming from such a source it
had had a depressing effect. The young hound had
everything; and he had taken an almost sadistic pleasure
in hinting at his sexual experiments. And the supplanted rival had had to keep quiet. After all he had
asked for it.

Father Melody after a quick searching inspection of
the curate's haggard face and discontented mouth
decided it would be kinder to come straight to the point.

'I've had a letter about you,' he said stretching out
one foot so that the toe of his shoe shone in the circle
of light on the rug.

'Oh, God,' groaned the unhappy curate, covering
his eyes with his hands. 'Not another.'

132

'Have there been others?' Father Melody's voice was mildly curious.

'Bill Conway got one, addressed to the bishop.'

'I see.' The old man chuckled, causing Father Moran to lower his hand and look at him anxiously; but the sunken eyes in the shadows were, as far as he could make out, benign. 'Tell me what Greasy Bill did about it?' He tapped the rug with his toe and smiled.

Suddenly Tom found himself pouring out the whole story of Bill's visit; and his suspicions about the behaviour of the employer in Galway. It seemed easy, and anyway what had he to lose now?

'I see,' murmured Melody again. 'It's like a ghost with no head and several voices. The point is, is it true?'

'I don't know what the letter said,' countered Tom. He wiped his damp palm on his knee.

Father Melody put his hand in his pocket and produced an envelope. The curate looked at it. He had not told the old man about Marie; had talked merely of vague accusations; of another man involved who had also heard something and had made trouble; of Bill's probable attempt to silence him. It was after all an old story, and could be denied, especially now that Langley was left in possession of the field, and unlikely to stir up any more trouble.

He reached out and took the letter from the parish priest's dry white hand. This was not going to be easy; but he could decide while he read it. It was written on cheap ruled note-paper in an uneducated hand. It was specific. Names, dates, times: someone who knew.

He leaned forward towards the light of the fire as he read it, and the old man watched his dark sensual face closely. The wide mouth twitched and softened, then drew back in a grim angry line. A vein swelled in his temple. Father Melody folded his hands over his stomach and waited.

Tom Moran held the letter down between his knees and stared into the fire for a few moments.

'What are you going to do about it?' he said in a dry choked voice.

'That depends on you.'

'It's not quite what I expected. Short and to the point.'

'They very often are, especially the fairly accurate one.' The curate jerked his head round aggressively, but the old man went on, unfoiled, his low voice swelling a little. 'I have some experience of those things. It's surprising how often they're right, when they're not crazy, and even then - ' the voice trailed away, and one small white hand was detached from the other and raised in front of his chest, a ghostly benediction in the gloom.

'Do you mean you've got other letters about me?' Tom felt his neck swelling with indignation. What a filthy lot of bastards they all were! That Langley with his theories of erotic satisfaction; it was disgusting. He felt self-righteous and revolted; emotions mixed, and for the moment undirected.

'No,' said Father Melody quietly, 'not about you.'

'In that case - ' he leaned forward, his wrist doubled back, the letter poised for a burning between his fingers.

'I wouldn't do that if I were you.' Father Melody's voice was soft, almost sad. 'Not unless it's totally untrue.'

The tense wrist remained rigid. Then abruptly it relaxed, the hand was withdrawn and laid down on top of the letter in his lap.

'I rather suspect it is true, Tom. Am I right?'

The curate looked down at the shining toe and thought incongruously of the ancient custom of kissing the Pope's foot. He felt his head throbbing, and the blood racing through his disturbed body. His responses were still mixed: pieties and suppressed lust. But he could not bottle this thing up over-night. It was still a relief to talk about it.

'There was something,' he mumbled. 'It was over before this young man arrived on the scene. Bill was clumsy. I'm surprised at his making a move like that.'

'No doubt he underestimated his man. It sounds exactly like what our Bill would do. But clearly the man in Galway is a zealot, and charged in. Hardly a

clerical type. Bill probably dropped a hint, and
neglected to give precise instructions, for fear of
compromising himself. I always thought he was too
clever by half.' He chuckled again, dismissing the
bishop's secretary and all clerical intrigue with an
impatient wave of his hand. The shining toe was withdrawn from the pool of light. 'What is really important
now is your attitude. What do you want to do? It's
over, you tell me. Do you want to carry on? Or clear
out?'

Calmly, clearly without emotion the choice was
spelled out for him. It had seemed easy when things
began to get difficult. He believed in the Church,
accepted its dogmas, assumed that he had a genuine
vocation. One could he knew possess all these things
and still make an ass of oneself, morally and intellec-
tually. He had assumed that a good confession and a
firm purpose of amendment would restore him. Now,
in the presence of this warm but disenchanted voice he
was not so sure. Would he ever succeed in regaining
that physical equilibrium - such as it was - that he had
known before?

'It's difficult getting back into harness again, Tom.
A certain balance, even if it's only a negative one - is
upset. We really come to terms with what we have
given up. Abstinence is better than moderation. We
know all the answers. Which doesn't make it any easier
at all.'

Tom looked down at his big beefy anointed hands,
one of them clenched over a sheet of cheap note-paper,
and then raised his head and stared at the shadowy
white face opposite him. Naturally an old parish priest
should know these things; but somehow he had never
expected to hear them from Father Melody. The old
boy sounded as if he knew what he was talking about.
Was it possible that he too - ?

'No,' he said dully, 'it doesn't.'

'Do you think you can go on?'

'With my head, yes. I've never bothered much about
the finer points of theology or canon law.' No, he did
not hate the Church because he had broken its laws.
He assumed, unfashionably, that it knew more than he

did. And yet, could he, did he really want to tame his rebellious body in the service of an ideal? It did not seem so easy now. In his confusion he did not know which of them had upset him most: Marie, or her ardent young lover.

'And with your heart?' enquired Father Melody gently.

Tom Moran looked over the old priest's shoulder to where beyond the window the line of amber lights twinkled on the horizon. His heart had not been engaged. And yet, to whom, to what did it belong?

'I don't know,' he said sulkily. 'I never thought of myself as anything other than a priest. A bad one, maybe, but still - '

'We're all bad ones. The important thing is to go on from day to day, year after year doing the ordinary things. You're not required to be a saint. Indeed that would be a distinct embarrassment to everybody, as well as highly romantic. But the odd thing is that the ordinary things are the most difficult.' Father Melody leaned forward, gripped the arms of his chair and slowly got to his feet. 'Which is why so many halfbaked saints leave the church.'

'I never thought of leaving. I suppose I just didn't think at all while this thing was going on. Now I don't know if I'll be able to carry on.'

The old man looked down at the angry, hurt, selfpitying face of this simple young man and suppressed the desire to pat him on the head. This he knew was not time for emotion. What the fellow needed now was cold steel.

'Get up,' he said abruptly. 'We're going out.'

'Going out!' Tom stood up, frowning and peering suspiciously. 'Where?'

'Oh, not very far. We're going to do one of the ordinary things. Come on.'

CHAPTER TWENTY-TWO

In that country parish it was not yet deemed necessary to lock and bolt the church at sun-down for fear of burglars. They went in on the sacristy door and found themselves surrounded in the dark by the mingled smells of incense, candle-grease, damp walls, floor-polish, and the sweetish waxen scent that impregnated all of Father Melody's clothes. It was an odour which his curate knew well: the redolence which the male body acquires after years of celibacy. To-night it struck him as immensely desirable and slightly disgusting.

Father Melody did not switch on the light and a mouse scuttled away in the darkness. Making his way unerringly he crossed the sacristy and pushed open the door leading to the altar. The small church was dimly lighted from a single electric bulb in the porch under the tiny wooden gallery which housed the harmonium; and which was never built for the noble organ that Father Melody sometimes dreamed about.

The old man genuflected and glanced around to see if the curate had followed him. He did not bother to look into the body of the church. His instinct told him that there was no one there. They were alone, facing the flickering red light of the sanctuary lamp, which still burned in that old-fashioned place. In spite of the sweeping liturgical changes which had turned the old ritual of the church upside down the parish priest had not yet installed an altar table to face the congregation; and the bishop, who hated any suggestion of change, had not yet insisted.

'Look,' said Father Melody, pointing to the lamp which had burned in that place for over a century to remind the faithful of the Presence in the tabernacle. It threw a dim wavering shadow on the far wall that

reached up into the darkness of the roof. 'I suppose
you believe in what that implies?'

Father Moran was startled. He had never questioned
himself about his beliefs; nor had he had any great need
to: this little flame and the curtained tabernacle which
it guarded were part of his heritage. In just such a
church had his people proclaimed their faith in their
own traditional way for a century and a half. And
before that on Mass rocks in the hills during the penal
times. And before that again in ancient churches now
destroyed or taken over by the new dispensation. A
long history of simple rock-like faith in good times
and ill; through wars, famines and revolutions;
stretching back into the dim almost mythical past when
this flame and this tabernacle had burned and inspired
the dark ages of Europe. A longer journey than the
walk from the presbytery.

'I mean,' went on Father Melody speaking in his
normal voice, 'does it affect you emotionally?'

In Maynooth Tom had been warned against emotional
Christianity; and encouraged to pursue the logical
subtleties of Aquinas: advice which no one in his class
had taken literally. Intellectual faith was not common
in the ranks of the Irish clergy who were apt to follow
their hearts first, and ask questions afterwards. It
was their great strength, and for a few a great weakness. Yes, he had persevered and submitted himself
under the influence of a powerful, primeval emotion.

Yet his native caution led him to hesitate. Was it
a trick question? And still he knew that the old man,
once assured of his determination to stay and battle
it out, would protect him. It was an unwritten law
among the clergy; except in the case of public scandal.

'Yes,' he said slowly, 'it does, I suppose. Although
not so much now as it used to. But it could, it could.'
And in his heart he knew that the old awe was still
there.

Father Melody made no reply; and for a few minutes
they stood side by side at the end of the altar, like two
actors waiting in the wings for the lights to go up. In
a sense they were players engaged in a tremendous
drama which touched upon the deepest and most secret

impulses of mankind: ministers of an ancient, terrible and hopeful message.

'It isn't enough simply to inspire awe, ' said Father Melody, as if he had been reading his thoughts. 'Or to feel it. Although of course it's a help. I envy you. I never had it. ' And with this surprising statement he touched the curate's arm and went back into the sacristy. Father Moran followed him, wondering what was the purpose of this seemingly aimless visit. But the parish priest did not enlighten him as they made their way back to the house through the wicket gate which opened on to the presbytery garden: an over-grown patch of brambles with a sodden path cut through them arched by gnarled trees that dripped under the vague and ominous sky.

Back in the house Father Melody motioned him to sit down and went to a side-board in the dining-room to fetch a bottle of whisky. Alone in the study Father Moran was assailed by the enviable smell of calf-bound books and old dry parchment; and the waxen scent of the curious old man who spent most of his days in this dark silent room. Was he happy?

It was a strange thought. One never imagined him as being anything except himself; and happiness after all was a very relative state of mind. No doubt he was content, and more than a little selfish, as old bachelors tend to be.

'Here, ' he said, gliding back into the room with a bottle and two glasses which he managed with the dexterity of a head waiter.

The curate took his glass and waited for the old man to pour out a few drops for himself. He had always been abstemious.

'There's a jug of water over there, if you want it, ' he said, waving vaguely into the shadows behind him. Tom decided to drink it neat.

'Slainte, ' he said.

'Good health, ' replied Father Melody primly. He was not an admirer of the Irish language, which he argued was at best a pre-fabricated affair, the mental continuity of which had long been lost. 'I suppose you're wondering why I brought you out like that?' He sat down in his chair, crossed his feet, and nursed his glass.

'Well, yes, I am.'

'There are some people who are impressed by the ritual of the Church. It has its uses of course, and its symbolism is very significant. But essentially it means little. What you see in a small country church like ours is nearer to reality. If that unromantic reality means nothing to you, then you had better get out. But I think it does to you, and not only because at the moment it suits your book to have me think so.'

The younger man's chin hardened; and he looked at his host angrily.

'I don't give a damn what you think,' he snapped. 'This is not an examination of faith. I have that.' He shook his head, and went on bitterly: 'I wish to God I hadn't sometimes.'

'Quite. It is an awful burden at times. It would be nice to be able to throw the baby out with the bath-water. Are you sure you'll be able to go on?'

'I want to, and that's the truth. But I don't know just at the moment if I'll be able to.' The voice was bitter; the eyes confused and dissatisfied.

'Because, no doubt, you now feel you know something of love.' The old man's musical voice was unusually flat and neutral; and even Tom in his disconsolate state could discover no hint of irony in it.

'Well, is it such a bad thing to know something of this human love we're always preaching about? Maybe it removes a lot of complacency.' He was making a last throw, working up a defence he did not really believe in himself. But no man, even one so uncommitted to the feminine principle as Tom Moran, likes to feel that he has been smoothly and effortlessly supplanted. Now he was angling for sympathy.

'That,' said Father Melody incisively, 'is a load of shit.'

The curate's mouth dropped open, and he stared at his superior with a kind of stunned admiration. Never had the old man seemed so human to him as at that moment when he was calmly and with Rabelaisian vigour demolishing one of the most cherished of romantic notions.

'We must fall in order to understand the sinner. I know, I know. It's supposed to be a sign of humanity. But for God's sake don't ever confuse lust with love. Any man can fall, but it doesn't make him in the least better or wiser or more understanding. All this nonsense about 'love' is nothing more than raging egoism, a sense of possession taken out of the shop and transferred to the emotions. Most people love one another as they would a field or a piece of furniture. With others it is merely lust sanctioned by the custom of the country. That human love that you mention, and which we're supposed to be always preaching about, is an entirely different thing. It is neither romantic nor passionate, it's acceptance of yourself and of other people. There is no need for a priest to go through the motions of a romantic novel to learn that. His vocation is to serve. Any other interpretation of what we do is not only heresy, it's drooling nonsense.' Father Melody paused and refreshed himself with a sip of whisky.

'But there is love between people, isn't there?' put in Father Moran, anxious to demonstrate that he was listening attentively. 'What is known as ordinary human love.'

'Of course there is.' There was a hint of impatience in the reply as if Melody knew that they were merely playing with words, decorating rather than revealing a problem on which they were in essential agreement. 'You either understand that or you don't. If you really loved this woman, you wouldn't have interfered with her in the first place. I take it you had no intention of marrying her?'

'Well, no,' admitted the curate ruefully, shifting uncomfortably in his chair. 'But supposing I had?'

'I don't suppose you'd be any better or worse than any other man. She'd get four or five years out of you, which is as much as any of them get. Women call these few years 'happiness'. After that you'd stick together because you'd got used to each other, or because of the children, or because you wouldn't admit that you'd made a mistake. That very often is the

most powerful basis of a supposedly happy marriage.'
The old man gave a dry chuckle, and brushed his lips
with his crooked finger. 'As it was, you had a bash,
and are now feeling the physical effects of it. They
can be very disturbing, as I know.'

'You know?' The black eye-brows shot up.

'I was young once too, Tom. I know what it is to
share in human failings. And it didn't make me any
better, or more charitable.'

A log dissolved into ash in the fireplace. Another
illusion gone. Did all the passion, pleasure and
experience in the world end in a solitary room?

'Which is what I meant when I said that I had some
experience of letters like that one,' the old man went
on steadily. 'I was a curate in the palace at the time,
when Dr. Dooley was bishop. He got some letters
about me, and unlike our blind friend now reigning,
read them himself.'

'My God!' Tom Moran swallowed hard and
instinctively clutched the pocket where he had put away
his particular letter. 'Women?'

'No, Tom, not women.' Father Melody stood up
and moved to the centre of the room where his desk
was. The curate watched him with wide staring eyes
as he took a bunch of keys out of his pocket and unlocked
one of the drawers. The sweet waxen scent was stronger
than ever, and the young man felt nauseated. Tom had
little understanding and less sympathy for the particular
problem which he supposed his parish priest had had
to live with. The thought of it had always disgusted
him; although he knew in precise detail from his study
of pastoral theology what its physical manifestations
were. His own furtive experiments seemed relatively
innocent compared with this.

Melody turned round and held up a piece of paper,
looking down at his junior with an ironic smile.

'I have kept it, just to remind me. I advise you to
do the same. Would you like to read it?'

'No, I would not,' Tom exclaimed harshly.

'Old Dooley was sympathetic and very understanding.
I don't know what I'd have done without him. But then
of course he was a kind of saint, in spite of being a

bishop.' The letter was put back in the drawer and locked. It seemed to Tom that the beautiful lilting voice came from a very far distance; almost as if he was hearing it from behind a grill. 'The boy is married now, and has a son a priest in this diocese. God's ways are strange, are they not?' There was a pause as Father Melody came back to his chair and sat down, folding his small white hands placidly in his lap. 'You may find it so too, Tom, as time goes on.'

'Did many people know about it?' The smell of his own sweat; acceptable now as something familiar and healthy.

'Yes, everybody did, as they always do in this country. But we put up a front. And in those days things were not discussed as they are now. But I could see it in their eyes, even those who did not fully understand. They have an infallible instinct for scandal. Yes, they knew about me. Just as they know about you.'

'What!' The even modulated voice had been flowing over him like half-understood music. Now he jerked to attention and stared. 'What?'

'You'll get over the restlessness. The remedy is old but effective. Work and prayer, especially work. But the other thing you'll have to live with for a long time, and that won't be easy.' Father Melody took up his glass and sniffed it. He really disliked whisky; remembering the bondage that that too had imposed in its own way.

'What won't be easy?' There was a frightened crack in his voice; for in his heart he knew.

'Living with people who know that you are in no way better than the rest of men. Working with them, doing the ordinary day-to-day things. Trying to accept them.' The glass was put down again and the hands folded.

'Have you accepted them?' With fear came unkindness: as always.

'No. But I hope that you will do better. After all your position is a more acceptable, and certainly a more popular one. Don't leave because of sex - it is the weakest of all excuses. If you can't face up to the other, I don't think I'd blame you. It isn't easy.'

The curate stood up and towered above the small

ivory-faced man, his big fists clenched, his wide mouth drawn back over his strong slightly wolfish teeth: a man bereft of comfort.

'I don't believe it, ' he insisted, trying to convince himself. 'Not all of them. They couldn't know. '

'Of course not, ' replied the other inexorably. 'But you and I know the kind the people are here. They know all right - most of them. The writer of that letter is not the sort of person to keep things to herself. It's a woman's hand, by the way, they usually are. That sort of thing spreads. You didn't see it because you didn't want to . But God in heaven, man, you don't think you could carry off a thing like that in this country without anybody knowing!' Father Melody's voice rose and he threw out his hands, palms uppermost, two flashes of white in the gloom. 'What about the parents? I bet they knew. '

Father Moran nodded. He could not put that into words.

'Naturally. They put up a front. So will all the others. And most of them will think you're one hell of a fellow. It's a game. But remember you're playing for your own soul - and for theirs, day after day. It's something you'll have to face, Tom. '

'How did you face it?'

'It was a challenge. I rose to that part of it, as old Dooley knew I would. He told me exactly the same thing as I have just told you. But I never learned to love them. I have never got behind the front. You will do better, if only because - ' he stopped, twisted his head and looked around at the window. A moment later someone knocked loudly at the door. It was an ominous sound in that quiet shadowy house. Father Melody got to his feet, but the curate had moved before him. At that moment he had to move. Anything was better than this horrible fusing of the past and the future.

Miss Price stood on the step, her bicycle propped against the wall. A sick call. The ordinary day-to-day business.

'It's Mrs. Fogarty, ' she blurted out breathlessly. 'She rang up looking for you, and she said you were to ring back immediately, and as Father Melody hasn't a phone I biked over, and Father she sounded awful upset. I hope to God nothing is wrong.'

Father Moran had already grabbed his hat and coat and was putting them on when the parish priest came out of his study. He had heard Miss Price's message and he looked at the younger man sharply. He had been led to believe that the affair was ended. Had Tom been telling the whole truth? Clearly he did not want any more discussion on the subject at the moment.

'I have to rush, Father,' he said from the door, while Miss Price's eyes darted watchfully from one priest's face to another. She knows, for one, thought Melody. 'Would you give a cup of tea to Miss Price?'

The point was taken. The curate did not want her in the house when he got home.

'Of course. Come in Miss Price. You must be frozen after your ride. Miss Scally will get you anything you want.'

Regretfully the housekeeper sidled her way between the two men and went down the hall in the direction of the galloping hoof-beats and the plopping guns.

'What is it?' said Father Melody, knowing that he would not be given any information.

'That is something that I have to find out,' said the curate grimly, taking out his car-keys. For a moment he hesitated, caught the old man's eyes, saw the anxiety behind them, opened his mouth to speak, and then dashed out into his car.

Father Melody stood looking after the car as its head-lamps lit up the twisted branches and swept off down the road towards the yellow lights strung out across the dark wide plain, and wondered what would happen to the young priest so very different to himself, and equally at odds with life. He shivered in the cold damp air and thought how very difficult it was to be really corrupt.

He sighed and went back to his books. Perhaps some day he would discover a little evil there.

CHAPTER TWENTY-THREE

In the chalet by the lake Brian and Marie were making some discoveries of their own.

He had a passive streak, an almost feminine capacity for affection. She, instinctively reflecting her father, was a great deal more active than she liked to pretend, and was adept at using the real tenderness which she felt for those few men who had really attracted her as a weapon with which to possess them more completely. Karl, who had developed her latent sensuality with a cold iron thoroughness, understood this perfectly, and left her before she had time to mature into a person, instead of the personification of feminine curiosity which he had first admired.

She did not think of that now as she lay by her lover, delighting in his complete subjection. To her it was love; this discovery of a deep quivering sensuality, taken and received with equal abandon. There was nothing she felt that she could not now say to him; except that words seemed a poor substitute for the questing mouth, and the warm intimate hands.

'There,' she murmured, running her fingers lightly over his damp chest.

The body beside her grew tense, then relaxed and stirred lazily, stroked the back of her head, and sighed in acceptance. It was graceful of limb and fine of skin; sinuous, accomodating and passionately responsive. Where she had asked herself earlier, had he learned to adapt himself so cunningly to the ebb and flow of mutual pleasure? Now it did not matter. They had gone beyond such futile questioning. Whatever their past experiences had been they had merely prepared them both for this miraculous fusing of kindred desires.

She caressed his thighs, and felt his hand tightening on the back of her neck. The warm scent of his body,

146

sweat mingled with talcum powder, filled her nostrils as she moved her lips down over the soft hairs on his belly, and felt his manhood throbbing against her cheek.

Marie rose with a lithe snake-like movement and fastened herself on him, swallowing his manhood in one long shuddering assault; and he gave himself completely to her, calling her name and throwing out his arms in a ritual gesture before drifting into sleep, while she lay beside him, watchful and unsated.

She took his moist hand and pressed her lips against the hardened palm; coiled her limbs about him, and watched the dead sky through a chink in the curtain. It could not be more than ten o'clock, she thought drowsily. The night was young. Excitement coursed through her body again as she thought of the future. They would have to be reasonably careful for a while. A premature discovery would upset the rhythm of their love - she could not conceive of their relationship in any other term - and cast a shadow on the long hallowed journey which they would soon embark upon together.

He murmured in his sleep; and she pressed his hand gently against her breast, restraining the impulse to cover his still body with kisses. He was hers, hers, and he loved her. Tenderness weakened her limbs and flowed over her like a benediction. But she would wait and be thankful for the pleasure he had given her; a pleasure which was not entirely physical. She smiled in the darkness as she thought of the silly prejudices so many people had against marriage. Perhaps they were right. She remembered her parents. What innocents they must have been at the beginning; allowing themselves to be destroyed by the social aspect of their contract. No wonder people were wary of married love when so many were ill-mated. What did they know of the pleasure which she had just experienced? How very foolish it was to expect people to understand one another when they did not know their own bodies.

Brian stirred and whispered her name.
'I'm here. It's early yet. I love you.'
'It's wonderful. I don't want it to end, ever.'

'It won't. No, no.'

'Yes.'

'No. Are you ready?'

'Yes. Oh, Brian.'

He pulled her to him, and once again there was no thought of conquest in their minds, as he entered her slowly and surely, reaching for love in long blinding thrusts and finding at the end that he was stranded on a desolate shore, clutching helplessly at an ebbing tide which receded into its own bottomless depths. Yet he was grateful for the warm tide that had washed over his so briefly. This was love; a rich bequest which he had never bestowed so gratefully before.

'I'm thirsty,' said Marie, raising herself on her elbow and rubbing her cheek against his shoulder: smooth summer marble on a winter's night.

'So am I.' He climbed out of bed and reached for his shorts, groped his way into the kitchenette, found two glasses, filled them with water and returned to find that Marie had switched on the bed-side lamp. She clutched the sheet over her breast and smiled as she took the glass of water. In the dim light Brian looked splendid, his pale torso rippling as he moved, the tight white briefs emphasising the heavy masculinity which she thought of as peculiarly her own. He looked down, following her admiring gaze, and sat down with a sheepish grin on the end of the bed.

'You'll catch cold,' she laughed.

'So will you.' He had a curious desire to get away, and put it down to a faint nagging sense of guilt. He supposed it would take time to get rid of that.

'There are only two things to do in this place, make love or get dressed.' She put the empty glass on the night-table.

Beginning now to really feel the cold, he agreed with her and reached for his shirt.

'Come here,' she commanded briskly, throwing back the blanket and holding out her arms. Her breasts were high but voluptuous; the brown-pink nipples standing out with startling clarity against the silky flesh. Just as Father Moran had found the smell of celibacy attractive and slightly repulsive, so now

148

Brian, tired from love-making found this blatant display of feminity at once disgusting and exciting. He allowed her to draw him to her and closed his eyes as she clutched his hips and kissed the inside of his thigh.

'We should have made love with the light on,' she murmured with her cheek against his buttock.

Against his will he felt turgidity stirring his loins and drew back, holding his shirt in front of him.

'You'd like that?' He pulled it on, discovered that he had forgotten his vest, and had to take it off again.

'Wouldn't you?'

'Mmm.' He was dressing quickly now, and she watched his nakedness disappear with a pang of regret. It was true that this place was useless for the kind of intimacy she wanted. Too cold, too furtive, too temporary. They needed plenty of time, and the full approval of society.

'Well, that will have to wait.'

'How long?' He paused, pulling on his socks and looked at her.

She was brought back to reality, a great deal more insistent than the cold.

'Not too soon, I'm afraid.' Shrewd now again, back to the careful logic which in fact had never deserted her. She was aware of the laundry smell which she would always associate with this place. The small heater in the corner stirring up the damp. It warmed the room sufficiently for the clothed; but was little comfort for the naked. 'Hand me my bag.'

He picked it up and reached for his tie, threw it over his shoulder and gave her the bag. She thought his movements had taken on an added grace gained from their unrestrained love-making. He felt clumsy.

'I wanted to give you this,' she said, taking out a letter. 'It's for your boss, the old bigot. I typed it this morning, and Daddy signed it during lunch. It makes things quite clear.'

He finished knotting his tie and took the letter from her with a show of reluctance.

'Thanks.' He left it down on the chair, unopened. 'What did you mean by "not too soon"?'

'The circumstances. They might think I was rushing
it for reasons of my own - the marriage, I mean.
We'll have to wait a bit, Brian.'

'Christ.' He broke a shoe-lace and looked at it
viciously. 'Will we always have to plot and plan like
this? I'd like to murder the whole fucking lot of them.
Do they ever do anything but count on their fingers?'
He took a careful step forward as if he had lamed himself.

'Not much. They'll give us no peace this way. You
know that.'

'And then they say the times are changed,' he burst
out bitterly as he put on his jacket. 'We're all supposed
to be so much more broad-minded. Not much sign of
it round here.'

Brian stood in front of the heater to warm his backside, and looked at Marie wonderingly.

'I suppose we'll be doing the same when we get
married,' he said thoughtfully. Brian felt curiously
lonely and vulnerable; and thought of Father Moran.
He had enjoyed that conversation.

'That's different.' Marie shifted her position with
ease, since she was speaking of something which at the
moment she believed in with all her instincts. 'We're
in love. What we do when we're married is our own
business. God knows we've had to fight hard enough
to get it.' Her face darkened with self-pity; and she
looked suddenly older and a little frightened. She
clutched the blanket to her breast and stared at him
appealingly. 'Kiss me Brian, please, now. I need it
all the time. I can't bear it when you're near me like
that, and yet so far away.'

Guilt rekindled his desire; and he was going to her
with outstretched arms and a set lustful expression,
when, like Father Melody, he turned his head and
looked at the window, listening.

'There's someone outside,' he whispered tensely.

'Oh, my God.' Marie huddled down in the bed and
covered herself with the blanket.

'Don't tell them I'm here.'

The rap on the door was sharp and insistent; and
Marie felt a tremor of something very like sensual

150

pleasure as she cowered in the bed and listened to the
voices at the door.

'Is Miss Fogarty here?' The voice was breathless,
light and high like a boy's.

'No.' Brian sounded calm and decisive. 'But I
know where she can be found. Who wants her?'

'It's her father. I mean her mother. She's after
ringing up the hotel and telling us that we'd find her
here. Her father is after taking bad. Where will I
get her?'

There was a jingling sound; the clink of coins.

'That's for yourself. I think she's over in the club-
house. I met her as I was coming over here.'

'Will I get her there? The manager said Mrs.
Fogarty sounded awful worried.'

'All right, all right. And if she isn't, she's in one
of the houses behind the hotel. No, don't. I'll go and
find her myself. Go back and tell the manager that.'

'O.K.' The young voice sounded knowing. 'Don't
forget or I'll be killed.'

Marie was already out of bed and fumbling with her
clothes when Brian came back.

'I heard,' she whispered. 'It's Daddy. He's dead.
I know he is. And only a few hours ago he signed that
letter for me. Oh, Brian, what'll I do?'

'Hurry up and get back to the car. How the hell did
she know you were here?'

'How should I know?' She sounded weak and lost as
she pulled on her stockings. 'Except that they know
everything. They always do. Oh, God, why did I come
away. He'll be dead when I get back, I know he will.
And she hated him. She hates me too. Oh, Brian, I'm
afraid.'

'So am I.' His voice was suitably hushed, but angry.
'I told Moran we were meeting here tonight.'

'Yes, yes, I know. You told me.' What way did
she look? There was not a looking-glass in the room.

'They're up to something. Do you want me to come
with you?'

'Yes. No. I don't know.' She stepped into her
shoes and pulled on her coat. 'How can they be up to
anything? If Daddy is - ' she bit her lip and started to

151

weep. He had never seen her crumple before. She
had always seemed strong, imperturbable, incapable
of a sudden collapse like this. Even in her alarm on
the night he had discovered her with the priest she
had been defiant. Had the bastard warned her mother
of their meeting?

'I am going with you,' he said crisply. 'I want to
find out if this is the truth. And if it isn't - '

'I don't know what you mean,' she said wildly,
making for the door, slashing at her hair with a small
silver comb.

'Go on.' He picked up his own jacket and gloves.
'I'll follow you, and wait outside the house. If you need
me, come out.'

'Yes.' She paused in the door and looked around.
The lake was flat, and black, like a sheet of tar. On
the blotted horizon the lights of the town glimmered
faintly, like cats eyes on a misty night. It was cold
and bleak; dark and silent under a turgid sky. Stones
and boulders were ashen grey; hedges vague and
mysterious like watchful bodies; trees, drooping and
shapeless with no moon, no stars to give them definition.
A night without shape, colour or life.

'Hurry,' he said as she stumbled down the steps
and began to walk quickly towards the lights of the
hotel. He watched her fade into the formless night;
and thought how quickly moods, passions and relation-
ships shifted in a country where fundamentally nothing
changed, and death was the ultimate excitement. It
was a little like the tarry lake at which he found himself gazing; its surface altered with the phases of the
moon and the vagaries of the sun; but its outlines
remained the same, and its hidden depths were touched
only by bleached bones.

CHAPTER TWENTY-FOUR

A few days of sullen rain and the river rose higher,
while the sky came down and seeped into the horizon.

The two old friends went to the graveyard fully
equipped to brave the elements, with stout black
umbrella, trench coats, water-proof over-shoes, and
extra thick combinations lining their armour in the
war of attrition with nature. It was too wet to sit on
the stile, so they kept on the move; round and round
the gravel paths between the sodden wreaths, the
streaming head-stones and the limp funereal trees.
How restful for the dead, nice and snug and cosy with
six feet of clay between them, the Church militant,
and the wicked wet world.

'Shocking day,' remarked Miss Price grimly. 'In
the old days you'd really gain an indulgence coming
here in weather like this. But now it's hard to know
where you stand in the next world.'

'We didn't tidy our graves,' retorted Nelly sourly.
She was in a bad mood; and to hell with indulgences.
It was not the weather, Miss Price knew. They were
both immune to that; and had often come here on their
errand of mercy in a snow storm. Happy days.

'But we had the intention, Nelly. Sure no one could
put a fork into the ground on a day like this.' She
sniffed and looked bleakly about her. Empty paths.
Not a single neighbour to see them giving good example.

'It might clear up a bit yet.' Nelly peered out from
under her umbrella at the pregnant sky. 'It's shocking
the way moss gathers on the head-stones. Poor auld
Nick Wall is nearly wiped out. I'm going to take a
scrape at him if it's the last thing I do to-day.'

'It'd be a real charity, Nelly, and he without a soul
in the world after him.'

This charitable thought brightened them up a bit,

and they increased their pace. The two ladies did not
confine their pious ministrations to their own dear
departed. Very properly and generously they considered that they had a duty to look after the resting
place of those who were neglected through a lack of
relations, or the unchristian behaviour of those they
had left behind them in the vale of tears. Although
they never boasted about it, Margaret and Nelly knew
that their grave-yard was the best kept in the district.

But to-day other more mundane matters were
pressing on their minds with the weight of clay. They
paused in their perambulations by the gate where the
wall was higher and afforded some shelter against the
elements.

'And to think I turned down a position in good
society to waste the best years of my life on them
stinking Fogartys. The dirtiest crowd of cut-throats
that ever came up out of the gutter. Good God, with
the way things are going in that house I'm ashamed to
say that I'm living under the same roof as them. '
Nelly gazed at the neat trim respectable cross that
marked her parents' last resting place and derived
some small comfort from its good taste and well-bred
restraint. There was always that to cheer one.

'Oh, but the poor old man, and he on his last gasp, '
protested Miss Price charitably. 'Sure the undertakers
have the lining measured for his coffin, as it is.
Satin, I suppose. It'll be a first class affair. Not that
it'll make much difference. ' She looked out across the
field where true democracy reigned. Satin, silk, or
the cheap materials of a third class lining were all the
one there.

'Isn't that the only reason I'm staying? It can't be
said of me that I walked out on anybody on their death-
bed. Even if the old bugger had a mind like a sewer.
I wouldn't like to be in his shoes when he faces the
man up there. ' She pointed a stiff fore-finger at the
streaming lining of her umbrella.

'All the same, he wasn't the worst, Nelly. ' Already
they spoke of Pat Fogarty in the past tense; and could
therefore afford to say a good word for him.

'He was fairly open-handed, I'll say that for him.

Never a one to count the rashers in the kitchen. Not like her nibs, scattering holy water with one hand and picking the pockets of the poor with the other.' Nelly gave vent to a most unladylike snort. 'The old faggot.'

'Well, she has the money now. Isn't that all she wants.' Miss Price's voice was bleak. Such was life.

'Mmm.' Nelly's low thoughtful growl caused her friend to glance at her sharply. Miss Price twirled her umbrella excitedly, and drops scattered about the gravel, an extra bonus added to the steady drizzle that encompassed them. Nelly knew something; and was mulling it over in her mind.

'How is Marie taking it, Nelly?' she enquired delicately, clearing her throat and dabbing at her cold lips with gloved fingers.

'Don't talk to me about that one. Of all the sluts -' Nelly shook her umbrella fiercely, and drops whirled about her like a halo. 'Didn't she have to be hauled out of a hut on the lake-shore last Wednesday night when her father got his bad turn. And who was she with? Her new boy friend, of course, the travelling man from Galway. Wasn't he cocked outside the gate in his car when I was coming home from the church, bold as brass and smoking a cigarette. What do you say to that, Peg Price?'

Nelly shifted her umbrella from one shoulder to another, like a sentry presenting arms; while her friend blessed herself three times.

'Glory be to God and his blessed mother. How did you find that out?'

'Isn't Bernadette Scully's daughter a waitress in the hotel? This boyo has one of the huts taken - I suppose he couldn't bring his woman into the hotels - and Loretta Scully saw her ladyship parking her car in front of the hotel and sneaking off to the hut. And if that wasn't enough, the old one rang up, cool as a cucumber on Wednesday night, and asked them to get her daughter out of the hut and tell her that her father was dying. Did you ever hear the like of that in all your born days?'

'So Mrs. Fogarty knew,' whispered Miss Price breathlessly, forgetting the stiffness in one of her knees brought on by the insidious damp. 'How did she find out?'

Nelly pursed her lips and frowned. That was something she would dearly like to know herself. It was an affront to her vanity to discover that anybody had an intelligence system equal to her own.

'Oh,' she said airily, 'I know that too, but I'm not telling. It's too horrible.'

Miss Price was too absorbed with the heart of the matter to linger over this obvious evasion.

'Do you think there's anything between Marie and this fellow? I mean, you know.'

Nelly gave her companion a pitying look from under her umbrella, raised specially to give point to her expression. Really, there were times when Peg was a pain in the neck. As if everybody did not know that there was only one way in which men and women could be kept from improper intercourse: and that was rigid segregation.

'Of course there is,' she replied impatiently with all the hoary faith of her buried fathers. 'A girl that'll throw herself at a priest and make him break his sacred vow of chastity and obedience won't stop short of you-know-what with a big bold stallion like that Langley fellow.'

'I know that she tried her best with my Father Tom. I don't suppose the thought would ever enter his head if she hadn't flaunted herself in front of him.'

'Arrah, go on out of that, girl,' exclaimed Nelly. 'Of course it did. Isn't he a man, and a big red-blooded man at that, stuffed to the gills with your prime cooking? But I'll say this for him, he's a good priest, and even if he did fall with a bang, it was that one's fault. It's always the women that get the priests into trouble, the dirty sluts.'

'Too true,' nodded Miss Price sagely. Beyond that she was not prepared to go. The situation was too delicate. She had known for some time that Nelly must have taken the initiative and dropped a line in her left hand to someone in authority about Father Moran and Marie. How else would she have known on that Sunday when Father Conway called, that the bishop knew all

about it, and that her man was on the mat? And
there had been that visit to the parish priest last
Wednesday since when Father Tom had been looking
very disturbed and white about the eyes. Had not
Nelly dropped a hint to her last Sunday that Father
Melody also knew? How could she have known that if
she had not dropped him a line also? In her heart
Miss Price was glad that Nelly had acted as she had.
Who knows, she might have saved the curate's soul?
Nevertheless she resolved not to reveal young Langley's
visit, much as she would have liked to do so. A little
stoking up of banked fires helped to brighten the atmosphere and make life more cheerful; but only if
there was no risk of herself getting burned. She hoped
and prayed that Father Tom was over his trouble. It
had been exciting while it lasted but enough was enough.
Besides there was still the intriguing matter of the
Fogarty family affairs to keep the spectre of boredom
from the holy ground. She decided to concentrate on
them.

'What's going to happen now when the old man dies?'
she said in the wondering voice she used when she
wanted to humour Nelly. 'Do you think that pair will
get married?'

'Like shot.' Nelly rose to the bait eagerly. Much
as she would have liked to crow over her influence
with the bishop and Father Melody, which although
anonymous, was still power, and therefore balm to the
spirit, she was also more concerned with the situation
in Fogartys. After all she had her nice cushy job to
consider. 'That is if the old one lets her. She hates
her like poison, you know. She was always her father's
child, and the old faggot was left out in the cold with
them two. But when he dies she'll have control of the
money, and then Miss Sly-boots Marie will have to toe
the line or get out.'

'Isn't it shocking the way these people carry on!'
Miss Price squeezed her lips and shook her head dole-
fully. 'Imagine a mother hating her own daughter! I
wouldn't mind her taking against the old fellow and the
sort of stinking pinchy-pants he was. But her own
flesh and blood! The Lord deliver us!'

157

Nelly ignored this piece of naive sentimentalism; and kept to the point, stamping on the ground to rouse her circulation.

'The atmosphere in that house you could cut with a knife. I've heard Marie and the old one having it hot and heavy in the drawing room about the travelling man. And the poor old man lying upstairs fighting for breath, and he the colour of a corpse three days dead.'

'Merciful hour.' Miss Price peeped out from under her umbrella. The rain was getting heavier, and her feet were like lumps of ice. 'What are they going to do now?'

'They're going to fight to the death,' said Nelly grimly, jerking her arm and scattering rain-drops in all directions. 'Over the money. That's what it always boils down to with them people. And to think that I've stayed all these years under a roof like that. Well used they were, the Fogartys, to carpets and coal-fires a few years ago! It's enough to make you puke. Of course I won't stay a minute longer than it takes them to bury Pat Fogarty six foot under, I have that much christian respect for the sick and dying.'

'God almighty, the rain is getting worse, Nelly. Do you think we ought to move?'

But Nelly was deaf to all appeals to comfort. She had worked herself into a frenzy of penitential probity.

'I wouldn't stay in the house one minute longer but for the prayers I say morning noon and night to purify the place. I'm sacrificing myself, that's what I'm doing. Body and soul offered up to keep evil away from the door.'

'Dirty hounds, the lot of them.' Miss Price stepped out from under the shelter of the wall and peered at the gate. 'We'll go home this very minute and I'll light a candle in the church.'

'No, you won't,' snapped Nelly, still in her mood of spiritual exaltation. 'We're going to scrape the moss off auld Nick Wall if the Shannon rises and sweeps over us. Maybe the old fool will pray for us where-ever he is.'

There was nothing for Miss Price to do but follow the determined figure down the rain-lashed paths. She would see to it that the parish heard of this day's wet work first thing in the morning.

The rain made the moss amenable to trowel and fork; but they were hampered by their umbrellas; and all in all it was sticky toil. Yet they stuck to it grimly: two avid sisters of charity brightening up the relics of mortality.

'Oh, look.' Miss Price leaned against the headstone to recover her breath, and prodded Nelly in the rump with her trowel. 'Look at the way the rain is whirling round Mulligan's angel. Wouldn't you swear the wings were moving?'

'It's a wonder you didn't see it taking off,' Nelly commented with heavy irony. 'Come on, you're only down as far as his date. The auld wife is below him. Angels ever bright and fair, how are ye.'

'How long do you think he'll last?' Miss Price was out of breath, and every bone in her body ached. But some face had been put on the Wall memorial. 'Old Fogarty, I mean.'

'Any day now. I wouldn't be surprised if he passed out on Christmas Eve. It'd be just like what'd happen. Well, for once in their lives it might turn their thoughts to God on Christmas day. Although I doubt it.'

'Me too, Nelly, me too.'

CHAPTER TWENTY-FIVE

'How did you get over the Christmas?' Brian, longing
for a cigarette, put his hand to his pocket, felt the
packet, and hesitated. The atmosphere did not seem
propitious.

'I think I could do with one too,' said Marie with a
wry smile. 'After all she can't eat us. And the nurses
smoke like furnaces. Oh, for God's sake, it's too
ridiculous.' She held his hand in hers as he proferred
the lighted match, glad of the opportunity of making
contact again after a long succession of solitary days
and nights, waiting and watching for the inevitable.

For Pat Fogarty had not died as quickly as Nelly
had prophesied. Now almost a fortnight later he still
lingered; dumb, motionless, almost a vegetable; only
an occasional anguished flicker of an eye to indicate
that the paralysed brain was still capable of some
faint recognition. It was far more horrible than death.

'Well?' Brian lifted his chin and blew smoke down
through his nose in an effort to appear imperturbable.
It was not a very good impersonation, but Marie loved
him for it, especially as she knew that his hands had
been trembling as he lighted her cigarette for her.
Complete self sufficiency would have been a bit off-
putting; but this attempt to give confidence to both of
them was flattering.

She sighed and closed her eyes with a weary little
smile.

'We had chicken for dinner, which made a change
from the eternal turkey. No wines, no plum pudding,
no cake, and of course as you can see, no candles or
decorations.' She opened her eyes and looked round
the room.

It was the first time that Brian had been in the
Fogarty's drawing-room. He had an impression of

160

softness, heat, muted colours and bright reflecting
surfaces. A great clotted silence cut through by tiny
sounds that had more effect than the hysterical scream
of a siren. The click of a door, the muffled creak
of a loose board under a carpet, the gentle ticking of
the clock on the mantelpiece, the dim thud of pigeons'
wings, like the flapping of damp sheets, in the beech
trees lining the avenue outside: all insistently emphasising the death-like silence of the house. And it
occurred to him in a sudden flash of inspiration that this
was how life ended: eternity opening with a sigh, like
the far-off beating of wings among silent trees.

He stirred in his chair, pressed his knees together
uneasily and looked at the girl seated opposite him,
smoking quietly and looking into the fire. She was
paler, more withdrawn and a great deal gentler than
he remembered her.

'I suppose you had the usual Christmas,' she said,
picking up the conversation as if it were a thread which
lay slackened between them. He felt a faint tug at his
heart; and looked at her questioningly.

'The usual.' He looked away again quickly as he
remembered the traditional rites which hitherto he
had always enjoyed; but which this year seemed suddenly
altogether irrelevant. 'It wasn't much of a Christmas
this year,' he went on, amazed to find himself so shy.
It must be the overpowering atmosphere of this house;
so rich, comfortable, and dead. Brian was not the
first man to discover that a lover in an improvised
bed can be very different when surrounded by her
household gods.

He looked over his shoulder uneasily at the door,
which some time before had closed behind the disap-
proving back of Mrs. Fogarty. Marie, misinterpreting
his gesture, got up quickly, opened the door, looked
into the hall, and closed it again.

'Don't worry, she's not there.'

'I didn't think she was.' He was vaguely shocked.
'Why, does she usually listen?'

'Everybody listens here.' Marie shrugged off the
awkward moment as lightly as she could. 'I'm sorry
about the way she acted. She's been like that since - '

she sighed and sat down on the arm of the sofa. He knew what she meant. It had been easy for Marie to explain to Brian how her mother had come to send for her that night in the chalet. Not knowing where her daughter had gone Agnes had rung up various people to find out if they knew where she was. Father Moran was one of them. Thinking that Pat was dying he had thought it his duty to tell her that Marie was meeting Brian that night in the Lake hotel. The seriousness of the old man's condition had stifled any further doubts that Brian may have had. It did not occur to either of them that Mrs. Fogarty had in fact rung only Father Moran, assuming that he would know where her daughter was: a revealing state of mind.

But Agnes had seized her advantage. It was a horrible thing that Marie should have been out in such circumstances on the night when her father had nearly died; a turn which she was quite sure had been brought on by the effort of signing the letter Marie had forced him to do earlier in the day. She hoped that her daughter would not disgrace herself again. She had done enough harm as it was.

For a few days Marie had been conscience stricken. Perhaps all that was true; and she had over-reached her father. But as the silence deepened between her mother and herself and Christmas loomed ahead she could not stand the atmosphere any longer. She had begged Brian to visit her on St. Stephen's Day. He had been willing enough to come - it was something that would have to be faced someday - and assumed that Mrs. Fogarty had consented to see him.

Yet he had not been too much surprised when the old lady confronted him silently in the drawing-room and walked out, giving him a look of such terrible malignity that he had drawn back and bumped into Marie who was standing behind him. Somehow he had not expected Mrs. Fogarty would give him a welcome: he had imagined that she would simply absent herself upstairs. But her expression, so full of implacable dislike as to be almost insane, had unnerved him for a while. Then he realised the price Marie had to pay for the comfortable facade of respectability behind

162

which she existed.

'I should have told her you were coming,' she was saying in a low voice as she tapped out her cigarette on a shell on the coffee table. 'But it's been impossible since that night. Now she has a grievance, and she's playing it for all it's worth. I should have told you too, but I was afraid you wouldn't come. It was terrible. You see she has this awful instinct for disaster. She knew I was expecting someone to-day, and no doubt felt sure it was you. So she stayed here, just to make it as awkward as she could for both of us.'

'But it's so stupid, Marie, especially at a time like this. Why does she do it?' He was not entirely surprised at the opposition: it was the timing of it that shocked him. They were in the presence of death; and that was a time when traditionally all enmities were laid aside. It was a ritual; a drama in which all the characters knew their parts, and were aware also of the end in sight.

But Mrs. Fogarty, a woman he had thought of as rigidly conventional, was not playing her part. Something must be very wrong.

Marie did not reply immediately. Watching his face she knew he was trying to work out something in his mind. She let the silence lengthen between them, until he became uneasily aware of it, started when the clock struck half-three, and then looked at her sheepishly.

'I'm sorry,' he said, rubbing his forehead with his fingers. He was sweating and could have done with a drink.

'I suppose it's because I'm part of her property,' she went on thoughtfully, brushing her thick silk skirt over her thighs. 'Have you ever thought of how money will always destroy love if it can, because its the one thing it can't control?' This was a subject on which Karl had frequently expanded. She had not listened very carefully at the time; but some of it had stuck. 'Every bit of property lost leaves one a little more vulnerable. People are afraid of that. I think my mother is.'

'But that's horrible,' he burst out, opening his fingers and holding them out rigidly over his knees.

'People aren't property.' He could understand a well-off family being suspicious of an alliance with someone who had nothing. His motives might not be entirely disinterested. It was reasonable enough to question that. He had never gone further, and asked himself why it should be questioned.

'No?' Marie's mouth twisted into a bitter little half-smile as she leaned forward and stubbed out her cigarette in the sea-shell. 'I think the whole point is that they are.' She straightened up and gestured round the room with her hand. 'Far more than all this.'

'You don't have to put up with that sort of thing for the sake of security.' His voice was firm, his eyes steady with faith in his own ability to preserve his privacy intact. Certainly he was in enemy territory; but as yet he had not worked out exactly why.

Marie got up and walked over to the small table beside her chair where her handbag rested on top of the pile of books. She picked it up, sat down and clasped it to her lap.

'It may come to that,' she said slowly, playing with the heavy gold clasp. Another tiny sound. 'You see, I don't quite know what is going to happen if Daddy dies. I may be left out in the cold.' The clasp gleamed dully in the firelight and he found himself staring at it before he raised his eyes to look at her. He was smiling now. This was easier.

'I told you before I wasn't marrying you for your money. The question is, if you are left with less than you have been used to, would you be willing to marry me?' In fact it was something she had not thought about; and this ought to have made him pause and reflect. But it did not. He was too taken up in the aura they had created about themselves.

'Yes, of course,' she said quietly, her fingers tightening about the clasp. And she believed what she was saying at the moment. This cut and thrust was part of their involvement with each other. 'Although I have a feeling that Daddy will not leave me completely stranded. He said something the day after he became ill. All the same it might not be too much.' She smiled but he did not respond. It occurred to him that they were like two casual acquaintances discussing somebody else's problems. This was not his scene, not his background. In a house like this the script was prepared in advance.

'Let's not make plans now,' he said as lightly as he could. 'We'll think of something. If it's nothing else than getting you out of this plush jail, it'll be worth it. Christ, I don't think I'd ever want to live here.' He looked at the velvet curtains, the artificial flowers - which he took to be real - the plump satin cushions, the gleaming silver and the soft deadening white carpet, and frowned.

'Not even for my sake?' she said, pulling down the corners of her mouth and raising her eyebrows. And then before he had time to reply she opened her bag and took out an object wrapped in a green silk hankerchief. He watched her as she undid it carefully and held up a tiny transistor radio, hardly bigger than the outstretched hand on which she held it.

'I should have thanked you for your Christmas present, Brian. It's lovely. See, I've got it wrapped up so that it wouldn't get scratched.'

It was a polite statement; and it embarrassed him. He was well aware that it was not a very suitable gift in the circumstances; but he had bought it before her father had fallen ill - or rather had made the first down-payment on it, and could not think of anything else to buy for her later, even if he had the money. And this he told her now, quite frankly. She shook her head and looked at him with an appealing smile which he had never seen on her face before, and did not recognise as a glance of pure affection. But it affected him profoundly; and for the first time since he had entered her house he felt the old physical tension; for him in that atmosphere a liberating sensation.

Smiling, she held the little radio up to her ear; and suddenly with obscene clarity the deadening silence was shattered by a high wailing sound, which seemed to rise into the air like a serpent, poise swaying for a moment and then collapse in a muffled sound of grasping fingers and clutching silk. It was the sound

of a tenor saxaphone. Marie had snatched the
transistor from her ear, covered it again with the
hankerchief and stuffed it back into her handbag. For
a moment they sat on edge staring at one another; and
then they both glanced instinctively at the door. But
no further sound disturbed the silent house: no door
thrown open, no foot-fall on a creaking board, no
voice raised in protest.

'I must have switched it on without thinking. I
never thought it would come on like that.'

'Can we get out of here this evening, Marie, even
if only for an hour? We could have a drink in the hotel.'

She looked at him with a childlike expression of
longing for a few moments, and then shook her head.

'No, Brian, I'm afraid.' She put her bag away and
stood up, her tall, high-breasted figure silhouetted
against the livid sky outside. 'You see it might happen
again.' She was rubbing her hands slowly over her
hips; and he realised that for the moment at any rate
nothing could be done.

Without quite knowing how he found himself standing
by her side looking out at the fading garden. When he
came in it had been as vivid and clear-cut as an etching
on glass; now it was blurred and formless, waiting,
like them, for another sun to rise and renew its life.
He took her hand and pressed it, feeling a terrible
loneliness and sure that he knew the cause: a girl's
fear that she would not perform a simple human task
for a dying relative. It was darker and more complicated than that; but as yet he was but faintly aware
of those depths.

They did not hear the door opening silently behind
them nor the small white-faced figure in black pausing
on the threshold and looking at them. It was only when
Mrs. Fogarty moved across the room and they saw her
reflection in the glass of the window that they sprang
apart and spun round to face her. Marie gave a little
gasp and clutched her throat with her hand.

Her mother said nothing. She looked from one to
the other with a wet-eyed stare, her hands folded in
front of her, her thin shoulders raised; motionless and
accusing. A coal fell in the fireplace: there was no

166

other sound except Marie's quick breathing.

It was she who recovered first. Brian could tell by her voice that she was angry and embarrassed. He himself felt guilty and soiled; like a little boy caught masturbating.

'You might have knocked, ' she said in a high toneless voice.

'You might have told me that you were inviting this person to my house. '

'It's not your house yet, ' Marie shot back at her.

Mrs. Fogarty made no reply to this; but her bloodles mouth twitched as she transferred her gaze from her daughter to the young man.

'I think you'd better go now, Mr. Langham. My husband is very low. I doubt if he'll last the night. I want to send for the priest. '

She had gone too far. There was something smug and cold-blooded about her reference to her husband which Brian found repulsive. He could not believe that she could have come into the room in such a way if Pat was really dying. And her antagonism towards Marie seemed out of all proportion to what a mother might be expected to feel towards a daughter who did not share her own standard of morality. In these matters he knew most mothers kept silent, whatever they might think.

But he did not know what to say to her; and stood silent and awkward staring into those dark unfathomable eyes. It was Marie who took the offensive again.

'I don't see why Brian shouldn't stay. I'm quite sure poor Daddy wouldn't mind. After all I've told you already, we're going to be married. '

Mrs. Fogarty ignored her daughter and addressed herself to Brian.

'There are some things about my daughter which I think you should know, Mr. Langham, ' she went on in her hoarse trembling voice, which if nothing else indicated a kind of desperate courage. 'But this is neither the time nor the place to tell you. '

'I know all about Marie, ' said Brian hotly. But the seed had taken root. What did the woman mean? Slowly but surely she was placing them at a disadvantage.

'I don't want to be told anything about her by you. '

'In that case you'd better go, hadn't you?' The voice was steadier now. Mrs. Fogarty was clearly a woman who was at her best when confronted with opposition. Perhaps she invited it.

Brian felt a hand upon his arm. Marie had moved closer to him, and her fingers dug into the tweed cloth of his jacket, warning him to follow her lead. It was something he was only too anxious to do. Without another word she moved with him towards the door, slipping her arm through his until they got to the hall. She was white and close to tears but her voice was steady.

'Ring me tomorrow. There's nothing we can do now. We'll just have to wait. '

'I don't understand, ' he protested vaguely. 'I don't understand. '

'I do, ' she answered grimly, 'only too well. Go now quickly. I can't bear it. '

CHAPTER TWENTY-SIX

The following Monday when he reported for work after the Christmas break Brian was told that his services were no longer required.

The proprietor called him into his office and informed him himself. Mr. Farrell was a dark neat man with a face like a frog. The heavy dissatisfied mouth, drooping at the corners, settled into its familiar mould of peevish solemnity as he waved Brian into a chair and looked at him over the rims of his spectacles.

'I have bad news for you I'm afraid, Langley, ' he said fingering his Pioneer pin affectionately. He was not a total abstainer; but he believed in giving a good example to the working classes. 'A nephew of mine has failed his exam in the college of surgeons, and wants to come into the business. He always wanted to, but his mother thought she'd like to make a doctor out of him. I knew he'd never make it, he always wanted to come in with me, but ladies have to be humoured sometimes. So I've offered him your job as a start. It's unfortunate - nothing personal, you realize - but there it is. '

'Has this anything to do with the complaint you told me you got from Fogarty?' Brian looked him straight in the eye. Farrell stared back steadily. It was something he never had any difficulty in doing. He always knew he was right.

'No, no, of course not. My nephew Joseph only made up his mind over the Christmas. '

'I have a letter from Mr. Fogarty to you saying that he never had any cause for complaint. He was very upset when he heard it and insisted on giving me a letter. I didn't give it to you because I thought all that had blown over. ' It did not make much difference now;

but Brian watched Farrell's face closely. No sign of surprise; but Brian got the impression that he was expecting to hear of it.

'That was kind of him,' he said mournfully. 'A decent man, Pat Fogarty. Lord have mercy on him. I suppose you saw his death in the <u>Independent</u> this morning?'

'I heard it last night.'

Farrell raised his bushy eyebrows; but made no comment.

'I was about to ask you this morning if I could go to his funeral tomorrow instead of Limerick. Now - ' he shrugged and grinned wryly.

'Of course, of course. As a representative of the firm - '

'Well not that exactly. You see I'm engaged to be married to his daughter.' It was something he hated to say; but he could not let the greasy little bastard off without some show of spirit.

Farrell pursed out his liverish lips, crooked a finger in front of them and cleared his throat.

'I hope you'll be happy,' he said primly; and for the second time Brian got the impression that he was expecting that too, and was not greatly impressed by it. 'There is of course a month's salary.' Farrell made it appear like a compliment; a gracious bonus which he was bestowing out of the goodness of his heart. 'I have left it with Miss O'Flaherty in the office. If you want any recommendation at any time don't hesitate to call on me.' He puffed out his cheeks and settled his spectacles on the bridge of his fleshy nose. 'I am not without influence in business circles, as you know. A word from me might go a long way.'

Either way, thought Brian, as he got up and went out to collect his money.

And that was that. A very smooth routine. Was there a veiled threat in Farrell's boast of influential connections? And his cool congratulations on the engagement has been followed by a reminder of a month's salary. Was there some hidden knowledge behind that? He would soon find out.

It was too early for the pubs; so he took a bus and

went home. The office was in Eyre Square; his mother lived in Nuns Island in a small red-brick semi-detached house behind the Poor Clare convent. It was raining and he did not feel like walking through the damp grey streets of Galway on a Monday morning, used as he had been to a car. That belonged to the firm and was no longer his. He began to make an inventory of his belongings as he sat in the bus on the short journey to Dominick Street.

The paucity of possessions did not depress him; but the manner of his dismissal did. He was sure that his relationship with Marie had something to do with it. Someone was working behind the scenes; someone who even now, after he had made his peace with Father Moran, was determined to let him know that any breaking of the unwritten code would not be tolerated. The first threat had come very shortly after his unexpected visit to Fogarty's house following that ribald conversation overheard in Sligo. Marie had proved that she knew nothing about it; and it was reasonable to suppose that her father was innocent also. Father Moran had been convincing; and Brian had believed him when he denied any part in the affair, but indicated that he thought he knew who was behind it. There remained the mother. Remembering that livid face, those implacable eyes as she stood facing him silent and accusing Brian could well believe it of her. But why?

He found himself outside his own front door. Instinctively he looked up and down the street. The neighbours would be wondering what he was doing without his car at this hour of the morning. Well, the news would travel fast enough; but he would not be there for the breaking of it. He let himself in and ran upstairs to his room, which he shared with his brother, Jim, who was studying medicine at the University. Fortunately during the holidays he had a temporary job as a bar-man in a pub run by one of his father's old employees, and had already gone out. His mother did her shopping after nine o'clock mass, and was rarely back before eleven.

There was barely room to dress in the narrow

space between the two iron beds under the large ebony crucifix with its gilt figure of the dead Christ. He got out his suitcase from under the bed and put it on a chair. He changed into a white shirt and his good blue suit; opened the brief-case which he had brought back from the office and transferred the over-night things into the larger case; got out his best overcoat, picked up a couple of paperbacks, and hurried down stairs.

He left a note for his mother on the kitchen table; and then realising that he would have to take an umbrella - fortunately she had two - to save his best wear from the rain, added a p. s. to say that he would return it.

Then he let himself out; and hurried back to Dominick Street to catch a bus for the station. There was a train leaving at noon which would get him into the town at half-past two.

The hour and a half he spent waiting for his train turned out to be more interesting and somewhat more disturbing than he had bargained for. One of the paper-backs he had brought with him had been casually picked up from the rack of some hotel lounge on an idle evening. It was the notebook of a French poet Brian had never heard of; but it made a change from the usual diet of spy stories and whodunits with which he passed the time. It had never occurred to him that literature could have a practical influence on life. He had left school early and gone out to earn his living. There had been no time for serious study; but he had an en-quiring mind which had already made him independent of most of the accepted prejudices in which he had been reared. Religion hardly touched his life except as an external ritual; one of the customs of the country which no longer made any immediate appeal to him.

Now, he opened his book and glanced through it, seated between the blazing fire and the greying slosh of coffee on the table beside him.

Fear, he read, is the primeval emotion in man, a creature wholly animal in his instincts and acquisitive-ness. Possessions give strength; and the sense of property is deeply rooted in man's sense of inadequacy in a hostile environment. Love which commands the

attention of the world in a thousand ways is the first
and most private of man's possessions; and a lover
who stands naked before the elements is exposing himself to the brute instincts of his fellows. A propitiatory
show in face of the danger outside often accompanies
the manifestation of this most magical and vulnerable
of human emotions. The desire to please, often taken
as a show of tenderness, is rooted in fear. Take my
private pleasure from me, my little taste of immortality,
and I am as nothing. The love which gives all and asks
for no reward is already haunted by death: a reflection
in man of the deities he has invented to personify the
vast silences by which he is surrounded. From the
beginning the most vivid of man's emotions, sexual
pleasure, has been involved with the defences built up
to sustain it; and of these in modern times the sense
of property is the most widely sustained. Property
allays fear, but it does not banish it, since it is based
on man's insecurity. The romantic notion of love
conquering all as a measure of its own justification is
false. Man shows courage in survival; but in love,
joined as it is to the sense of possession, he reveals
his primitive fears. Hence the vast body of laws,
codes and rites evolved to protect this emotion so
intimately concerned with the survival of the race. It
is impossible to disassociate what we call 'love' from
the sense of property and therefore of defence.

The train came in and Brian stood up and stuffed
the book in his pocket. The thoughts he had been
reading were interesting; and more to his taste than
the dogmas which he had been taught. But they did
not seem to him to apply to his own situation. He was
in love; and that was that. Later he was to recall
them in the usual vague way one does when something
that is half-assimilated stirs in one's consciousness.

At that time, as the train rattled by the flat Galway
fields towards Athenry and Ballinasloe he had other
things to think about. Mrs. Fogarty had called him
'Langham'. Was this deliberate? And what did she
mean when she said: there are things about my
daughter which I think you ought to know?

CHAPTER TWENTY-SEVEN

The smell of death - a mixture of fresh linen, candle-grease and waxen flowers - was quickly obliterated in the Fogarty house by the hoard of relatives who descended upon it after the funeral. They were not exactly merry; but there was a subdued excitement under their self-consciously prim bearing and conventional expressions of sympathy. All of them were aware from their own experience that a bereavement is like a stab in the flesh, which opens for a short painful instant, letting in the cold air of eternity, and then slowly, inexorably begins to heal. Life goes on; and it is twice as sweet at wakes, with their long history of orgies.

All of the relatives were less prosperous than the Fogartys, and most of them would not meet again until the next family bereavement. Many of them had never been in the house before and were anxious to count the place while the going was good. On the pretext of washing their hands and fetching fresh glasses and cups for one another, they managed to inspect every nook and cranny in the place, and every inch of the grounds. 'It's getting a bit stuffy. I'm bringing Molly out for a turn in the garden'. They were impressed by what they saw and more than a little envious. What did anybody want with all that stuff? Such a pile of pictures, furniture and silver they had never seen in their lives; and the carpets alone must have cost a fortune.

They were divided, as was the custom, into two camps; the Fogarty cousins proper and Agnes's own relations, the Naughtons; and there was little love lost between them. Marie was soon surrounded by her father's people who clearly imagined themselves to be a cut above the opposing faction by virtue of Pat's visible success; while Agnes held court among her own clan, who regarded her husband's relatives as low, vulgar and grasping to the last degree. Marie, looking about her with a cool observant eye, could see nothing to choose between them: they all looked drab and uninteresting to her. But she was grateful for their presence. They were a buffer between the past and the very different future. There was a sort of damped-down vitality about them which was not unattractive; and a few of the men had looked at her with a unmistakeable, sly invitation in their eyes. Tall young cousins, red-faced and bursting with health, and redolent of the same sort of sexual virility which her father had once possessed - it was clear that two or three of them would not have minded a still closer relationship with the richest branch of the family. But as the evening wore on and the house began to reek of whisky, stale powder and masculine sweat, she felt a kind of panic rising in her which took the form of a hysterical urge to burst out laughing. It nearly reached breaking point when one of the male cousins, passing cups of tea to his mother who was regaling Marie about the scholastic achievements of her family, contrived a second time to touch her breast with the back of his large hairy hand. She rose, made an excuse which was charitably interpreted as a desire to go to the lavatory, and fled to her room.

Was Brian at the funeral, she wondered as she kicked off her shoes and lay down on the bed. It was intolerable to be separated from him at a time like this, just when she needed him most.

'Are you all right?' The voice was low, husky and urgent. It came from the door; and as she swung her legs off the bed and groped for her shoes she heard a faint click, and smelled the sharp tang of whisky. A shapeless dark bulk loomed against the white door.

'Who is it?' she called out in a shaking voice.

'Me. Pat. I came up to see if you were all right.' She remembered the voice; and his red face and hairy hands flashed vividly across her fevered imagination. Pat Fogarty, her father's nephew; and his spit and image as a young man. She remembered thinking of the resemblance to early photographs the first time he had brushed against her in the drawing-room. What was the idiot doing here? No, no, she thought, no, as the carpet creaked under his weight and the heavy form took a step forward.

'Go away,' she said wildly, unable to find one shoe. She was certainly not going to get down on her knees now and search for it. She twisted round and switched on the bedside lamp. He put his hand up in front of his eyes, and drew his lips back over his teeth with a hissing sound. His hips were on a level with her eyes, and with horror she saw that he was aroused.

'What do you want?' she demanded sharply, trying to achieve a sarcastic tone. But she was not really thinking. Her heart was thumping rapidly and her fingers dug into the satin coverlet of the bed. There was still time to jump up and make for the door; but she had only one shoe. Her toes were cold.

'Don't be like that,' he said, taking his hand from his eyes and looking at her with a crooked smile. The corners of his mouth were damp with spittle. She remembered now; he was about thirty and was a school teacher. God help the senior girls under that fellow, she thought wildly. 'I know how you feel. I felt that way myself the night my own father died. Your Uncle Jim, don't you remember? You were only a small girl then, but I remember you. I was almost out of my mind that night. I know how you feel. I could see it downstairs.' He had clasped his hands in front of him and was pressing them against his fly.

'What way do I feel?' she said stupidly, getting to her feet and looking round for her shoe.

'Aw, come on now, Marie, I know, I know.' His voice was low and coaxing; and she could imagine him wheedling a greyhound bitch in the same tone.

'Don't do that,' she snapped as she felt his hand on her arm. 'I'm going down.'

But before she could make any sort of move, with or without her shoe, he had reached out and switched off the light, and grabbed her about the shoulders. What was one to do now, she thought, as she struggled weakly in his rough but not entirely brutal embrace?

176

Scream and bring all the mourners galloping up the stairs?

He had clumsily unbuttoned himself and was clawing at her skirt. She could smell his hot whisky breath on her neck as she struggled silently to free herself. The room was filled with the furtive slipping noises of rumpled clothing, crushed satin and low murmuring words.

'Don't, don't,' she whispered feebly as she felt herself going under. But the weight thrusting itself upon her had by now discovered its own power; and she realised that nothing short of a screaming fit of hysterics would save her. As she felt his wet mouth, and struggled with his damp hands as they sought their object with amazing skill and speed she had a momentary vision of twenty up-turned faces in the drawing-room staring at her open-mouthed with pleasurable shock. There was nothing for it but to submit.

But there was also a rising tide of excitement. The obscene words muttered in a half-wheedling tone as he bore down upon her had an incantatory magic of their own; like the recital of some ancient litany: an urgent fleshy echo of the moaning chants she had been listening to all day. And after all what did it matter now? Nothing mattered much in a situation like this, except to get it over as quickly as possible. As the brutal phallus pierced her flesh she shuddered and tightened her grasp about his neck. His urgency increased so that for a moment all fear of danger and discovery was blotted out in a rising fever of confusion.

'They asked for it,' he muttered hoarsely and in-explicably into her ear just before his movements became more frantic and demanding; and all thought was erased in the memory of other quick couplings in this room. A hard thrusting body very like this one; lustful and completely lacking in tenderness; also pre-occupied with time and the fear of discovery. Images flashed and exploded in her mind as she lay in a sweat of angry trepidation and half-awakened responsiveness. She almost expected to hear the telephone ring and Tom Moran's voice in her ear; and then as the heavy body shivered and tautened and the mouth closed about

her nipple she had a sudden vivid glimpse of her
father's face bending over her as a little girl, his
gentle hands stroking her body until she fell asleep.
And now this blood relation, this youthful double of
his uncle was slumped on her breast his lust assuaged,
his hairy loins slack and sated. She thrust him from
her with a harsh little cry, digging her nails into his
chest.

'Christ,' he swore, 'what's come over you?'

'Get out,' she hissed, pushing him off the bed so
that he had to clutch at the slippery satin cover to
prevent himself from slumping onto the floor. 'Quick,
quick.'

'You wanted it,' he grumbled in a hurt voice as he
began to fumble with his trousers in the darkness.
'Don't tell me, I know.'

'Oh, for God's sake hurry up and go away.'

'You wanted it,' he repeated in a curious little boy
tone. She could imagine his pouting lips and sulky
eyes. It was comic. Then she remembered that that
was one unfailing way of getting rid of them.

'God if you could only see yourself,' she mocked.
'You make me laugh.'

'What's the matter? Cut that out.' His voice was
really hurt now, with a blustering undertone of anger.

'You don't even know how to do it,' she insisted as
she groped on the carpet for her shoes.

'You should know,' he shot back bitterly.

'Yes, I do,' she hissed back. 'Run down now to
your mother, like a good little boy.'

'You fucking bitch.' But already the voice was
further away, the shadowy bulk melting into the door-
way. 'We all know what you are.' Then he was gone.

Yes, she thought wearily, as she switched on the
light, found her shoes and sat down on the stool in
front of the dressing-table to pull her clothes together
and brush her hair. Yes, no doubt they do, it was
the sort of thing they would scent out. And then as she
gazed at her pale-faced image in the looking-glass the
full weight of what he had said struck her. My God,
I'm branded, she thought. A loose woman, a slut, an
easy lay. That's what they think, the bastards. She

put down the brush and stared at herself in astonishment.

She stood up abruptly and covered her cheek with her hands. She must get in touch with Brian immediately. She had not been unfaithful to him: this thing had been forced on her at a time when everybody was emotionally aroused. Men did it whenever they got the chance; why should it be different for women? But she realised that she could not go on like this. Soon now, and the quicker the better, she would have to erect her own defences. Otherwise as time passed she in her turn would become a joke.

She looked round the room wildly and inhaled the smell of sweating hair and whisky breath. This is how it would be if she did not move quickly and decisively. And then the most horrible possibility of all struck her with the blinding force of an idea never before understood or even sensed. She clasped her hands to her stomach in the immemorial gesture of a woman terrified of her body. This time, unlike all the other times, she had been caught unawares, and had made no preparations. She looked at the locked drawer in her dressing-table and closed her eyes. It was just possible that Pat Fogarty, the dark personification of the family image, had achieved something which she had as yet granted to no man. And for the first time that day she wept bitterly for herself and for all women.

CHAPTER TWENTY-EIGHT

When Brian telephoned next afternoon she had recovered her self-possession and most of her hopefulness. Another day had dawned.

'How are you?' Marie asked in a low voice.

'Not bad. How are you?' His voice sounded hoarse and dry; and indeed the night before in the hotel bar he had smoked too many cigarettes and drunk too much whisky. 'I was at the high mass.'

'Were you, I didn't see you?' She was pleased and grateful. He had come for her sake; and was staying for the same reason. She felt an upsurge of happiness.

'Oh, at the back of the church. I have some news for you.'

'What is it?' she said cautiously. 'Good or bad?'

'Bad mostly, I'm afraid.'

She felt a tremor of panic. What did he mean by that? Several different possibilities flashed through her mind. Had someone talked again? Had Pat Fogarty been in the hotel after leaving last night?

'Oh, God.' She sighed wearily into the receiver. 'I seem to have heard enough of that. What are you doing now?'

'Nothing. Are you free this evening?'

'Yes.' This was better. The enquiry was slightly diffident: no hint of menace. 'Can you come out?' She would have to get this thing settled quickly. Just as well that her mother was sitting in the drawing-room, listening to every word.

'Will it be all right? I mean - ' his voice trailed off.

'Of course it will,' she said firmly. She must never be exposed to another Pat Fogarty. It was time to make a stand. The love front must be erected. 'Will eight be all right?'

'Yes. But are you sure?'

'Of course I am. Right?'

'OK. See you.'

She left down the receiver and went into the drawing-room. The aura of Pat and his cousins still hung heavily about the place.

Agnes Fogarty sat by the fire with her rosary clasped in her hands. Those restless fingers with their loose rings were for the moment stilled. But she was not saying her prayers. It was clear to her from her daughter's whole attitude that morning that she was determined to make trouble; and Mrs. Fogarty was prepared for it. Marie must be taught a lesson once and for all. Otherwise, there would be no standing of her.

'Who was that?' she enquired mildly.

'Brian Langley. I've asked him out this evening.' Marie lit a cigarette, and poured herself a glass of sherry from the bottle left on the tray for late visitors.

'I see.' Mrs. Fogarty freed one hand and clenched her fist. The firelight glittered on her loose engagement ring. How long ago that seemed now; and how much had she learned of the hollowness and corruption of human nature. But her face was still set in its mourning mould; pale, serene, brave and composed. She saw that she would have to handle this carefully.

'Your Aunt Lily was talking to me about him yesterday. Did you know that her husband has a niece working in Farrells - the mineral waters, I mean?'

'Has she?' Marie smoothed her black silk dress and sat down. She did not like the colour and was determined to get out of it as soon as she could; but she knew that it emphasized her slimness. She pressed one hand against her stomach - an instinctive gesture which did not escape her mother - and sipped her sherry.

'He lost his job on Monday,' said Mrs. Fogarty flatly. But she clutched her rosary again to give her courage. Could it be possible that there were complications already? But no, surely Marie could not be that careless in this day and age. 'He was let go,' she went on, hammering her point home.

'Was he?' Marie looked at her mother sharply; but

there was no gleam of malice in the dark hooded eyes;
any more than there had been a hint of triumph in the
voice. She knew that she had to be very careful.
Calm, cool and self-possessed her mother was dangerous.

'He might not find it so easy to get another job. At
least that's what Lily thinks. She didn't say why.'
Having let drop this innuendo Mrs. Fogarty lifted the
cross of her beads and studied it attentively.

Marie made no reply. Long experience had taught
her to adopt a prudent silence when her mother hinted
at anything. Her fingers tightened about the stem of
her glass and she stared down into its tawny contents.

Her mother cleared her throat and began again.
This thing would have to be thrashed out before Langley
arrived. Mr. Farrell had been very understanding
when she had phoned him herself after she had discovered Marie and Pat together with that letter. There
were a great many things Brian's employer did not like
about him, principally the fact that he did not go to
Mass every Sunday. It did not surprise him at all to
hear that the young man had insulted a priest, and
showed no sign of contrition following the first warning
he had delivered to him on Agnes' advice. Besides he
knew Mrs. Fogarty by repute for many years; and did
not underestimate her influence in those circles where
they both did business. And now that her husband was
dying she was likely to be playing an even more active
role in the business. He had his eyes on a deal with
them for a monopoly of their trade; and if that meant
the end of young Langley he was willing to take the risk,
especially since it was quite true that his nephew was
anxious to come into the business. It was all very neat
and satisfactory; and he and Agnes had parted on the
telephone with expressions of mutual esteem.

'I don't like bringing this up, Marie, so soon after
your father has gone to his reward. It's been a terrible
time for us all.' There was a faint rattling sound as
she lifted her hands and pressed her fingers against
her temples. Marie looked at her impassively and
waited. 'But you force me to it. You don't seem to
realise it but this young man is altogether unsuitable
for you.' She wove her beads round the fingers of both

182

hands like a chain and clasped them together on her
lap.

'Surely I can judge that for myself. I'm not a child.'

Mrs. Fogarty sighed and knitted her brows. In her
opinion that was precisely what her daughter was:
childish. She had looked forward to a child who would
make up to her for all the agonies of the marriage bed;
only to discover that Pat had thwarted her there too.
Now he was gone; and she felt the stimulating sense of
power quickening her blood. If she could never have
the love of this child, she could at least control her.

'You know very little about the world, Marie, although
like all young people nowadays you think you do. You
have led a very sheltered life, and have always had
everything you wanted. A girl like you needs someone
to look after you, who understands your ways. Above
all someone who won't be reliant on you. All this may
sound very old-fashioned to you now, but one day you'll
realise the truth of it.' Here Agnes was perfectly
sincere. She knew her daughter's weaknesses; had
long ago sensed that she had inherited her father's
temperament in very full measure; and judged quite
rightly that such an inheritance was even more dangerous
in a woman than a man. Langley was certainly not the
man to handle her daughter once the first fine careless
rapture had worn off. He was too romantic, too highly-
strung, as he had proved by his behaviour the night he
had come bursting into the house to confront Father
Moran and all of them. For Agnes and her husband
had been under no illusions about Marie's connection
with the priest. If Langley had been a sensible man he
would simply have absented himself, to kick up such a
fuss betrayed an instability which would expose all of
them to a constant war of nerves.

'All of this means of course that I should have nothing
to do with him because he has no money.' Marie drained
her glass quickly and put it down, clearing her throat
and shaking her head. 'And now has no job either. I
wonder how that was managed.' She looked at her
mother boldly; but Agnes did not flinch. She knew that
silence was the greatest of all weapons. What was un-
expressed could never be proven.

'I, of course, don't know what happened,' she said
quietly. 'Your Aunt Lily has no hold on her tongue.
She has a story about embezzlement, but I wouldn't
put much store by that.' She threw out this line carelessly on a dying fall. 'The fact remains that he has
nothing, so far as I know. What do you propose to live
on?'

Marie felt her face reddening; and took a deep
breath to help her control her temper. Could it be
possible that Brian had created all that fuss to cover
himself? She looked at her mother with cold fury. No
matter what happened she was not going to knuckle
under to this. The threat was now explicit. Her
mother was in control of the purse-strings; and she
was not going to subsidise this union.

'We'll think of that later. If you want to close the
door in our faces that's your affair. Brian and I are
getting married no matter what you say or do, and
there isn't really any point in discussing it.' She made
to get up, but with a sudden gesture of her chained
hands, which she raised together with the cross dangling
between them her mother restrained her.

'You can hardly get married immediately any way,
can you?' she said carefully. 'It would hardly be decent,
with your father hardly cold in his grave - '

'A lot you care about that - ' broke in Marie, stung
by the thought that her mother had somehow sensed the
added complication of the awful scene after the funeral.
If there was no way to escape this monstrous strangle-
hold except by leaving the house, then she knew she
would have to go.

The same thought occurred to her mother, wise in
the ways of the world. Now that the house was hers,
and the business too - she had taken care that Pat made
a will to this effect when he had his first slight stroke
- she did not want to be put at a disadvantage at once.
To throw her daughter out because she wanted to marry
a penniless man would merely draw attention to all that
had gone before. Not only would she be accused of
heartlessness and rapacity; but in all likelihood the
background to the whole affair would be dragged in by
kind neighbours; the episode with Father Moran, and

184

one or two others that Mrs. Fogarty knew about.
Marie would be discredited; and in the process some
of the dirt would rub off on her mother. Better that
this thing should be settled quickly.

'You hardly know this young man,' she said,
ignoring her daughter's outburst. 'And how well does
he know you?'

'What do you mean by that?' Marie knew immediately
that she had allowed her alarm to show in her face.
Years of watching every reaction had taught her the
bleak secret that the knowledge of self-betrayal always
comes too late.

'What should I mean?' said her mother innocently.
She could afford not to press her advantage now she
knew she had scored. 'It happened very quickly.
Your backgrounds are very different. Even if you had
complete control of your affairs - ' she paused to let
this home truth sink in - 'this young man might not like
the idea of being dependent on you for his livelihood.
He may be a very independent type for all I know. On
the other hand he may be very interested in your pros-
pects. Either way it is not very satisfactory.'

A cold afternoon sun bathed the room in a clinical
light. Every line and hollow on Mrs. Fogarty's face
was picked out with remorseless clarity: she looked
old and withered and very tired. Marie, staring at
her intently, was glad that she was not facing the light.
Was this what a loveless life did to one? A pre-
occupation with ways and means; a vision of life as a
chess-board on which men and women could be pushed
about as if they were made of ivory; a cold surrender
to the sense of property.

Agnes, who was used to her daughter's antagonism
and was more than able to combat it, saw something
else in her face and for the first time flinched before
it. All the failures of her married life rose up and
confronted her in the person of the living fruit of it.
She clutched her rosary in her dry hands and stiffened
instinctively. She knew what was coming.

'I happen to be in love with him, Mummy,' said
Marie slowly, as if she were speaking to someone
slightly retarded. 'I don't suppose you'd understand

that, would you?'

Mrs. Fogarty collected her forces for one last effort.

'I understand more than you think,' she replied
bitterly. 'Why the hurry to get married? Has something gone wrong? Is that what you call love?'

Marie opened her mouth to speak, and succeeded
only in gasping. For a blinding moment she understood
what it felt like to condone murder in the heart: it must
always arise from a desire to be free, to assert one's
own right to survive. At that moment she was nearer
to her mother than she had ever been before, except
perhaps when she lay panting under the brutal weight
of Pat Fogarty. But the moment passed, crushed by
the burden of the years as her mother's fragile
sensuality had once been shattered by the weight of
another Fogarty. In how many marital beds had murder
been conceived?

There was really nothing that they could say to each
other. But Marie, frightened now had to say something.

'What in God's name do you want?' she cried,
throwing out her hands.

'It was very nice of Mother Theresa to write such
a nice letter,' replied Mrs. Fogarty in a perfectly
normal voice. 'And a Mass card too. After all these
years.'

But she had not gone mad; nor did Marie think she
had. She was well used to this. It was simply that
Agnes' keen ears had detected Nelly coming with the
tea.

CHAPTER TWENTY-NINE

Brian passed a hand across his forehead and squeezed his eyes shut when Marie had finished. He felt tired, dispirited and bitter.

He pressed his fingers against his eyes causing a little universe of shooting stars to explode in the darkness of his skull, and tried to remember something he had read recently. Something about love being allied to fear, and mixed up with the sense of property. It certainly was in this case. And then he remembered something else - a quotation he had learned long ago in school.

'You will answer: the slaves are ours' he murmured, taking his hand from his eyes and looking bleakly at Marie.

'What's that?' she said, startled by his strange tone. Brian was not much of an actor, and his voice was stiff and self-conscious.

'Nothing. Just a line out of something I learned in school. Shakespeare, I think.'

Marie relaxed and stroked the side of her leg nearest the fire. While waiting for him to come she had heaped coal on the fire, drawn the curtains, switched off the centre light and put on the pink-shaded standard lamp at the back of her chair. It was an instinctive gesture; an attempt to shut out the harshness of the world beyond, wrapped in a sinister January fog. Alone she would never have dreamed of doing such a thing: the silent house with its heavy furniture was oppressive enough. She felt trapped and wanted to share her sense of captivity.

Brian took out his cigarettes and offered her one. She shook her head and watched him blankly as he lit one, threw the match into the fireplace and took up the glass of whisky which she had poured for him. The

187

ritual biscuits lay untouched on a silver tray on the table behind the sofa. She could dispense with these for a visitor like this.

'What does she want?' he said wonderingly. 'It's more than opposition in the usual sense. Mothers are always on the look-out for a good match for their daughters, but not many of them carry it this far. I don't understand it. Even if she knew everything about me, I still don't get it.' He clenched his teeth and drew back his lips over them, making a faint hissing sound as he expelled his breath.

'I think she does know all about us, Brian, that's the whole point. And she can't bear it. Oh, I know she feels she has the whip-hand now, and wants to make the most of it. But it's more than that. I think she can't bear to see anybody happy and well-adjusted in love.' She paused and stroked the side of her nose, a curious masculine gesture she had picked up from a lesbian nun of great charm who had once taught her English. 'You know, if you had been a dried-up stick who looked as if he made the sign of the cross over himself every time he had an improper thought, I don't think she'd have minded at all.' She chuckled wryly and ran her eyes over the big loose-limbed body sprawled on the low sofa.

'We look too pleased with ourselves, Brian,' she went on in a half-serious tone, responding as always to the physical impact of his presence which always gave her courage.

'I'd be better pleased at the moment if I had a job.' Man-like, he took his pleasures more lightly than she; and found it difficult to understand such an attitude.

'How much money have you?'

'About sixty pounds. That won't last long.' He shook his head ruefully.

'I came into an insurance policy when I was twenty-one. A little over a thousand. I still have eight hundred of it. That would keep us going for some time, wouldn't it?' She leaned forward eagerly, clasping her hands and searching his face.

'Us?' He lifted his head and stared back at her through drooping eye-lids. Inside their own little universe there were already complications reflecting the greater ones outside. His voice was wary.

'Well, we can't go on like this,' she explained enthusiastically. 'You'll have to get a job and it might take some time. And if she continues to act this way, so will I. We'll have to get out of here. You don't know how a person like that can poison everything she touches. I'm afraid, Brian, truly I am.'

'So am I.' He looked over his shoulder at the door. Although Marie had told him that her mother was gone to bed he still felt nervous in this room where only a week ago Mrs. Fogarty had made such an unexpected appearance. Did she, he wondered, really want to get out of all this; or was he merely drifting, waiting for something to turn up? He felt a sharp spasm of irritation and frowned into his glass. He sensed the narrowing of the walls.

Marie frightened by his sulky apathetic appearance got up and went to him quickly. She took the glass out of his hands, held them in her own for a moment and raised one of them quickly to her lips.

'Don't do that,' he said roughly, snatching it away.

'Brian,' she pleaded, 'we won't get anywhere analysing things like this. It'll only end up with a sort of barrier between us, and that's exactly what she wants. Don't you realise that the only thing they can't take from us is this? No one can create this except us. I'm not ashamed of it.'

'Don't.' He sat up and took her hand away from his loins. But he could not control his slow sullen response. Indeed at the moment it seemed to him that this really was all that was left to them.

'Please.'

'No, not here.'

She stared at his flushed face for a moment and slowly got to her feet. She leaned her elbows on the mantelpiece and stared at her reflection in the mirror. Did she really know him at all, she wondered. Had the whole thing been a game from the beginning? A desperate gesture of revolt against the strictures she felt surrounding her?

He stood up and came to her side, his eyes steady,

his mouth set and determined. And some of the
mystery was solved, as it always is when a man repels
a facile emotion based on a purely physical appeal.

'I can't think straight about this, Marie, while I'm
situated like this. I'm out of a job and fed up. Suppose
I take your money, what then?'

'It means if you don't that they get the better of us,'
her voice was quick and persuasive. 'She's done the
worst she can. If we weaken now she's won. Can't you
see she's relying on this? That was the whole point in
leaving you without a job. She thinks you'll get up on
your dignity and refuse to have anything to do with me
because you have nothing.' She reached out and
clasped his arm convulsively.

'I thought you couldn't buy love,' he said slowly
looking at her white face in the looking-glass.

'Nor can you. But you can destroy it that way. And
that's what they want. Not love, not even affection,
just because it can't be bought. If you really loved me
you'd take that eight hundred - ' she broke off, conscious
of her impassioned inconsistency. What were they
struggling with if not for an understanding beyond words?

'I can love you without it,' he said calmly, turning
round and pressing his shoulder against the marble
ledge. 'I'll get some sort of a job. So long as I can
keep myself I can go on seeing you.'

At that moment she sensed victory; all the long
night of uncertainty swept away in a surge of gratitude
and surety. But she controlled her impulsiveness.
Both of them were learning a little wisdom.

He touched her hand and looked down at her with a faint
smile. In their love making there had been no restraint
and no shame. Both of them knew that that was a rare
thing; and while they realised that it was not the whole
of a relationship, they also knew that without it they
would be only half-alive. Beyond the intimacies of
mouth, tongue and genitals there lay a vast unknown
territory inhabited by the ghosts of all the people who
had made them what they were. And they both sensed
now that it was here that they could go astray.

'So we go on as we are, for the time being,' she said
humbly, feeling the warmth of the fire at the backs of

her legs flowing up through her body in a warm reassuring glow.

'For the time being.'

'It means you'll be away.'

'Yes, I'll have to look around. There may be something in Galway. If not I'll try Dublin.

'Have you anything in mind?' she said thinking of
several Dublin firms with which Fogarty's did business.

'Why?' he asked gently; beginning to think that he
knew her better than he thought. Was she really
prepared to accept him as he was, without trying to
make him over into something more available, more
convenient? Stripped of most of the ties which drew
them apart they could afford to be truthful.

'All right,' she nodded, 'I won't interfere. I'll just
have to wait.'

They looked at each other and knew a measure of
freedom. But moments of intoxication do not last long.
Marie suddenly remembered what had happened to her
yesterday, and shivered. She was not free after all.

'What is it?' He took a step nearer, put his hand
under her chin and tilted her face back. Tears swam
into her eyes, as she realised that she must deceive
him once more.

'I'm afraid,' she whispered, making no effort to
control her tears. 'You won't be here. It's horrible,
Brian. I feel sometimes as if I were in prison.'

'I know, I know.' He stroked her hair gently,
allowing himself to drift on the warm tide which he
felt was engulfing them. But he knew very little; and
was only vaguely aware that they could not escape now
from the hidden influences which had shaped them.
He sensed the negation of love all about them; the
perversion of it, so that it might be the better controlled
and if necessary destroyed. They were not free; and
in time all those pressures would combine to make
them conform in their own way to the power which had
been wrested out of fear.

But now there was only the loneliness, the sense of
being together in spite of everything, the knowledge of
something forbidden, shared, accepted and desperately
indulged. It bore in its flowering the seeds of its own

191

destruction; but this mercifully they did not know.

'Can we get out of here?' he muttered, remembering the hotel room, cold and impersonal, the bar, full of garrulous hearties of both sexes, the silent watchful streets, the uncertainty of to-morrow.

'Oh, God, yes, please. Anywhere. Can we go to the lake place?' She stepped back and knuckled her eyes like a child. And indeed in spite of her veneer of sophistication there was something childlike about Marie; here her mother was not altogether wrong. But while Mrs. Fogarty put it down to a wilful lack of responsibility, a shrewder and less biased observer might have divined in this carefully poised girl a curious innocence. She had been born with a greater capacity for love and pleasure than most people; and her nature had very early on found itself at war with the primitive, property-ridden society in which she was reared.

Silently they crept out of the house, in pursuit of what some would call sin, and others a primal innocence. They melted into the fog and disappeared like two criminals.

CHAPTER THIRTY

The fog lifted and the weather turned bland as it sometimes does in January. A pale winter sun washed over
the plain touching the yellow fields and the purple river
with a subdued magic. Objects glowed in a luminous
haze, and seemed to bend under the shifting sky. A
whisker of thorn bushes running on top of a low hill
was smudged with diffused light; church steeples turned
silver and half-melted into the cornflower sky: a cart,
a motor, a snaggle of cattle passing along a country
road were surrounded by a sort of pastel halo of
shifting light as they moved against the open horizon.
It was a foretaste of spring, brief and treacherous.

Brian went home to look around for a job to keep
him going; and surprisingly enough got the offer of one
in two weeks time. A colleague of his in the mineral
business had moved to a better job with a firm of
cigarette manufacturers; was now being transferred on
promotion to Dublin, and put in a strong recommendation with his area manager. Brian was interviewed,
made an excellent impression, and informed a week
afterwards that he could take up the position at the
beginning of February. It seemed hardly possible at
the time; but as his friend remarked that was the way
things went: you either hit the bulls-eye on the first
shot or you went on missing for the rest of your life.
The personnel manager who interviewed him, an
elderly Englishman with a weakness for good manners
and a horror of brashness, was impressed by his air
of quiet self-assurance. Customers he knew were
more often than not put off by the eager-beaver types
who infected everybody with their anxiety to impress.
And a firm jaw, broad shoulders and a suggestion of
latent potency always helped sales. Brian although he
was spared the more obvious effects of high pressure

193

salesmanship did not entirely escape the cattle-mart.
A commercial he had long ago discovered must have
something to display besides his wares: he must sell
himself.

His telephone conversation with Marie that evening
cost him twelve shillings. He was excited and confident;
she garrulous, as women are when they approve of
something for the wrong reason. She had no intention
of allowing Brian to continue in that job indefinitely;
but she did not think it wise to tell him so at that stage.
He would come to visit her in a few days time when he
had bought himself a new outfit, assured his mother of
his good fortune which she still found hard to believe,
and got to know his new colleagues a bit better. Marie
listened to this sympathetically. It would give her
time to adjust herself to a new situation, lately arisen,
but not yet fully grasped. The tide was turning at last
and the boat she knew had to be carefully steered.

She remembered her mother's caution when it
became apparent to her that Marie was not going to
give up her latest boy-friend. Better that these things
be settled quietly. The corrupt values in which she
had been reared were pliable. The cloak was always
available to those who held the strongest dagger.

A week after her father's death Marie had received
a letter from a firm of Dublin solicitors, asking her to
call at their office in Clare Street at her earliest
convenience. The communication was unexpected but
the implications of it were not. On more than one
occasion her father had told her that she would not be
left unprovided for in the event of his death. What she
did not know was that he had left instructions with his
bank manager to get in touch with those solicitors if
anything should happen to him, and inform them of it.
This had been done; and the first effect of it lay on the
desk in what she still thought of as her father's office.

Slivers of yellow sunlight bisected the blue carpet;
the money was heaped in neat five pound bags and
bundles of notes with the dockets of each vanman placed
on top of them at the end of the desk. Miss Rafferty
was typing in the outer office. The storeman was
calling one of the packers. The big feeder truck was

194

pulling out of the yard with a loud vibrating diesel snort. Business was usual.

Marie sat down at the desk and read through the letter again. She did not want to go to Dublin at the moment so she took up the telephone and put through a call. As usual in Dublin offices no one was in. Could they ring back? She gave the number and name and began to count the money. An hour afterwards someone rang to say that the gentleman who was dealing with that particular matter was out to-day. Could she ring to-morrow. Marie was used to this sort of thing. As the means of communication multiplied it became increasingly difficult to get in touch with anybody.

Mutton broth, cutlets and bread pudding for lunch. Neither Nelly nor her mistress believed in pampering the palate. A smell of grease was disagreeable, but safe; oysters and pheasants were suspect. Bacon and eggs or a boiled egg for high tea - it never varied. Rosary and gossip in the evening; Mass in the morning; and a careful watch on the weather in between. The suffocating sameness of it day after day struck Marie now with renewed force as she was left to nurse her longing for her lover in private. A sense, even an illusion of union, a happy mingling of limbs, a deep private pleasure given and shared, it did not seem too much to ask.

The next day she rang the solicitors after her mother had left the office and at last got her man. He hummed and hawed when she asked him to come down to the town; a trek to the provinces he implied was somewhat outside his range of understanding. At length she got him to agree to a meeting at one of the local hotels for the following day. Had it something to do with her father's estate? Yes. And the legal gentleman put down the telephone.

He turned out to be a young man in whom the dry creaking old voice of his profession had been prematurely developed to an abnormal degree. Marie came to the conclusion that it was not his only abnormality; for not once did he give her the impression that she possessed any sort of sex. She could not help wondering what this chunky red-headed young oaf did when he was human - if ever.

But it did not matter. The news he brought was sensational. According to her father's will drawn up six months previously Mrs. Fogarty was to be paid back in full for the original investment she had made in the business, a matter of fifteen hundred pounds. Marie had no idea that her parents had started on so little. Mrs. Fogarty was to be provided with an income of six hundred a year; and any additions to it were left to her daughter's discretion. The remainder of his estate, including a considerable amount of house property adjoining the store and office, was left to Marie. It was a great deal more than she expected; for even she had not realised how deep the breach or how bitter the unspoken quarrel had been between her parents. Pat had got his own back in the only way open to him. It was an action which the local moralists would understand.

'Can I get you a cup of tea?' asked the solicitor, blandly winding up the legal manifestation of an obscure human tragedy. He would have plenty to do in the next few weeks getting this client - he did not think of her as a woman - to sign all the relevant documents; but for the moment he felt the need for a little reckless refreshment.

'No, thank you.' Marie looked at the tight-legged young man with distaste. She felt no sense of elation, but a curious feeling of despondency which she did not attempt to analyse. All she wanted to do was to get away as quickly as possible. It would take her some time to get adjusted to this new and in some ways alarming situation. She would have been surprised to learn that she was humble about it, like a true believer on whom some unexpected grace had fallen. For Marie had not escaped the heritage of her generation: love, marriage, sex and religion might be treated lightly and without any great prejudices: but money, never.

She drove back to the office, white-faced and slightly numb. Miss Rafferty was convinced that she had received some bad news; and wondered if there had been another Lovers' quarrel. She could never understand how girls like Marie Fogarty, who seemed to have everything that the world could offer, always seemed to be in trouble. She had never in her life questioned the ability of all the money she banked every morning to bring happiness to those it controlled.

CHAPTER THIRTY-ONE

While Marie was with the solicitor Agnes Fogarty had
an unexpected caller. She opened the door herself as
she usually did when she was alone, on the ostrich
principle that the less Nelly saw the better. At first
she did not recognise the small very fat woman in the
brown tweed coat who displayed a set of ill-fitting false
teeth and called her by her Christian name.

'Why Winnie,' she exclaimed covering her surprise
with an equally false grin, doubly insincere since her
own teeth were all sound. 'How are you? Come in.'

'Pat had to come to town to a meeting. The I.N.T.O.
you know. He's on the national committee. So I thought
I'd call and see how you are after the trouble. It's
when it's all over that it really hits you. The empty
house and all, God help us.'

The two women eyed each other suspiciously in the
hall for a few moments. Agnes hardly knew her sister-
in-law, and what she saw of her she did not like.
Winnie Fogarty smelled strongly of turf smoke, which
Agnes always associated with poor relations in the
country. The wives of gentlemen farmers smelled
like successful business women - of good soap, discreet scent and clean underwear. But the reek of turf
suggested smoky kitchens and the inability to rise
above the station in life to which God has called one.

In addition to this private prejudice she knew in a
general way that Winnie had never had tuppence to
jingle on a tombstone. Pat's brother Jim, now mercifully deceased, had never made much of the thirty
ancestral acres which he had inherited, except to
bring an odd bullock to the fair and drink the proceeds.
Of their three sons two were in England 'at the building',
and the third, Pat, had somehow got himself through
training college and was now teaching in a country

198

school near his home where he lived with his mother.
But Agnes had not been able to place him among the
nephews at the funeral: they were all vaguely alike,
except for one who bore a frightening, and to her
obscene resemblance to her late husband. Could this
have been young Pat, she wondered uneasily?

The two women seated themselves warily on either
side of the blazing coal fire, and carefully avoided
each other's eyes. Winnie was not asked to remove
her coat; a polite hint that her hostess was not
anticipating a long visitation. Agnes had already taken
full stock of her sister-in-law's cheap black beret,
shapeless tweed coat with its sagging hem-line, cotton
gloves and worn shoes. If her son gave her a decent
allowance out of his salary she was certainly not
making good use of it.

'Gorgeous place you have here,' said Winnie, looking
round her with slow-eyed thoroughness. 'Not that that's
much comfort when the grief is on you.' She clicked
her teeth, making a sound like a distant typewriter,
and slipped one of her swollen feet half-way out of her
shoe.

'Will you have a glass of sherry?' Agnes glanced
pointedly at her sister-in-law's bared heel and squeezed
her lips. She was pretty sure that this untidy slob had
not come to hold her hand in mutual lamentation over
the dead.

Winnie clutched her bosom as if she had had a sudden
heart spasm and shook her jowls fiercely.

'Wouldn't touch it if it was to save my life. The lord
knows I saw enough of that in my time. And it isn't
over yet.' She lowered her eyes and shot a hooded look
at her sister-in-law. Agnes was twisting one of the
rings on her bony fingers and staring out of the window.
She gave every impression of being at a loss for words.
Winnie twisted round on the sofa and peered at one of
the tables in the corner, wriggling her foot back into
its shoe as if preparing to take off. To Agnes'
astonishment she did, heaving herself up with a loud
sigh and waddling across the room where she picked
up a framed photograph, held it close to her eyes and
then turned round and thrust it out in front of her. 'I

noticed it the minute I came in after the funeral,' she said in a breathy voice. 'Your poor man when he was young. I often heard Jim say that our Pat was his twin double at the same age.'

Agnes clasped her hands together tightly and could not repress a shiver of distaste. So that was who the young man was. It was as if the ghost of those horrible early days had come back to haunt her.

Winnie came back to the sofa and sat down with a gusty sigh, clutching the photograph in her lap.

'The very spit and image,' she murmured. 'He must have given you a bit of a turn when you saw him. A brilliant boy too. Won all sorts of scholarships without any help from anybody. Not a penny.'

Agnes, staring at the photograph with a sort of fascinated uneasiness, did not know what the woman was getting at. She was well aware that Pat had been in the habit of slipping a surreptitious hand-out to his no-good brother from time to time. What she did not know was that the last application just before Jim died and his son graduated from the training college had been refused. All that had gone before was forgotten; this last slight was remembered. Winnie nursed her resentment in silence. In her muddled mind it seemed to her that the richer Fogartys had prospered entirely on the strength of exploiting their less fortunate relatives.

'I have heaven stormed to keep my boy from the bottle. You and me know that that's a family failing with the Fogartys. It would be awful if anything happened to Pat now at the height of his profession.' She raised her two chins and gave Agnes a cold meaning look. 'He wouldn't be the first brilliant boy to go to the wall out of bad company. It's shocking what example will do.'

'You must pray.' Agnes looked down at her empty hands and felt naked. 'We all have our crosses to bear in this life.'

'True for you. But some have heavier crosses than others, and no Simon of Cyrene to give them a lift of the load.' Suddenly as if she had turned on a little private tap in her forehead, tears sprang out of her

red-rimmed eyes and ran down her yellow cheeks.
'I hope to God he'll be all right to-day at that meeting
for he was in a terrible state the other night. The
way he carried on, like a maniac, I'll never forget it
in all my born days.' She sniffed, wiped her nose with
the back of her hand, and transfixed Agnes with a wild-
eyed stare which gave her slack features a sudden taut
look, as if her rigid eyes had pulled them mysteriously
together. 'What happened to my boy here on the day
of the funeral? What did your daughter do to him?'

'What?' Agnes drew herself up with a jerk and
thrust out her head with what the other woman took to
be antagonism.

'You needn't tell me you didn't see her rubbing up
against him, and she making him pass the tea, moryah,
and then taking him out of the room with the whole
family staring after them. Didn't Lily Fogarty and her
daughter tax me with it afterwards? They were watching
the whole performance and so was everyone else.'
Winnie clutched the photograph to her heaving stomach
and there was a faint crack which neither of them
noticed.

'I don't know what you're talking about,' said Agnes,
playing for time.

'Oh, don't you.' Winnie thrust out the photograph
and waved it like a weapon. 'I suppose you don't know
your own daughter and the sort she is. Doesn't the
whole world and its wife know about her. Didn't Lily
tell me - ' she broke off and covered her tracks by
leaving it to the imagination. In fact Lily, another in-
law, had excused herself and followed Pat upstairs on
the day of the funeral to 'wash her hands'. He, as she
had hoped, was not in the bathroom. She locked herself in, listened for sounds, and shortly afterwards
had heard someone come out of the bedroom at the end
of the corridor, a room which she knew from her
formal inspection of the house, to be Marie's. Opening
the door, her innocent business finished, she had come
out just as he was rounding the corner, and making for
the stairs. Half-way down he realised that he was
being followed, glanced back, and Cousin Lily, a
mistress of the art of enquiry, had read everything on

201

his face. This by various polite circumlocutions she
had conveyed to his mother later; and Pat had seen
them whispering together and looking at him. But all
this Winnie had no intention of telling Agnes.

'And in the very presence of death too,' she went on,
giving the cracked photograph another shake. It might
have been a holy picture she was holding up to defend
herself against the powers of evil. 'What am I going
to do if my Pat gets drunk again and comes out with the
sort of story I heard him raving and shouting about the
other night when he came rolling into the house like a
madman.' She paused for breath, and with one of those
lightning changes of mood and expression which are
second nature to those who feel that life has insulted
them, her eyes clouded over and she slumped back on
the sofa clutching the picture to her bosom. 'Not that
I blame him, the poor innocent gossoon, after what
happened to him in this house and the corpse hardly
out of the bed.'

Agnes was beginning to recover her composure.
Distasteful this encounter might be; but she had a
feeling that out of all this evident spite and muddled
self-righteousness some little grain of truth useful to
herself might emerge. But long experience had taught
her never to admit anything until all the facts were
clear.

'Well, what happened to him?' she said bluntly.

'If you only heard him,' whispered Winnie, still in
her smelling-salts mood. 'The things that came out of
that boy's mouth. If he gets into that state again and
lets it out in public, I won't answer for what I'll do.
And it's all your daughter's fault.' She threw the
photograph onto a cushion and pulled herself up, hard-
eyed now and shaking with indignation. 'Do you know
that one invited him upstairs, got him into her bedroom
on false pretences, and then threw herself at him like
one of them fallen sluts you'd hear about on the Dublin
quays. She ought to be locked up, so she should.'

Agnes looked over her shoulder at the door, and
composed her features for battle. On the surface of it
this would appear to be a cover-up operation; but one
never knew. Why was Winifred telling her all this if

she had no plans to turn it to her advantage? Pre-
occupied as always with the motive behind every action
she had never given much credence to the equivocal.
She had no understanding at all of the tangled under-
growth of sexual frustration of which she herself was
a sterile shoot.

Pat Fogarty had struck out in a fit of guilty rage.
'You don't even know how to do it. Run down to your
mother, like a good little boy'. These taunts had gone
home; and all the more forcibly since he knew that he
had been observed. He had brooded over the episode
until his thwarted uncertain masculinity had erupted
in a drunken stupor - the only force of release he was
capable of - and he had sobbed out the whole sordid
story on his mother's shoulder. But like many drunks
he preserved an instinct for self-preservation.
According to him Marie had lured him to her room and
seduced him. The nasty little boy had struck back;
and his mother, at last finding an outlet for her many
grievances, had sprung to his defence. Now she had
something to fling at the high and mighty Agnes and
her pampered daughter; and fling it she would before
they took it into their heads to accuse her. For
Winifred did not trust her son an inch. Suppose he had
followed the girl and forced himself on her? There
had been one or two other episodes of a like nature in
Pat's career; and this time his mother was determined
to teach him a lesson by airing the whole thing within
the family circle. She had come ostensibly to show up
Marie for what she was; and Pat still smarting under
the lash of her superiority had not discouraged his
mother. But Winifred who was not as stupid as she
looked was determined to turn the matter to her own
advantage, irrespective of how it turned out. If she
could get something out of Agnes, well and good; if not,
she would go back and tell him that the Fogartys were
thinking of reporting him to the police. That might take
the young buck's thoughts off the girls for a while.

'Now listen to me, Winnie, ' said Agnes in her
softest sodality voice, 'I don't know how much of all
this is true, but you and I know what men are like when
they have drink taken - '

'It is true, every word of it,' declared Winnie stubbornly. 'I know Pat. He hasn't been the same since that day, and what am I going to do if he lets it get on him and takes to the drink properly? He could lose his job like that, and then where would I be after all my hard work, and never a helping hand from those that have to throw it away?'

'And what do you expect me to do about it? Your son is old enough to take care of himself.'

'No he isn't. Whatever that one did to him he hasn't been the same since.' True Irish mother that she was it never occurred to Winifred that the idea of a big hefty fellow of twenty-eight being taken advantage of by a woman might strike some people as ludicrous. It did not strike Agnes that way either. If she had had a son herself she would have felt exactly the same about him.

'The least you might do is to make some restitution for the way Marie got at him,' went on Winifred sullenly. She knew that the game was up; either Agnes knew nothing of the affair or she was even more of a two-faced faggot than everybody said she was.

'Restitution?' Agnes had now got what she wanted; and she was determined to give nothing in return. All the same a few more details might be of help. 'What kind of restitution?'

'I have my son's good name to think about.' Winifred was tempted. 'Supposing that Lily and her squinty-eyed daughter start going round saying - '

'Saying what?'

'What she said to my face. That your daughter went the whole way with my son after she got him drunk.'

Agnes who had been leaning forward, listening intently, drew back with a set face, like a woman who had just seen a rabbit caught in a trap of her own setting. And indeed in a sense the trap had sprung. Winifred might be able to scare her son into a more reasonable acceptance of conventional standards; but she would get nothing out of her sister-in-law. As if she realised this her eyes spurted tears again and her vast bosom heaved with all the sorrow of an overpowering but not entirely dis-interested maternal passion.

'He's all I've got left in the world,' she sobbed. Agnes let her sob, until with another instant volte-face she pulled herself together, sniffed and looked about the room with contempt. 'But I might be better off than you are with all you have. At least my child has some decent feelings left. He's ashamed of his living life, so he is. And with the kind of conscience he has, a thing like that could destroy him. It's well known that a woman like that can ruin a man's life. What did she say to you about it?'

'This is the first I've heard of it.'

Winifred stifled a sigh of relief. That meant that the girl had not repulsed him. Probably even encouraged him as he said. Her heart lifted with the hope that her boy was not the maniac she sometimes suspected him of being. But she was not going to throw in the towel as easily as that.

'I bet it is,' she blustered. 'She could hardly boast of a thing like that to you. Dragging my boy out in full view of all the family, and trying to take his good name away from him. And she his own flesh and blood, the spit and living image of her own father. Glory be to God, it's worse than anything.'

She could hardly have made a more unfortunate remark at that juncture. Agnes felt her blood curdle, and thought she was going to be sick. She rose abruptly to her feet; and Winifred, knowing that the interview was over, stuffed her shoe back onto her foot with trembling fingers. She had a vague sense of being out-manoeuvred; but exactly how she could not determine.

Agnes took up the photograph, observed with relief that it was cracked, and put it under her arm. She could now lock it in a drawer with a clear conscience.

CHAPTER THIRTY-TWO

Father Moran had been in the habit of getting odds and
ends at Fogarty's store. A yard brush, fire-lighters,
nuts and bolts and a heater for the sacristy came cheaper
there than at the retail shops. Finding himself in need
of a tin of paint to touch up a damp spot in the hall he
saw no reason why he should now take his custom else-
where. For one thing it might look like running away;
and any suggestion of that must be carefully avoided.
It was a risk he would have to take, and he was now
beginning to feel that he was strong enough to take it.
He could not go on avoiding Marie for the rest of his
time in the place; and besides he was curious about her
in a nebulous sort of way. He no longer thought of her
much - such women as troubled his thoughts were now
indefinite, a sum of femininity. And there was always
the chance that he would not meet her.

But he did. Just as he was paying the storeman she
came out of the office, hesitated for a moment, and then
walked towards him. The storeman with infinite Irish
tact disappeared and the two of them were left together,
searching each others faces for those traces of change
which people once intimate are always curious about.
He came to the conclusion that she looked thinner, paler
and older than he remembered her; she thought that he
looked fatter, paler and older than she remembered him.
Passion and lust have the same effects when they are dead.

'How are you keeping, Marie?'

'So so.' She frowned and looked into the yard thoughtfully. 'I want to talk to you,' she said suddenly. 'You
might be able to give me a bit of advice. Business advice.'

'I'm not very good at that, I'm afraid.' The office was
out. He looked at it and shook his head.

'All right.' She crossed her arms over her breasts
and cupped her elbows. 'My father has changed his will,

left the place to me. Mummy is out except for an
allowance. I'm worried. What would you advise me to do?'

Father Moran felt his priestly calling moving his
spirit. Be careful, it prompted; don't get involved.
Everything works out in the end; and turns to ashes.

'Oh, I wouldn't like to advise you on that, Marie.'

'Mummy hasn't been very nice to me.' She frowned
again and looked down at the ground. 'I hardly know
what to say to her, it's that bad.'

She's looking for support, he thought. Careful, careful.

'Do the right thing, Marie. Then you won't have to
worry.'

'Yes, but what's the right thing?' She looked up
earnestly, and now it was his turn to shuffle his feet and
stare at them.

'It varies with the circumstances.' Indeed it does.
He felt a sudden irritation. He had not gone into the
Church to give advice on wills. Father Moran had regained the safety of the establishment. If Marie needed
any proof that their affair had not disqualified him for
his duties as a country curate, she had it now. He was
to the manner born; but with an added shrewdness, an
extra caution. His future was assured. But she was not
seeking information on this point. It was simply that she
felt the necessity to talk to someone about it; and she did
not know how she would discuss it with Brian. It was the
greatest compliment she could have paid to her lover.
To Father Moran too. He was being treated as an old
acquaintance who might be expected to give an impartial
word of advice. But the moment passed unrealised
between them. The past might be dead; but it was still a
ghost.

'I suppose I'll think of something,' she said with a wry
smile. The priest looked over her shoulder at the packers.
He was anxious to get away. Well, it was understandable
enough. This aspect of the clerical character she knew
only too well. 'I hope you got what you wanted, Father.'

He picked up the tin of paint and brandished it in front
of her. This was what they should have been talking about.

She smiled and turned away, unaware that the words
they had exchanged, trite and superficial though they were,

had been prompted by something else - that instinctive
sense of the future which often prompts people to say
something, make a gesture which at the time appears
idle and meaningless, but which are a blind manifestation
of an inner foreboding. It might have appeared to Father
Moran that Marie had been trying to make a polite conversation, although he questioned the matter of it - what
had her father's will got to do with him? - but in fact
she was anxious and vaguely apprehensive, and would
have welcomed a word of advice from almost anybody.
But this he could not know now that all tension had
slackened between them. Besides which he had other
things to think about.

He got into his car with a friendly wave to the foreman and drove off, rather pleased with himself.

At that hour the narrow streets of the town were
clogged with a slow-moving line of cars, trucks and
vans moving along confusedly in the meandering rhythm
of the place; a vehicle parked in the wrong position
could hold up the line for ten minutes, while drivers sat
slumped in their seats staring out apathetically at the
passers-by. The guards were not in evidence; very
sensibly they left things to sort out themselves. And
that narrow secret old town had never been built for the
heavy traffic which now converged upon it at break-neck
speed on the new tourist roads. The people shrugged
and went about their side-long business - it was a
curious characteristic of the place that none of the
natives ever walked straight - and smiled their cynical
smiles. It would all be the same in a hundred years' time.

Father Moran at length got into the market square
and passed under the reeking walls of the castle and onto
the western road by the apple-white church. The river
was swollen higher than ever, greyer, quietly menacing.
The lights were on on the parapet of the bridge recalling
the flaming torches of another age. He passed by the
side of the church with the bending Byzantine towers
above, by the high barrack wall and the dripping trees
on the promenade, the swaying boats and the massive
cannon; under the lacy-white railway bridge and back
towards where he came from.

Half-way home, just inside the parish boundary, a

new house had been built. A conventional two-story concrete box with a small garden fronting the road, a garage, and a little Lourdes grotto set into the wall facing the square strip of lawn. It belonged to an engineer in the turf company: a Tipperary man who had just moved in with his wife and four children. Father Moran had seen them at Mass: a quiet inconspicuous family, all daily communicants. Three daughers and a son, ranging in age from sixteen to eight; the boy, the eldest, tall, gangling pale-faced and earnest like the father; the girls, plump twinkling and rosy-cheeked, like their mother. They had struck him as healthy, uncomplicated and friendly, and he had found himself thinking about them more than once. Perhaps the son would go on for the church; one of the daughters might enter a convent; the others pass into the civil service. Nothing spectacular; a decent, hard-working, god-fearing family.

They were in the habit of sitting in the front room with the curtains undrawn. At tea-time they were to be seen grouped about the table, talking animatedly, smiling often; in the evening the parents would sit on either side of the fireplace in the other room, one reading, the other knitting, while one or two of the children looked at television, and then went back to the dining-room where they grouped round the table studying their books. Father Moran had passed the house several times while out walking and was already familiar with their habits. It was a homely domestic scene; and he found himself lingering on the road outside every time he passed. As he looked at this apparently happy and united family he thought more than once of what Father Melody had said to him. 'I never learned to love them. I never got behind the front. You will do better, if only because - ' He knew now why old Melody had never accepted his flock. There was really no way that he could identify himself with them. In an age of much vaunted outsiders, the old priest really was one. But could the same be said of himself? These people had something which he could admire and encourage. They were very like the sort of family he would have himself if he had married. Everything about them interested him, and now more especially than ever.

He pulled the car slowly to a halt outside their gate. They were having tea; munching jaws, raised cups, dipping heads, a waving brown tea-pot; and behind them on the wall facing the window a gilt mirror and a mahogany clock on the tiled mantelpiece.

For some time now Father Moran had promised himself that he would call on them. It was in his line of duty. But with this family his thoughts went a little further. They were not natives of the place; would know nothing of the complicated issues of blood and ancient envy that made the natives so prickly to the visitors. It was not really possible to make friends with any of them: jealousy soured every attempt at a normal neighbourly relationship. But these people perhaps were different. He allowed himself to think of a night or two a week when he could relax and enjoy their company. Perhaps he could help the children with their lessons; talk with the parents about the weather, politics, the awful state of the times. Get to know them and warm himself at a family fire. Surely it was not too much to expect. These he knew he could accept, even love; and it was unlikely that their eyes would have the watchful look he imagined he saw on all sides now.

The mother got up and went out. One by one the others blessed themselves and left the table, the girls helping to heap the china on to a tray and fold the cloth. He pressed his forehead against the window of the car until his breath nearly blurred his vision. Suddenly the door opened and the mother stood framed in the light of the hall. Father Moran drew back and fumbled with the gears in a panic. But before he could start up a small white dog came racing down the path barking furiously and stood up on its hind legs clawing at the gate. Father Moran made a quick decision; got out of his car and held out his hand to the dog.

'That's a good boy,' he said in a coaxing voice. The dog stopped barking and began to wag its tail. The priest pushed open the gate and with the little terrier frisking at his heels walked up to the waiting woman at the door. Brown hair streaked with grey; smiling blue

eyes, pink cheeks and a warm smile. The husband
came out to join her in the hall, and as the welcoming
voices rose the children trooped out and stood shyly
in the background waiting to be introduced.

'Well, now Father isn't it nice of you to call. Come
in, come in. You'll have a cup of tea.'

'Ah, sure that would be too much trouble.'

'Kathleen, put the kettle on. Come in, Father, into
the room. It's a terrible cold evening. Would you like
some soda bread? This is my husband Tom, and this
is Tommy, and this is Fidelma - oh a bold lassie -
and Siobahn, the nun of the family. Kathleen is on
duty to-night, wait until she brings in the tea. Sit down,
father, sit down, won't you. Here on this chair. Wait
until I stir up the fire.'

Father Moran sat down and looked about him shyly.
The warm eager voices lapped about him like warm
waves on a summer day. Soon he had stretched his
legs and felt the fire toasting his ankles. The children
came and handed him plates of bread and cakes.
Encouraged by their artless hospitality he found himself talking freely, drawing them into the conversation
about their lessons, their games, their ambitions. He
was not aware of any inhibitions in their replies; and
the parents looked on fondly as little tentative links
were made, interest explored and a genial air of
mutual good-will established.

The priest smiled happily. He felt safe. The
troublesome, the deviant, the non-comforting seemed
very far away in this happy family atmosphere. It was
no harm no doubt to have met them; but wise not to
linger too long in their company. Father Moran was
fulfilling his vocation in the only way he knew. He felt
sure he would benefit by it.

CHAPTER THIRTY-THREE

Money has a curious pervasive power, not unlike the
mysterious grace which sometimes touches the souls
of the truly religious and preserves them from evil.
Just as those who are born with a certain fineness of soul
often emerge unscathed from situations which would lead
others to corruption, so too those born with a sense of
property are protected by their own faith and never seem
to fall into the sin of poverty. A second sense bestowed
upon them by the gods they worship leads their steps
unerringly on the straight and narrow path which leads
to security. Agnes Fogarty was one of those. She was
neither a very intelligent woman nor a particularly far-
seeing one; but not once in her life had she deviated
from the faith to which she had dedicated her life and
energies. All those qualities of heart and mind which in
others are fulfilled in affection, creation and love, were
in her lavished on the pursuit of money, respectability
and that bestowal of favours on others which often accompanies a fierce sense of self-protection. She had the
reputation of being a deeply charitable woman; and indeed
she contributed to many charities and rarely allowed a
poor client to leave her door without some little material
reward - in itself a thanks-offering to the god of fortune.

When she tackled her daughter about Pat Fogarty, the
younger, she did not yet know that Marie now held the
whip-hand over her; and could if she wished have put her
out of the house. Since Agnes could not and never would
have believed in such an eventuality her faith was strong
and her spirits high. She started with the advantage of
complete self-assurance, made even more formidable in
her case by the care she always took never to go too far.

'I want to talk to you a moment, Marie,' she said
quietly on the evening of Father Moran's visit to the store.
They were alone in the house together; Mass was

over; Nelly was still out and Marie had had her chat on the telephone with Brian who was coming on the following day. Agnes judged that the moment to strike had come.

Marie who had planned to have a bath and go to bed early with a novel heard the request with misgivings. Whenever her mother indicated that she wanted to talk for a few moments it boded no good.

'Well,' she said sharply, feeling a great deal less assured than she sounded, 'what is it?' She remained standing inside the door, an indication that she was in a hurry. But Agnes settled herself in her chair and pointed to the sofa with a peremptory gesture.

'I'm going out,' said Marie, changing her plans abruptly.

'You're doing no such thing. I want to talk to you. It's important. Now sit down.'

Has she heard, thought Marie, as she came into the room slowly and took her seat on the edge of the sofa. She had not yet got used to the idea of being independent, and did not quite know how to go about using it. And Agnes did not look like a woman who had accepted the idea that she was living under a roof which was no longer hers.

'I heard you talking to that fellow on the phone. Coming here to-morrow is he? How long more do you expect me to put up with that?' Agnes smoothed her skirt with dry steady hands. When she was on top of a situation she did not feel the need for her rosary.

'I don't expect you to put up with it at all.'

'What do you mean by that?' Mrs. Fogarty narrowed her eyes and looked at her daughter's exposed knees.

'Just that. It's really none of your business, and I wish you'd stop talking about it. What have you got against him anyway?'

'None of my business!' Agnes selected that part of the reply which suited her best to answer. 'That's a queer thing to say to your mother.'

'Well,' insisted Marie, 'what have you got against him? He's just as good as anybody I'll ever meet round here, and he has a good job again now, better than the one he had with your friend Farrell.'

'Oh, he's able to put himself over, all right. I don't doubt he's talked himself into it. A smooth boy.' She paused and gave her daughter a meaning look. 'So long as he doesn't lose his head and blow up.'

'Is that all you want to say to me?' Marie leaned forward and prepared to propel herself out of the low sofa.

'No, it is not.' Agnes held out her hands, spread the long bony fingers with their close-cut nails and studied them attentively for a moment. Water gurgled in the heating pipes. Outside in the garden a song thrush called: 'go out, go out, go out'. 'I had a visit yesterday from Winnie Fogarty, your Uncle Jim's wife. You may not know her very well, but she told me that you know her son Pat better than I thought. In fact - '

There was no need for her to go on. The expression of blind panic on Marie's face told her everything. Instead of the feeling of triumph which a woman consciously aware of the part she was playing might have felt, Agnes, who possessed a wide range of conventional maternal attitudes, felt sick and furious. Was there no depths to which this daughter of hers would not descend? Whatever advantage Winnie might have been hoping to gain from her information Agnes had never doubted her for a moment.

'I can see that it's true,' she said in a harsh strangled voice. 'Oh, God in heaven, to think that I had to sit here in my own house and listen to the story that one had to tell. Oh, the shame of it! And you hardly back from the graveyard after burying your father.'

Marie did not recover herself as quickly as her mother, who thought her past all shame, had expected. For a few minutes the physical shock overwhelmed her and prevented her from thinking clearly. She was still worried by the fear of pregnancy, and that over the past few days had caused her to take an even more melodramatic view of the whole episode than she might otherwise have done. The very thought of it sickened her. And now here was her mother, implacably opposed to Brian, in full possession of the facts. Her bowels loosened with fear and disgust, and for a moment she thought she would faint. Only her mother's face, yellow and filled with self-righteous loathing, gave her back the courage to fight.

'I don't know what you're talking about,' she replied in a high toneless voice, sinking back against the cushions more out of a need to support herself than to appear indifferent.

'I think you do.'

'Is that so? Well for your information I never know what goes on in those old hags' minds. I leave that to you.' Marie's voice was spiteful; but she was still far from the control she was desperately trying to achieve. Was this a plot, she thought wildly? How could anyone have known? And then the implications of it struck her and she became furious. It did not give her cunning, the one thing she needed now, but brought her back to the immediate reality of defending herself.

'Yes,' went on her mother bitterly, 'I'm the one who has to listen to them all right. Clean up the mess as usual after you - '

'You mean to tell me you defended me instead of showing the old bitch the door,' exclaimed Marie furiously. Her mother's dart had struck home.

'What she had to say had to be listened to so that I could try and deal with her. She was very sure of her facts. Besides she's my sister-in-law, your aunt, and I couldn't very well turn her out of my house.'

Marie said the first thing that came into her head.

'It isn't your house anymore,' she blurted out, gathering herself together and sitting up white and stiff on the sofa. Her mouth was trembling but her eyes were hard and angry.

Her mother stared at her as if she were mad. Such an outburst hardly called for an answer. Perhaps the girl was unbalanced. She had often thought the same about Pat.

'I didn't want to tell you,' went on Marie speaking rapidly, 'but I can see that you'll stop at nothing to get your own way. Daddy made a will and left everything to to me, including this house.'

Mrs. Fogarty drew back in her chair and her eyes seemed to shrink. But her voice was steady as she defended herself automatically.

'I have your father's will. He made it only two years
ago and I saw it witnessed. He wouldn't be fool enough
to leave you in control of anything.'

'Oh, wouldn't he? He wasn't such a fool as you think
he was. He made another will six months ago. I saw
the solicitor the other day. You can ask them about it
if you like.'

The two women looked at each other; their expressions
stripped of all conventional deceit now that the moment
of truth was upon them. What Mrs. Fogarty read in
her daughter's eyes reminded her of something she had
thought she would never experience again - her husband's
dumb accusation, half-guilty, half-contemptuous. She
sought refuge in her nerves.

'So that's what you were getting him to sign that day
I came in on you, you cold-blooded little bitch. I knew
you were up to something. Well, let me tell you you
won't get away with that. Your father wasn't in his
right mind and I'll - '

'You'll like it or lump it,' said Marie coarsely. 'I
told you this will is six months old. You aren't even
listening to me.'

Mrs. Fogarty made as if to spring out of her chair;
her hands clawed at the arms, slipping over the smooth
velvet as if she had lost her sense of direction: a
woman suddenly stricken. Her eyes glazed and her
mouth dropped open. Marie in her turn was reminded
of her father on the morning they had found him lying
on his bedroom floor. But the moment passed. Mrs.
Fogarty recovered herself and looked out of the window,
aware for the first time of the sound of the thrush.
She did not know what call it was; nor did she wonder
if it was usual for birds to sing so late on a winter's
evening. Her whole body was numb with shock; but
her mind was active. Could it be possible that God had
saved her through the agency of this child whom she
sometimes thought of as not belonging to her?

'I'm listening to you,' she said slowly, with a twisted
smile, 'but I'm not thinking of wills at the moment.
I'm thinking of what your young man will say when he
hears about you and your cousin Pat.'

It was out now, and Marie realised that this was

what she had been vaguely dreading for the past few days. Her blood had warned her, and she felt curiously relieved. At least now she knew what she was fighting.

'You'd do that?' she said gently.

'It's my duty. I don't want that fellow to kick up another row and make a disgrace of us all over again.'

'He won't if you don't tell him.' Marie recovered and shifted her position. 'Especially since it's a pack of lies.'

'Winnie has proof. Not only what Pat told her himself when he was drunk, but you were seen.'

Another family ghost rose between them. Marie remembered what she had said to the guilt-soaked aggressor. 'Run down and tell your mother'. But who had seen them? Not that it mattered now.

'It's not the sort of thing your young man would like to hear,' went on Agnes remorselessly. 'Which is one of the reasons why I've warned you against him from the beginning. He's not suitable for you, and never will be. I'm not so ignorant in these matters as you think I am.'

Oh, yes you are, thought Marie; that is precisely what you are. If they had been closer she might have given this judgement further thought: it was nearer to the truth than either of them realised.

Marie took a cigarette from the box on the table before her and lit it to give herself time to think. There was no doubt about it, her mother could ruin everything if she really wanted to. Brian could hardly be expected to understand that her cousin had forced himself upon her: she would be discredited for the one act for which she had notresponsibility. Or had she? If she had been different would it ever have happened? In spite of herself she shivered. Now more than ever she needed him.

'And what good would it do?' she said, almost speaking to herself, staring at the smoke drifting up- wards from her lap. 'Especially when it gets out about the will. It would look a bit like you trying to get your own back, wouldn't it? And remember, I'm independent now. Things are changed.'

Agnes saw the direction of her thoughts, and remained silent.

'I may as well tell you I got quite a shock when I heard about the will, ' Marie went on carefully. 'I had a feeling that Daddy would not leave me completely helpless, but I never expected this. I thought we might have come to some sort of arrangement. '

'An arrangement?' Agnes spoke the word as if it were foreign and of dubious meaning.

'Yes. I know how much the business means to you. I thought perhaps we might divide it between us, sort of half-and-half, and this house to remain yours. I don't think Brian will want to live here anyway. But of course if you want to poison his mind with gossip - ' she broke off and flicked ash carelessly on the carpet.

Agnes looked at her daughter with a certain puzzled respect. It was an arrangement which she could understand perfectly; but not one which she believed her daughter would ever have thought of if the circumstances had been different. In this she was mistaken. Marie had thought of coming to some accommodation with her mother; but her hand was being forced. It was something neither of them would ever know. At the moment both of them were fighting for survival, as they saw it. Agnes waited. This was something which Marie would have to put into words.

'You poison Brian's mind against me, ' she went on at last with the ruthlessness of desperation, ' and Daddy's will stands. Not a penny piece will you ever get out of me, except the twelve pounds a week he has left you. I doubt if you'll be able to run this house on that. ' She looked at her mother levelly, her brown eyes dark and smudged. 'Well, do you want to create a scandal, or don't you?'

'I never wanted to do that, Marie. ' Mrs. Fogarty's voice was low and determined. She was on home ground here. 'That is exactly what I want to avoid. '

'Well, then avoid it. It isn't as if you had any love for the Fogartys. I don't know what you and Winnie were up to, but I'm sure you can handle her in your own way. If not - ' she stubbed out her cigarette viciously on the wobbling shell. The position was now

218

quite clear. If her mother's objections were sustained
she would probably lose Brian and come in for a great
deal of money. For the first time in her life Mrs.
Fogarty was faced with the choice of paying for her
declared convictions or revealing her real ones.
There was no doubt in her mind which she would choose.
But appearances had to be preserved.

'Do you realise that this is blackmail?' she demanded.

'Yes,' said Marie bluntly, 'and begun by you. I
haven't the slightest doubt that you'd force me to give
him up or get out if I were relying on you for my living.'

'I was doing my duty.' Mrs. Fogarty's voice was
sharp. 'And now if I do it I'll be left with hardly enough
to eat. Trying to save you from making a fool of yourself, and this is the thanks I get for it.' Suddenly she
came straight to the point. 'You'll have to prove that
will to me. It's a shocking thing for a man and his
daughter to plot together against their own flesh and
blood.'

Marie relaxed; and looked at her mother with a wry
smile. It was a draw; but at least she had survived.
In her heart she knew that her mother despised her
for yielding up one iota of property to keep the man
she wanted to marry. In a way this made it easier.
Agnes always enjoyed dealing with fools.

'I'll prove the will all right, Mummy, don't worry
about that.'

Her mother made one last move. In the circumstances she felt she could afford it.

'Do you realise what you're giving up for this man?'

'Yes, I do. But I happen to think it's worth it.'
She got up, picked up her handbag from a side-table,
took out her compact and studied her face in the tiny
mirror. She had a smudge on her nose. She moistened
one of her fingers and rubbed it off. Her mother
watched her silently as she dabbed her nose with
powder and then shut the compact with a decisive little
snap. 'But I'll need your consent, as they say. And a
definite promise that you won't make trouble.'

'I haven't much choice, have I?' Agnes' voice took
on a whining note. 'To think that I'd be treated like

this at the end of my days. Why we wouldn't have a
roof over our heads if it wasn't for me. The way I
slaved and worked in that business. It isn't fair, it
isn't fair,' she wailed.

'You should have thought of that before you listened
to filthy gossip about your own daugher,' said Marie
with a self-conscious little laugh.

'Are you going to give this fellow any share in the
business?' Now that she had made her choice Agnes
saw no reason why she should not make a good bargain.

'I don't think he'd want it,' said Marie briskly. 'He
likes to be independent. We'll get married before
Lent, and if he wants to go out on the road for us
instead of the cigarette people that's up to him.'

'I see.' Agnes frowned thoughtfully. Perhaps
Marie was cleverer than she had thought. Could she
have known that if she had insisted on giving Brian a
legal share her mother might have proved less easy
to settle with? She would have to wait and see, and
secure her own position. It was she knew very shaky.
Marie having secured her silence could always go back
on her word. Where money is concerned Agnes knew
just how much family feeling was really worth.

'I suppose you think I might double-cross you?'
Marie had been thinking exactly the same thing. 'But
what guarantee have I that you won't do the same? Get
me to make a settlement and then come out with this
nonsense about Pat Fogarty?'

They both considered this; and came to the conclusion
that it was too complicated. In business matters some
degree of honesty is essential for success. Agnes
realised that an embittered partner would make progress
very difficult. If she was to be allowed to pursue her
chief interest in life Marie would have to be kept happy;
and there seemed only one way to do that.

'I don't break bonds,' said Agnes Fogarty simply.
'If we come to a sensible arrangement which won't break
up our business, I'll stick to it. I have built up a good
credit, as you'll find out if you take the trouble.'

And it was true. This was one declaration of faith
which she could make in all sincerity. Dishonesty does
not pay. It had been the ruling passion of her life; and

she could stand any examination upon it. Whatever
her husband's early dealings had been like - and she
suspected them of irregularity - she had always
believed in putting the ethics of good business first.
Before this simple faith all emotion, all prejudice and
all human confusion of purpose faded away. To get
you have to give.

'All right,' said Marie firmly, 'we'll work out something on a fifty-fifty basis, as I suggested.' She recognised the truth of her mother's statement; and now
that she was a woman of property herself realised the
wisdom that lay behind it. The god that watched over
them both was smiling.

CHAPTER THIRTY-FOUR

The sitting-room was large with two windows looking
out over the street. The ceiling was low, giving promise of hot stuffy days in summer and warm cosy
nights in winter. It was a room designed for thick
yellow-white lace curtains, heavy mahogany furniture,
an upright piano, and Belleek vases on the mantelpiece.
Behind it overlooking a small yard with a stunted
sycamore tree was a double bedroom; and four steps
down from that on the return of the stairs the bathroom
and lavatory. Upstairs on the second floor were two
more bedrooms, and a tiny airless hole for the maid.
On the ground floor behind the shop were the kitchen
with its flagged floor, and the dining-room. The shop,
a public-house, with its high ornate wooden counter,
and its pink china pint-pullers was closed. It smelled
of dust, stale biscuits, and cobwebs. But it was a
good size and had a high ceiling. Brian and Marie
planned to cut a hall-way through it from the door to
the stairs behind, and turn it into a dining-room.

The place, one of Pat's last acquisitions, was a few
doors down the street from the main store and offices.
He had bought it a few months before his death as an
investment, hoping in time to link it up with the other
two houses he owned alongside his business which
were turned into flats. Only a small sweet-shop run
by an ancient widow separated the two properties, and
it was Pat's intention to acquire this also when the old
lady died or retired, thus linking up the yards at the
back and giving him room for expansion.

When Marie was making the settlement with her
mother she handed over the two blocks of flats to her,
but retained this house for herself, Once when they
were driving past she had pointed it out to Brian and he
had said with a kind of nostalgic passion in his voice:

'That's the kind of house I'd like to live in. Reminds me of our old place at home. '

Marie had remembered the remark, inspected the house again, decided it had possibilities, and asked Brian what he thought about it. From the moment he had set foot in it there was no question of their setting up house anywhere else. His enthusiasm affected Marie who found as women in love always will that he had anticipated her own wishes. And indeed in a way he had. The new-rich opulence, the pseudo-Georgian setting and the expensive solitude which her parents had surrounded themselves with when they came up in the world, was not associated in her mind with either comfort or happiness. She hated the large rambling house in which she had lived from the age of ten; but did not entirely understand why these rooms above a shop in a narrow street appealed to her so powerfully. She assumed it was Brian's touching enthusiasm which influenced her; but in fact it was something else, something deeper and more instinctive in both of them.

In just such a house in a smaller less busy street had she been born in the days when Pat and Agnes Fogarty had first set up shop, and the world had been large, rosy and full of flouncy dolls and sticky caramels for her; in just such a house had Brian been reared in the days when his family had owned their own business. They were going back to where they started; and as they stood in the empty decayed sitting-room they were both assailed by memories of their childhood - the low ceilings, the flickering night-light, the cosy fires on frosty evenings, the unambiguous affections, the stilled terrors and the fleeting raptures.

For the past few week-ends they had been busy making their plans, spending long happy hours wandering about the rooms discussing colour schemes and improvements. They expected the place to be ready by Easter. In the meantime the empty house served as a convenient meeting place where they could be alone for an hour on the pretext of inspecting their future home. In that town everything sooner or later was turned into a pretext. But now it was easier; they were officially engaged, although out of respect for the dead the announcement had not been printed in the 'Irish Independent'; and they planned to be married quietly on the day before Shrove Tuesday in Dublin. For the past week or two Marie had been picking up bits and pieces of furniture in local second-hand shops; brass-wear, pictures, china, and a hideous Victorian sofa which she had bought because she felt that the wood-work alone was worth the ten pounds the weary dealer was asking for it. Her taste was not good; and Brian's was not much better. Here again they both reflected the background in which they had been brought up; horse-hair sofas, bamboo sideboards, potted plants, carpets thickly covered with monstrous roses, and lace curtains. They decided however to put up heavy silk curtains to shield their privacy from the prying street. Was there not something about 'lace-curtain Irish'?

On Sunday afternoons they brought a bundle of sticks along with them and lit a fire in the bedroom. Here for an hour or two they were free to make love, drawing on the marriage credit which was already lodged in the bank. On the last Sunday before their marriage Marie sat on the sofa and watched Brian squatting before the fireplace lighting paper under the wood. The decorators had moved in during the week and the house smelled of paint and fresh varnish. But as yet this room had not been invaded. As she looked about her Marie furnished it in imagination, and saw the warm nest into which they would soon move: a thick blue carpet, yellow curtains, solid oak wardrobe, and a large bed with a built-in bookcase and shelves at the head. Here they would have a little white radio for the eight o'clock news in the morning, and the weather report before they went to sleep at night. Someone was bound to give them one of those gadgets which woke one in the morning and boiled a kettle for tea at the same time. That would fit into one of the shelves also. And a fitted case for her shoes, she must have that too; and a cheval-glass, and a tall manly chest of drawers for Brian's shirts and socks; and a candlewick bed-spread to match the curtains; and a brocade covered seat for the dressing-table; and lots of bright sunny modern paintings to bring some colour into the wet days. She sighed happily.

Brian sat back on his haunches and looked up. His face was red from the blaze. The sticks were crackling and he had put a beech log on top of them.

'You know, I can't get over the way your mother has come round recently,' he said, sucking his teeth and shaking his head.

'Just as well, since we have to live with her until this place is ready,' said Marie. Brian had decided to keep his present job for a few months; and then perhaps, as Marie hoped, he would come into the business. In the meantime he would be away most of the week; but Fridays to Mondays he would be spending with the Fogartys. Agnes, whose acceptance of the marriage was now complete, had suggested this herself. Indeed once she had made up her mind to accept the young man she had done so with a good grace. Now that they were all committed to the business and its future a united front was necessary.

'I hope you weren't thinking of me when you made that settlement with her,' he went on thoughtfully prodding the fire, as men will, with a small twisted poker.

'What do you mean?' Marie sat up and stared at the back of his neck anxiously. She had given him an edited version of her arrangement with her mother; stressing the fact that she thought the will very unjust. Besides which it would make things almost impossible for them.

'Well, you might have. To win her round. Certainly it's done the trick.'

'It wasn't that,' said Marie sharply. 'I could have done what I liked. It's just that it seemed altogether too much. She's always lived for that business. It would have killed her to be cut off like that. Besides, well, I just couldn't do it.'

'Yes, of course it was the right thing to do.' Brian looked up again with a wry grin. 'But I wouldn't like to think I came that expensive. Have you thought about that?'

'No, of course not.' Marie's voice was indignant; doubly so since she had thought of it in some detail.

About a year before his death her father had had his business and property valued for insurance purposes by a well-known Dublin firm not amenable to bribery. They had produced the figure of one hundred and fifty thousand pounds odd. Marie therefore reckoned that Brian had cost her something like seventy five thousand pounds. But of course she would inherit everything when her mother died - that was part of their agreement - so that in fact she had merely invested that amount of money in him. It was a fascinating thought; but not one which she intended to share with him. How much was that sculptured mouth? How much those strong smooth legs? How much those hard muscular arms and shoulders? How much those private parts, most precious of all perhaps?

'Why are you frowning?' he got to his feet and stood in front of her. To cover her confusion, for it was obscene to think in such terms, she put her hands on his hips and drew him to her and kissed his groin through the thin flannel trousers. For a moment she thought he was going to yield, but he disengaged himself with a little laugh and sat down on the sofa beside her, his full mouth set with theatrical firmness. She had evaded his question.

'What are we going to do about the wedding?' he went on, leaning his elbows on his knees and clasping his big hands.

'Oh, that.' Marie looked thoughtful. They both wanted it as private as possible; but Mrs. Fogarty had indicated that she would attend. Marie saw the point; and agreed with it. Brian's mother and his sister and brother would also have to be present. It was a bit of a bore; but some gesture had to be made towards the state religion. And they were both aware that it was usual for the bride and groom to receive communion on their wedding morning. This presented problems.

'Do you really want to make a general confession?' said Brian, wrinkling his brow and staring into the crackling fire.

'God, no! That's not going to make either of us any better. I'd feel an awful hypocrite.'

'Me too. But what are the others going to say?'

226

Confronted with the assembled family Brian felt uneasy. It was so difficult to get the old people to understand that these things were essentially personal. For them religion had always been part of the immutable order of things.

'They won't say anything, if we go about it quietly,' said Marie who had given the matter some thought. 'You know how people pretend not to have noticed. If we say nothing they'll assume that we're both going, like everybody does. And then if we don't, I doubt if anybody will say anything afterwards. I mean I don't see much point in letting them intimidate us. Going to communion without confession just to please them would be silly. The whole thing is enough of a bore as it is, without getting into a panic and making things more complicated than they are.'

'I agree. Yes, I suppose that's the best thing to do. I wish to God we could get it over in a registry office. This church business is an awful cod. All that emotionalism.'

'Yes, but we'll have to go to Mass when we settle down here,' said Marie cautiously. 'That's one sacrifice you'll have to make as a married man.' Brian had been in the habit of going out of the house for an hour on Sunday morning, taking a drive out to Spiddel, having a drink and coming back to preserve appearances at home. Now he would have to take on some of the responsibilities of a man of property.

'I suppose so. There's an evening Mass, isn't there?'

'Three, in the three churches. It isn't so bad once you get into the habit, which is all it is really. I don't think there's any point in making an issue of it. After all neither of us cares that much anymore. I wonder if anybody really does. And you meet people, keep up with the news and that sort of thing. Although of course the sermons are diabolical.'

Brian nodded abstractedly. It was just something they would have to go through. He did not feel all that strongly about it. Besides there were other more important things to discuss. He clasped his hands tightly and gave Marie a quick sidelong look.

227

'Do you want to start a family right away?' he asked bluntly. Since the opposition had been removed, and their position more or less legalised they had become more relaxed; less awkward with each other. Now safe behind these walls, in this room which they had already furnished in their imaginations, they felt free to discuss those intimacies which hostility, uncertainty and their own lack of sophistication had hitherto surrounded with a false air of constraint.

'No, Brian, I don't think so,' said Marie slowly, leaning slightly against his shoulder, comfortably aware of the growing warmth which they shared. 'Not immediately. There's so much to do with the house, and you being away and everything. If we do start you'll have to give up that job.'

'Is that blackmail?' he answered with a grin, sliding his arms about her waist.

'Perhaps.' She smiled and caressed his thigh fondly. 'But I do want children. Two anyhow, a boy and a girl.' She spoke without embarrassment. Pat Fogarty had not after all complicated the issue; but it had been a frightful time. She felt in her bones that she was one of those women who start a family very quickly; indeed the Dublin doctor who supplied her with the pill had told her as much. That pleased her now and she spoke her thoughts out loud.

'Who told you that?' he demanded, his thigh stiffening a little.

'A doctor, of course. A man I go to in Dublin. How do you suppose I've been managing with you all this time?'

'Oh, that.' He was still a little tense. 'Who's this doctor fellow? Another old boy friend?'

'Don't be silly. This one is as queer as a coot. You'll be meeting him I suppose.' She laughed easily. 'I'm the one who'll have to worry there. From what I hear you're just his type.'

'Cripes, that'll be the day,' he said heartily, putting his hand over hers and pressing it into his flesh. 'Unless you think this is queer.'

'It's one way of saving on the pill.' Her hand was insistent now, her weight heavy against his side.

Excitement mounted in him, but as always he made the ritual resistence. That was silly too.

'Do you have to save it all the time?' he murmured teasingly, shifting his weight heavily, delaying the moment of mindlessness.

'Shut up, Oh, Brian.'

'Yes,' he whispered, 'yes,' taking her head in his hands as she slipped to her knees and the familiar frenzy began. The firelight cast a pale shadow on the opposite wall, moving quickly, a bobbing blur, then slowly dissolving and breaking apart.

'There are jokes about that,' he said huskily when it was over.

'Yes, I know,' she replied calmly, ruffling his hair. 'People are afraid. It's so damned silly.'

'Not for me.' He stood up and grasped her shoulders. 'But it's selfish. What about you?'

She put her arms about his neck and smiled tenderly.

'I am thinking about me, darling. You see I love you very much, and when you love someone it's wonderful. Nothing to joke about. Besides the sofa is so cramped. Kiss me.'

'I could, you know,' he said after they drew apart. 'I want to.'

'No, it's only until to-morrow night. I'll wait.'

He hugged her boyishly and kissed her ear.

'I hope to God it's a fine day. I've never been in a plane before.'

They were going to London for a week; and he was full of it. The Tower, Buckingham Palace, Madame Tussauds, the Changing of the Guard, the theatres, a look inside the Ritz - he was looking forward to it all.

'I must pick up some things for the sitting-room there,' she said taking his arm and moving towards the door. Arm-in-arm they crossed the narrow landing and went into the front room. 'I've got the address of a place where you can get the most marvellous sea-shells. Reasonable too. I want a collection of them for this room, pictures, ornaments for the mantel-piece. I'm mad about shells.'

'Yes,' he said vaguely, looking out of the window, while she prattled on about a piano, cabinets, curtains

and cushions. They would have to have at least one
religious painting somewhere; but she would see that
it was a modern bright one with some artistic value.
And a cabinet for that Crown Derby tea-set her mother
was giving them.

'Yes.' The street curved away below him, grey
and sleepy in its Sunday afternoon torpor. On just such
a scene had he often gazed out as a boy - a long narrow
row of stone houses behind the Spanish Arch. He had
known the people there, had been one of them. Would
the children play hopscotch here on the pavements
when the spring broke through? An old woman with a
limp waddling by, two little boys wrestling in a door-
way, a pale face glimmering behind a window opposite.
Above the uneven roofs, a huge shifting sky streaked
with red; and at the end of a steep downward alley the
burnished glass of the river.

She came and stood by his side. Unlike him she did
not know the people here very well. Like a favoured
soul who has been touched with grace she had always
been set apart from them by a larger dispensation of
good fortune. She was aware of it in a general way;
and had not come back here to make friends. That
would be impossible. Always she would be watched for
a fall from grace; and Brian too as time went on. They
possessed all the virtues of an ancient hieratic faith,
stern, commanding and implacable. They would have
to work hard to be human.

'Isn't it wonderful,' said Marie with a sigh, 'our
very own window to look out on.'

230